M000044097

Attack on Titan
End of the World

Created by Hajime Isayama
A Novel by Touji Asakura
Based on the Screenplay by
Yusuke Watanabe & Tomohiro Machiyama

Translated by Maria Maita-Keppeler

VERTICAL.

Copyright © 2016 Hajime Isayama, Touji Asakura. All rights reserved.

First published in Japan in 2015 by Kodansha, Ltd., Tokyo

Publication for this English edition arranged through Kodansha, Ltd., Tokyo

English language version produced by Vertical, Inc.

Based on the Screenplay by
Yusuke Watanabe & Tomohiro Machiyama.

© 2015 TOHO / KODANSHA / DENTSU / AMUSE / HORIPRO /
Hakuhodo DY media partners / JR Kikaku / KDDI / Yomiuri Shimbun /
The Asahi Shimbun / Nippan / GYAO / TOKYO FM

Originally published in Japanese as
Shousetsu Eiga Shingeki no Kyojin ATTACK ON TITAN and
Shousetsu Eiga Shingeki no Kyojin ATTACK ON TITAN Endo obu za Waarudo.

This is a work of fiction.

ISBN: 978-1-945054-08-2

Manufactured in the United States of America

First Edition

Vertical, Inc.
451 Park Avenue South
7th Floor
New York, NY 10016
www.vertical-inc.com

CONTENTS

Maybe the sun fell to the ground. For a moment, Armin considered the outrageous possibility. The ground heaved so violently he couldn't remain standing, and a deafening roar thundered from the other side of the wall like the world was breaking. Darkness consumed the blue skies, and a boiling hot wind blew as if from nowhere.

The sun had fallen. Nothing else could explain such an event.

Thrown into a panic, Armin tried for a moment to imagine the possibility. It wasn't long, however, before he and the three others with him understood exactly what was happening. The sweltering wind brought a spattering of pebbles, at first in sprinkles, and then increasing in force like rain. Since they were at the base of the First Wall, just glimpsing the top, over fifty yards up, was a challenge. They craned their necks until the muscles in their necks were sore, until eventually, the area above the wall came into view. Holding their hands up to protect their faces from the falling pebbles, and narrowing their eyes, they peeked cautiously, as if at a secret.

Finally, through the opening in the steam, the sand, and the smoke, they could see it. It was backlit. The dark silhouette moved slowly, eerily, almost as if it were teasing them. More pebbles rained down as it moved. The ground shook as if it had come to life.

The moment they fully understood what was happening, Armin and the others sank into despair.

We were being lorded over. Within our walls, or perhaps within our cage, we are nothing more than pitiful prey.

Their existence bowed to a power that could not be fought and was bereft of freedom and deprived of all hope.

In seconds, the wall was breached.

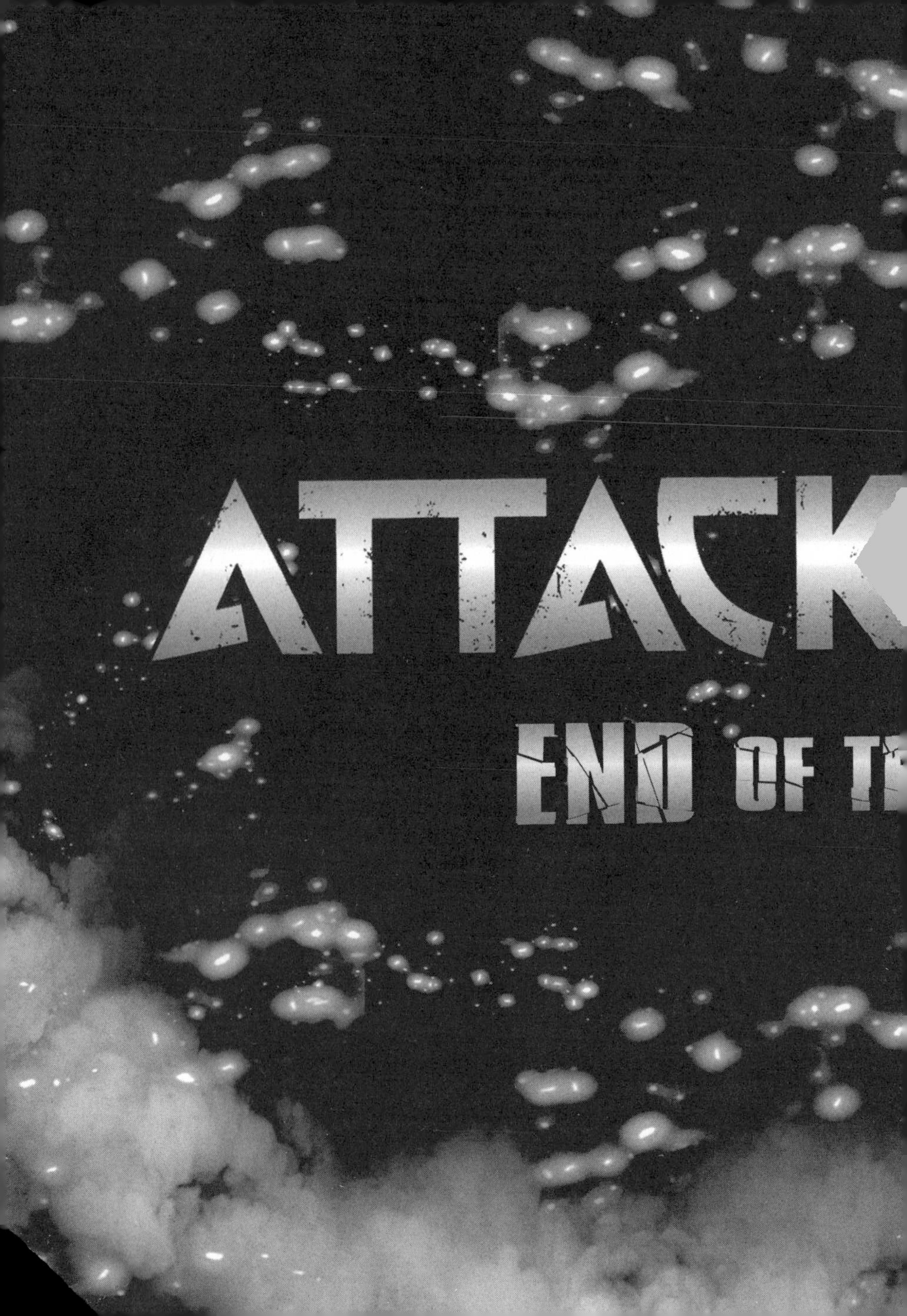
ATTACK
END OF

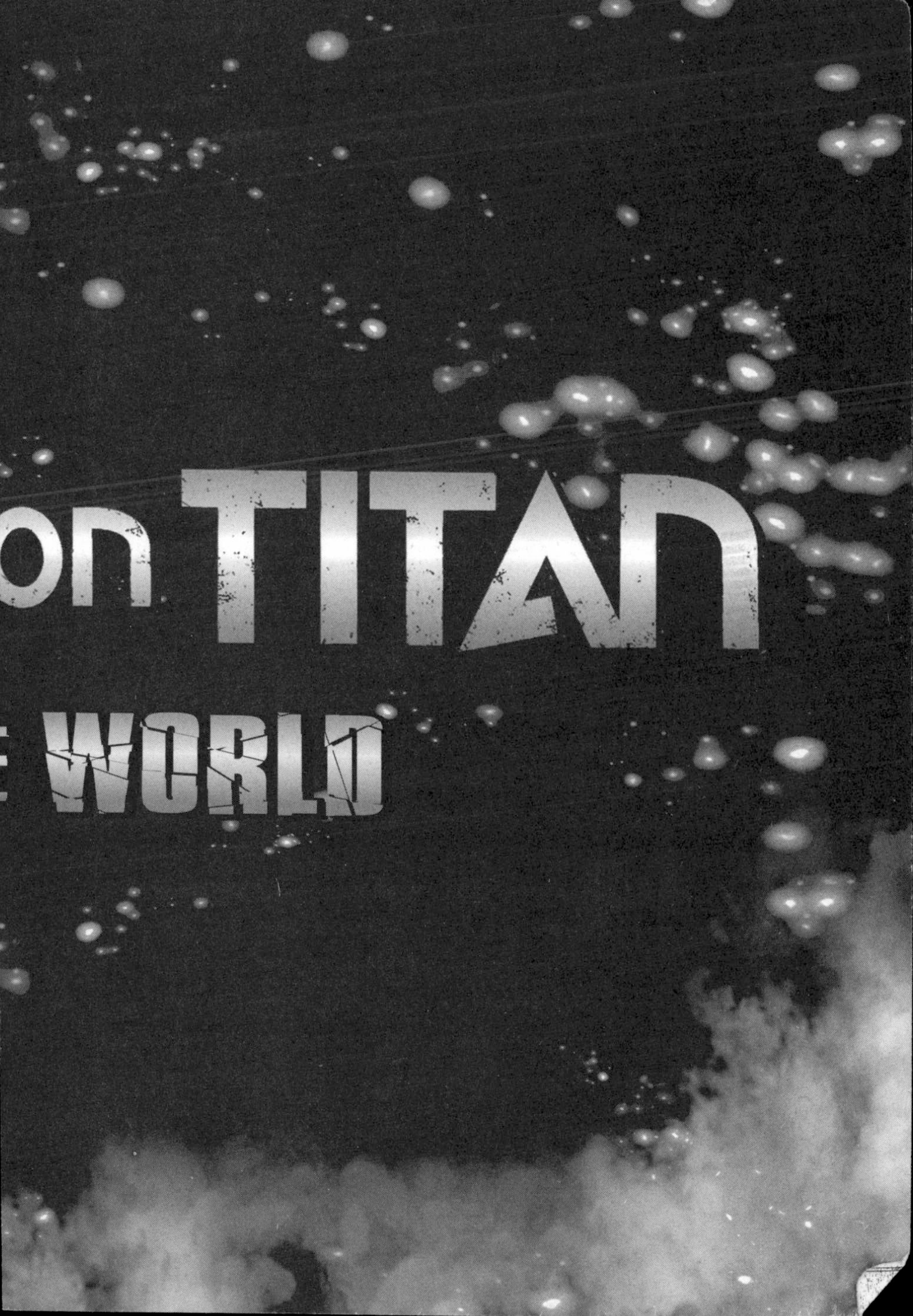
on TITAN
WORLD

I. LIMBO

The mainspring had broken after all.

Armin took a deep breath as he carefully operated the tweezers. With dexterity, he removed the broken mainspring, and while taking care not to put stress on any other part of the machine, he installed a new spring. He replaced the cogwheel and replaced the lid on the case. After confirming that everything was sitting normally, he wound the spring and observed the motion of the hand.

He had fixed it.

"Excuse me."

As he raised his head, he saw the shopkeeper of the fruit store standing before him, a plastic container in hand.

"I-I'm sorry." Armin stood up in a panic. "I hope I didn't make you wait."

"No, no, I just got here. Full tank please."

Armin brought the plastic container to the fuel tank and loosened the valve. Presently the glassy canola oil began to trickle into the plastic container, and a distinct, savory aroma wafted into the air.

As the oil flowed, Armin's world gradually settled back into reality. From the storefront, he could see the usual flow of people downtown. He could hear a sale advertisement shouted from the fertilizer store across the street, and fragments of price negotiations from the farm equipment shop next door. People weaved through the surging crowds, their eyes set on their individual tasks. It was the usual congestion and tumult of the poor, but lively, downtown.

Armin shook his head as he reflected upon what had happened. *It's always like this. Whenever I become absorbed in my work, I stop being able to see what's around me. I shouldn't even call myself a shop clerk.*

As the shopkeeper of the fruit store waited for his container to fill, he idly scanned the desktop.

"What's this?"

"It's a wind-up timer," Armin answered. "I use it to measure the time for canola oil extraction. It's more convenient than an hourglass. It wasn't working properly so I was fixing it."

"So you made it yourself?"

"Yes."

The shopkeeper winced as he looked at the timer. "It's not my business, but you should be careful about doing this kind of thing. Especially in front of such a busy shop… You don't know who could be watching."

Armin smiled slightly. "Well, the Military Police don't come to this area."

"No, no." The shopkeeper frowned. "For some reason, they recently decided to expand their range of activity. Just the other day somebody around here was taken away by the Military Police. I've also been careless since this is just a tiny southern town on the First

Wall. But recently everything has started to become so much more oppressive."

"I'll be careful."

Armin handed the filled plastic container to the shopkeeper.

"By the way," Armin said. "How is Eren?"

The shopkeeper's face darkened as he tossed his payment on the counter.

"He quit suddenly."

"He quit?!"

The shopkeeper nodded unhappily. "He's trash. He's useless. He seems to think it's his job to argue with customers."

Armin sighed. He could imagine the scene well.

"That hot-blooded kid might as well go join the Survey Party," the shopkeeper spat.

"The Survey *Party*?" It was a name Armin hadn't heard before. "Don't you mean the Survey *Corps*?"

"You don't know? The Citizen Survey Party." The shopkeeper's eyes widened in surprise. He pulled a piece of paper from the pocket of his stained pants. "Just recently there was an announcement during the meeting downtown. It was even posted to the notice board in the city center. You haven't heard about it?"

Scanning the sheet, Armin explained that his father had gone to the meeting in his place. When he finished reading, he promptly removed his oil-stained linen apron. It was good news.

When his father returned a few minutes later, Armin asked for somebody to cover his shift at the storefront and dove into the crowds downtown. Three streets away, where they began to thin, was the wooden cabin where Eren lived. Technically the cabin belonged to Armin's father, but Eren rented it through a man named Souda. Armin tried knocking but there was no answer. With no idea of Eren's whereabouts, he tried the weaving studio next to the cabin.

"Is Mikasa here?" Armin asked the woman standing in front of the studio. Mikasa appeared at the storefront a few moments later. She removed the work bandana from her head, releasing her flowing, black hair.

"Sorry to drop in on you like this, but do you have any idea where Eren went?" Armin asked.

"He said he just started working at the fruit store," Mikasa answered in a monotone as usual.

When Armin explained what he'd heard about Eren from the fruit store clerk, Mikasa's eyebrow gave an angry twitch.

"If he's anywhere he's there," she said. "On Missile Hill."

"*That* place?"

Mikasa nodded. "I'll go with you. I'll finish up here, one sec."

Missile Hill was named for a single undetonated missile that was left on top of the hill as if forgotten. It was a huge cylinder, nearly twenty feet long, that lay on its side deserted. The hill itself was a slight climb from the town of Monzen where Armin and the others lived. From it, one could see the entire town, the surrounding farms, the dazzling green pastures, and the complete view of the towering First Wall that stretched endlessly around the perimeter.

Despite the splendor of the view, because of the presence of the undetonated missile, very few people went near the hill.

"He really is here…" Armin said, surprised. Not only was Eren on the hill, he was lying casually on top of the missile, which, though said to be from the Great War era over a hundred years ago, might still explode.

At the sound of Armin's voice, Eren rolled over to glance at his friends suspiciously. He always tended to wear a bitter expression, but perhaps because he was truly unhappy to see them, Eren's eyes filled with reproach.

"What are you guys doing here?"

"Well, actually—"

"Why did you quit your job?" Mikasa demanded. "After you'd finally found one."

Eren scratched his head lazily. "They're so annoying, the customers—*do this, do that*. All high and mighty over one piece of fruit."

"You should have expected as much. People just want to make sure they're getting their money's worth with what little they have."

"They just want to push me around because they're stuck living their stupid lives inside this wall. They're all pathetic."

"That's not the point. You're living inside this wall just the same as the rest of them."

Mikasa's words seemed to spark something inside of Eren, who sharpened his already icy gaze. He slid smoothly down the gray body of the missile to drop down at Mikasa's feet.

"I'm different," he said, glowering.

"How are you different?" Mikasa didn't flinch.

"I'm going outside. Outside the wall. I'm *completely* different from all those people who live their lives inside the wall while pretending that they *aren't* surrounded by the wall."

"How are you going to go outside? Do you plan on climbing the wall?"

Eren glared at Mikasa in silence.

"Um…guys…" Armin quietly interceded. "I actually have something interesting to tell Eren." When he saw that he had their attention, Armin handed the paper clipping he'd gotten from the fruit store clerk over to Eren. Though at first Eren glanced at the letter with impatience, before long his eyes glinted with interest.

"Citizen…Survey *Party*."

Armin nodded. "So you didn't know about it either, huh? It's just like it says. It seems the prohibited 'outer wall investigations by citizens' might finally win the parliament's approval. It's a notice for the first troop recruitment. Anyone who's over fifteen can join. Why don't you try joining?"

Eren continued to stare at the letter hungrily.

"Inside the wall, land is limited," Armin went on. "There are a lot of people who aren't satisfied with their lives here, just like you. And even though there might be a better life outside the wall, the government's actions are so murky that we can't see any kind of progress with the Survey Corps. And the Titans…"

Armin paused as Eren lifted his face up and squinted into the wind that passed over the hill.

Armin continued, "Some people even think that the Titans don't really exist. In over a hundred years, the wall hasn't ever been breached, and aside from a group of government officials and the soldiers in the Survey Corps, nobody has seen the Titans. And the Survey Corps only ever leave through West Gate or North Gate, so we never even get the chance to see them around here."

"Outside…" Eren said to himself. "I might be able to see the

Ocean."

"The Ocean?" Mikasa, who'd fallen silent, asked him.

"It's the salt water that covers this world, so many times bigger than a river," Eren said excitedly. "Armin looked it up in a *forbidden* book."

"H-Hey, Eren." Armin instinctively checked his surroundings. "What if the Military Police hear us?"

As if they'd be in a place like this, the faint smile on Eren's face seemed to say.

Mikasa's expression had grown darker and darker since talk of the Citizen Survey Party had begun. From impatience, or perhaps confusion, she rolled her eyes. Overcoming her hesitation, she managed to speak.

"I...I want to see the Ocean too."

"Right?" Eren responded in his increasingly cheerful voice. "I'm going to join the Survey Party and go find the Ocean. And after that, I'm going to take you there too. It's a promise."

"N-No." Mikasa looked away.

"Huh?"

"Not like that. If you're going, *I'm going too.*"

"Huh?! What are you talking about? You're always—" Eren stopped speaking as he suddenly looked away towards the wall. And for some reason, rather than finishing his thought, he remained silent.

"Eren?"

Eren's eyes filled with some kind of disbelief as they stayed fixed on the wall. After a little while, he shuddered like he was startled by something he'd seen.

"It's shut," he murmured.

"It's shut?"

"Th-There was a small hole in the wall just now."

Armin, and without a doubt, Mikasa, had no idea what Eren was talking about. *A hole in the wall?* However, without giving Armin or Mikasa a chance to ask any questions, Eren took off running towards the wall. A cold wind passed over the hill, stirring up a strange tension in the air.

As Eren ran, he thought about what he had seen. His friends shouted at him from behind that his eyes must have played tricks on him, a possibility he couldn't deny. Still, for some reason, Eren didn't think it was a figment of his imagination. About halfway up the wall, there had been a rectangular hole, just big enough for a single person to pass through. It was only for an instant, but he thought he could see something like sky on the other side. However, before Eren could show his friends, the hole had closed up without a sound.

It was so strange.

He continued running for a while as he thought about the hole, eventually arriving at the foot of the wall. Eren hid his body in a thicket beside the road, where his two friends caught up to him.

"I'm telling you, it was just your imagination. There's no hole anywhere."

Ignoring Armin's words, Eren rested his eyes on the Garrison Regiment base, which stood about thirty feet from the wall. The narrow and long base, built of sturdy concrete, curved along it. Dozens of guns sat ready on the rooftop in the unlikely event that the Titans tore down the wall and invaded. However, fire had never spouted from their muzzles, and as to whether the Garrison Regiment could actually properly use the weaponry, Eren had his doubts. Could something like a cannonball even take down the Titans, who (as legend had it) were *immortal*?

Either way, as far as Eren could see, the only job of the so-called Garrison Regiment was to stay within the base and wear firearms at their hips. They were "good for nothing" if anyone ever was. The fruit store owner at least strove to make money and had a little more merit.

"Over there, there's a place in the barricade where the wire netting is torn," Eren said, dropping his voice a little. "I'm going through and heading for the wall. The Garrison will never catch me."

Armin protested all the more, but Eren continued into the thicket heedlessly. Evading the soldiers' eyes, he crept along the side of the base and made it to the barricade. As he had confirmed before, the wire netting was torn. Taking care to not get his clothes caught, he crawled through it.

"I'm telling you, this is a bad idea, Eren." Armin's voice shook with worry. "If you get close to the wall you could be shot without warning. We're already risking a huge punishment just for passing through the barricade that's supposed to stop people from getting to the wall. Any closer and we might alert the Titans. Let's turn around while we can. See? It looks like there's no hole after all."

"It *was* here," Eren said. "It's just closed now. And besides, if there *is* a hole in the wall it's a huge problem for the Garrison. They're supposed to be protecting the wall. If I find the hole I plan on telling those guys their wall has been breached!"

Armin paused, his face troubled.

Eren stared in silence up at the wall. The oppressive gray structure that stretched up to the sky was baked brown as if to call attention to the passage of a hundred years. Parts of the wall jutted out while others caved in, hinting that it had been built in such a way to fit with existing buildings like a puzzle. From up close, it gave the impression that it was extremely crooked, or even unstable. Ivy crawled over the entire surface and somehow made it look more ominous.

The air current had shifted. At the foot of the wall, the wind blew far stronger than at the top of the hill. Eren's hair, his clothes, and even the weeds swayed restlessly. Birds flew overhead and disappeared over the wall with incredible ease as if to taunt him. For whatever reason, they frustrated Eren immensely, and he bit his lip without thinking. The wind was cold.

Hachoo. At the tiny sound of a sneeze Eren turned around to find Mikasa sniffling. When Mikasa met his gaze, she lifted her red scarf to her mouth wordlessly. *Mikasa,* Eren was about to say when he stiffened.

"What are you doing there?!"

Armin and Mikasa whirled around in surprise. Three men approached from the barricade, their shoulders tense with anger. The intimidating gait. The firearms on their hips. The crest of two roses on their shoulders. They were from the Garrison Regiment.

Eren was still shaken as the soldiers advanced rapidly. Before he could offer an explanation, they grabbed Armin by the scruff of his neck and threw him down on the ground. Eren immediately felt the blood rise to his head at their violence, but he began to calmly explain that he'd come to investigate a hole in the wall. The moment another soldier tried to handle Mikasa in the same way, however, he lost control of himself. The cork that held in his emotions popped open without a sound.

With all his strength, he swung his clenched fist against the cheek of the soldier who was trying to seize Mikasa. The punch was too shallow and merely grazed his face. The soldier brushed his cheek and glared with eyes like ice at Eren, who didn't hesitate to throw one more punch. The soldier dodged the blow and grabbed him by the collar. Eren struggled as much as he could under the man's grip, but ultimately it wasn't more than a few seconds before he was pinned down to the ground, his shoulders heaving as the moisture of the ground seeped up against his cheek. The crushed weeds beneath his cheek had an earthy smell of defeat.

"Well, well, if it isn't Eren," another voice came from behind.

Someone new had arrived. Eren tried to turn over, but his head was held down so firmly he couldn't move.

"I just came to see what all the noise was about, and here you are… Hey, guys, you can leave this one to me."

"But—"

"Sorry, sorry, I know this kid. Do me a favor here, okay?"

At that point, Eren had a fairly good guess as to who the speaker was. The hand on his head lifted away almost reluctantly. And yet, for a little while, Eren remained on the ground. He didn't want to meet, even by accident, the eyes of the soldier who'd been holding him down.

"Look, it's okay now. Everyone's gone."

As Eren slowly got to his feet, he swept the dirt from his pants.

It seemed as if Armin and Mikasa were unhurt. Mikasa didn't have any stains on her clothes, so apparently, she hadn't been held down. He let out his breath.

"What are you doing in a place like this?" Eren's savior, Souda, smiled teasingly. "Don't tell me you're still pretending to be an explorer at your age?"

Souda was an older soldier in his mid-forties who had served with the Garrison Regiment for over twenty years. Perhaps because of his occupation, he had dark, sun-weathered skin, and a fit frame. His countenance was generally bright and cheerful, and he spoke with a distinct, deep voice that rumbled in the back of his throat.

"There was a hole," Eren said. "Around the middle of the wall."

"A hole?"

"There," Eren pointed to the place where he thought he'd seen the hole. "I saw it from the top of the hill. But it was filled right away."

"A hole, huh?" Souda murmured, and the smile gradually disappeared from his face. A crease between his eyebrows took its place. It looked as if he was thinking hard about something, but of course, Eren had no idea what. Still, he felt vaguely relieved that Souda, unlike the others, had taken him seriously.

"Armin, Mikasa, you saw it too?"

They both shook their heads.

"I see... Hmm?" Souda's eyes came to rest on a piece of paper poking out of Eren's pants pocket. "What's this? You got homework or something?"

"H-Hey! What are you doing?"

Souda took the sheet from Eren's pocket, unfolded it, and looked it over. Though he began by reading the words out loud, as he continued his expression clouded over, and his voice slowed until it finally trailed off altogether. Then he moved his head from side to side as if to shake something off.

"Eren." Souda folded the paper back up. "This Citizen Survey Party—don't do it."

"Wh-What do you mean?"

"You mean to join, right?" Certainty flashed in Souda's eyes. "It's exactly the kind of thing you would spring for."

"So what?" Eren retorted.

"I'm not going to say anything bad about it. Please just don't do this, okay?"

"Why would you say that to me? Feeling parental or something?"

"Actually, for someone without parents like yourself, I am a bit like a parent, aren't I?"

Blinking heavily as if his eyes were terribly tired, Souda sighed.

"Listen, Eren, your life is your life. It doesn't belong to anyone else. I only want you to live the life that you desire. But don't listen to what other people say. There's no need to try to carry what you think is your fate or your destiny on your shoulders. You could even go on working at the fruit store for the rest of your life if it's what you—"

"He already quit the fruit store," Mikasa filled him in.

Souda pursed his lips and then nodded.

"I wouldn't mind if you started working once more at the fruit stand, or even if you went to the farms. However, Eren...*however.* Just don't do this. The Survey Party is dangerous. All those guys are just amateurs, fantasizing about the outside world. They have absolutely no understanding of the real situation out there."

"That's why I'm going to go survey, no? I'm going to go survey because there's so much we don't know."

Souda scratched his head hopelessly as he cleared his throat. "Okay, Eren. Let's talk…"

Talk————

————

—

The word lingered in the air, but Souda was cut short.

Instead, a massive crash like Eren had never felt before shook the earth. He and the others fell to the ground. It had happened suddenly—far too suddenly. With no warning and no time for anybody to prepare, it came.

Eren had no idea what was going on. It was as if he'd been thrown into some kind of dream world. Or perhaps it was the opposite. Perhaps he had only just woken up from a dream. The thought occurred to him, and in some ways, it was the reality. Recalling the moment later, he would realize that the notion that he'd woken up from a dream hadn't been entirely off the mark.

Darkness suddenly cloaked the skies. It was as if some curtains had been drawn. A hot wind raged from above as pebbles and plumes of dust rained down, mercilessly pummeling Eren and the others. Nevertheless, fighting against the tremors, Eren slowly got to his feet. Because he wanted to understand what was going on, because he wanted to be aware of the circumstances in which he had been placed, he looked up at the wall.

Then Eren saw it.

He saw that it wasn't just regular pebbles falling upon them, but pieces of the wall, and that there was a strange mist mixed into the clouds of dust, rising—from *it*. He realized that the thick, log-like object that clung to the top of the wall was unmistakably a *finger*. And that the finger belonged to—

"A Titan," Eren murmured.

It was a real Titan, peering out over the top of the fifty-yard wall. The make of its huge face was so abominable that it seemed like the embodiment of terror itself. Forgetting even to run, Eren was petrified by its unnatural presence. The Titan's skinless face was covered in red, sinewy, muscle-like flesh. The surface pulsed and spewed white steam every few seconds. Its expression—if it could even be called an expression—was savage, fiercely enraged. Its pupils gleamed hauntingly under its deeply creased brow. With the Titan's every movement, pieces of the wall crumbled beneath its hand and fell around Eren and the others.

If Eren had never been taught of the existence of Titans and was instead told that the creature was a god descended from above to end the world, he would have easily believed it. A level of fear he'd never felt before devoured him. His blood stopped flowing to the tips of his hands and feet, and his limbs began to go numb. Again, the roar. The rumbling that felt like it would split open the earth. The downpour of the wall. Eren lost his balance.

"Wh-What is it doing?" Armin said weakly as he stared up at the Titan. Tears welled in his eyes.

"That thing…" Souda said. "The wall… It's kicking the wall… It's trying to break it down."

Eren and his friends stared at Souda, speechless.

"Run," Souda said without taking his eyes off the Titan. "Run, now."

"Wh-Where?" Armin's voice was no more than a whisper.

"Anywhere! If the wall falls, nowhere within the First Wall District will be safe. Make your way to Monzen and then towards the Second Wall, with all you've got! Get as far away from the First Wall as you can! Right now you just need to run, no matter what!"

"H-How many miles do you think there are to the Second Wall?"

"It doesn't matter, go."

"What are you going to do, old man?" Eren asked.

"As long as my strength lasts…" Souda stared at the foot of the wall. "All I can do is fight, isn't it? As hard as I can. Now go!"

Urging Mikasa forward, Eren and Armin began to run. Staggering against the great quakes created by the Titan, they slipped through the gap in the wire net and ran towards Monzen. They ran, and ran, and ran across the ground. They didn't have time to catch their breath, or to exchange any words. With their sights set on the Second Wall in the north, they just ran.

Souda left the wall and hurried towards the base.

As he got farther from the wall (and the Titan) the hot wind gradually faded away, and the light from the sun that had been blocked by the Titan's head returned. Still, the ground continued to shake violently every few seconds. By the time Souda reached the roof of the Garrison base, most of the soldiers were already preparing the guns for battle. Five soldiers flocked around each of the thirty-six cannons on the roof. Their hands shook, and their shouts swelled with confusion and terror.

Despite all the training they had undergone, they had no actual combat experience. Most of the soldiers had already prepared themselves for the end. Their faces were pale.

When Souda reached his assigned Squad 3-2 post, he found its leader, Kunugi, who had enlisted the same year, twenty years ago.

"Kunugi," Souda said, his voice breathless and rough. "That thing is breaking the—"

"I know," interrupted Kunugi, rubbing his sallow cheek. His forehead was shining with sweat. "Once the guns are loaded, we're aiming at the head and firing in unison. You too, stand ready. I already sent a messenger squad back to the main force… Man, what a monster. I guess it was a lie that they only grow to fifty feet. We underestimated."

Again, the earth shook.

The base, which was supposed to be sturdy, shook so hard that the joints in the guns grated and creaked. Souda could see the Titan's face much more clearly from the roof. He watched as it gripped the top of the wall with both hands and glared menacingly at the Garrison base. Souda took a nervous gulp as the Titan made its next move. It leaned back farther than before, preparing to kick the wall again. Its fingers clamped down on the wall.

It was coming.

The impact sounded like an explosion—it was different from before. A whirlwind reached all the way to the base. Souda gripped his firearm as the gusts passed. For at least ten seconds, the whirling explosion of fine sand and pieces of wall pummeled the base. When the force of the blast died down and Souda could finally see the wall, he was speechless.

Countless cracks spread across the base, and an uncanny light leaked through them. The wall was reportedly thirty feet thick, and the Titan had nearly destroyed it. Souda already believed it: *This is the end.*

Again, the Titan gripped the wall with its fingertips. It knew it had succeeded, but its expression didn't change; there was no triumphant grin, no softening of relief on its face. As its pulsing red muscles spewed steam, dispassionately, as if delivering a verdict on mankind, it moved.

The final swing.

The din of ruin.

Pieces of the wall went flying.

Souda crouched in the shadow of their gun to protect his body. It was no longer just pebbles, but rocks bigger than cannonballs that came flying. The wind raged. Several enormous rocks crashed into the Garrison base, one onto the gun right beside him. Some pieces even flew right over the base to mercilessly pummel Monzen. Souda saw pillars of black smoke rise up immediately from the town. He clenched his teeth at the calamity, and when he was sure the debris had passed, he turned around.

Kunugi, who had already gotten to his feet, was training his trembling gaze on one spot.

Souda looked.

There was a hole in the wall.

It was at least thirty feet high. Glaring sunlight shone through from the other side. The Titan that had made the hole was nowhere to be seen. It had disappeared, leaving only faint vapors as proof that it had been there. The word "Jaeger" flitted across Souda's mind for a second, but he'd think about that later. Souda, the wall, and mankind stood on the brink here and now.

"Troops! Aim all remaining guns at that hole!" the commander of the Monzen Garrison Regiment rallied the soldiers, who appeared to have lost their fighting spirit. They knew that he was only trying to preserve his dignity as commander and saw how he was shaking too hard to fix his eyes on anything.

"If the Titans come charging in…"

The base commander's words simply vanished without leaving a flicker of hope. The light streaming in through the hole had grown weaker.

It was time.

Tremors came from somewhere.

Each and every soldier understood.

They were here. The tremors were their footsteps.

It wasn't long before the first Titan became visible.

"What is that?" Kunugi blurted from beside Souda.

As if passing through a gate, the first Titan bowed its head slightly as it emerged from the hole. It looked very different from the Titan that had been kicking the wall. This one had a skin covering, if sickly and pale. Though its body resembled that of a human apart from its size, its arms were too long (on a human they would stretch to the knees), and its grotesque facial features were distorted. The corners of its mouth angled up as if it was smiling, but its pupils wandered aimlessly, and it was impossible to discern any coherent expression on its face. Its head was too large for its body and bobbed unevenly from right to left with every step. There was no sign of genitalia between its legs; dry skin stretched continuously over its entire body. It stood thirty feet high. While much smaller than the sixty-yard Titan that had been taller than the wall, the presence it exerted was more than enough to instill fear in mankind. The more the soldiers looked at it, the more they were consumed by a terror of the unknown.

"S-Squad 2-2! Prepare to fire!" a voice rose from the group on Souda's right. "Fire!"

They fired.

The rooftop shook. The first cannonball to be released cut through the wind with a buzz and headed straight for the Titan's head—it was a direct hit.

"Yes!!"

Cries of elation rose up from the Garrison. The head of the Titan was completely destroyed. Strangely, the Titan remained standing, but they could only conclude that it had been killed. Only the lower jaw remained of the head; the top had been blown off.

It collapsed.

They could do it. There was no reason to despair.

Before they could relax, however, a second and a third Titan emerged through the wall. The second Titan had a body that was somehow reminiscent of a woman. It was about thirty feet tall, with a slender waist, a thinner build, and terribly ugly features. Its eyes were practically next to its nostrils, and much bigger than those of a human. The third Titan was about twenty feet tall, but had a solid, rather well-toned body. Saliva dribbled steadily out of its large, sloppy mouth.

The loaded cannons began to fire at the two Titans. Souda's squad began to fire as well. The rooftop shook violently as they bombarded the monsters. White smoke rose from their bodies where they were hit, and shouts of delight, almost akin to anger, erupted amongst the soldiers.

Then something strange happened.

In an instant, the soldiers fell silent.

The headless Titan slowly began to walk.

Its thunderous footfalls echoed as if to drum up the soldiers' despair. White steam wafted up from its lower jaw, and as if rising up with the vapor, the Titan's face slowly but surely started to restore itself. It was almost like studying the makeup of life. Bone-like material formed out of the steam, and then the muscle tissue began to emerge, and finally, the skin. Moisture returned to its eyes, and hard teeth grew into its mouth.

It was the same with the other two Titans that should have been destroyed. Every part of their bodies miraculously regenerated and resumed functioning as if nothing had happened.

"So it's true... They don't die," a young soldier said, tears flowing from his eyes. "Th-There's nothing we can do..."

Four more Titans poured in through the wall. One of them trampled the wire barricade with incredible ease and started towards the heart of Monzen. If they continued towards town, the base artillery would no longer be able to reach them, and there was no other way to fight them.

Six more Titans came pouring in through the hole. The barrage continued, but with no sign of any success. Even after a direct hit, the Titans continued to advance step by step, growing closer and closer. Finally, one Titan came right up to the Garrison base. From somewhere came the sound of a pistol. The Titan hadn't been shot. A soldier had killed himself.

As the monster approached, its immense size was palpable.

Even though Souda was on the roof, he stood eye level with it. Compared to the other soldiers, he thought he was far more prepared, having lived his entire life for this very day. There was something he had to do, and his heart was ready to sacrifice everything for it. And yet—

He was afraid. Souda was scared because the Titan standing before him was the avatar of fear itself.

When the Titan finally came within a few yards, its throat could be heard emitting a voice. Though the groan could not be mistaken for "words," the timber was exceedingly close to a human's. It sounded eerily like it was laughing or mumbling to itself. A pungent, sour odor similar to that of vomit floated from its mouth.

The guns fired at point-blank range, aiming for its chest.

But it had nary an effect on the Titan, which slowly lifted its right hand and grabbed a soldier from two cannons over. Like a baby grabbing a toy, without hesitation, without care, it squeezed.

The soldier struggled to escape but could only move his arms. His comrades nearby frantically fired their pistols to try and rescue him, but to no avail. The monster brought its right hand to its mouth and chomped on the soldier. As if to show them, it chewed, dutifully and deliberately.

A scream echoed off of the wall.

Nobody could stop them. Souda lost count of the number of Titans that had made it past the wall. He didn't know how many surrounded the base, how many soldiers had been preyed upon, or how to understand any of it.

Souda apologized silently.

I'm sorry. There's something that I simply have to do. I know that I can't be forgiven for it no matter how much I apologize. I'm really sorry. But I have to accomplish this.

Ignoring Kunugi's calls to stand his ground, Souda abandoned his comrades and his post.

Eren looked over his shoulder again and again as he ran through the weeds that stretched to Monzen. The fourth time he turned around, there was an opening in the wall. Huge chunks of stone crashed down around him and his friends. Armin fell over, stunned, and had to be coaxed back to his feet, but otherwise they were unharmed by the debris. They continued to run. The seventh time Eren looked back, the Titans had made it through the wall. Eren and the others shuddered at the grotesque sight, but following Souda's advice, they continued to run. Or rather, it was impossible *not* to run from the Titans and their otherworldly presence.

By the time Eren and his friends reached the edge of Monzen, the town was in a state of utter chaos. Some people were grabbing their belongings, some were fleeing with only the clothes on their backs, and some were unable to do anything but watch hopelessly as the Titans approached from the wall. Screams, children crying, adults cursing—even the ordinarily deserted streets on the outskirts were crowded with people.

"It's out of the way, but we should take the back road on the east side."

Adopting Armin's plan they abandoned the street that passed through the town and circled around instead.

The eastern back road was slightly easier to run on than the main street, but still far more crowded than usual. Bumping into people, Eren and his friends called out to each other every time they nearly lost sight of one another. Breathlessly, bruising and scratching their limbs, they continued on.

Still, *it* came.

They had run halfway through Monzen on the far eastern side when they felt the quakes—a Titan's footsteps.

Eren could see it standing near the town entrance. It was too far away for him to catch all the details, but the Titan was very plump and had a squashed nose. It held in its mouth something like a cigar. No—it wasn't a cigar, but someone's leg. As his eyes adjusted, he could make it out. Dangling between the monster's teeth was a human leg still wearing its shoe.

"E-Eren…"

"Don't look, Armin."

The color drained further from Armin's naturally pale visage. Though Mikasa was trying not to let her fear show, she was clearly shaken. Eren could hardly think straight, either.

He looked around to find that the Titans were increasing in number. Three, four…six… No, there were too many. Everywhere in Monzen, as if they were plucking pieces of grain from the ground, the Titans tossed humans into their mouths.

"S-Sorry, Eren, Mikasa," Armin said, his pupils drowning in fear. "I-I have to go to my house. I'm worried about everyone."

"Hey, Armin!" Eren shouted, but his friend had already taken off.

Armin's house was adjacent to the canola oil shop and right in the town's central shopping district. Though Eren wasn't sure, it seemed like a dense area would be much harder to evacuate. He bit his lip and prayed for Armin's safety but continued along their original route with Mikasa.

Yet, the more time passed, the more Monzen began to resemble hell. Corpses lay unceremoniously on the road. Sometimes it was just a detached arm or leg, leftovers most likely. Clean fingertips and hands that looked like they might start moving ended in torn, splintered stumps stained an all-too-vivid red. A rotten smell began to fill the air, but of course, flesh didn't spoil so quickly. His own fear had summoned the stench, Eren told himself.

"Let's check out your house, too. It's on the way to the Second Wall."

When Mikasa agreed, Eren veered to the left. He had no family, but Mikasa's parents, who lived in their weaving studio, always took good care of him. Eren, himself, was concerned for them.

They ducked into a narrow alley and turned right, but as they took a left at the next corner—

Their feet stopped.

Their breathing stopped, too.

In an instant, Eren's body temperature dropped a few degrees.

The Titan's sickly, pale back stretched up farther than they could see. A gaunt pillar, its gigantic spine, shot up before them. Torn limbs and crushed skulls lay scattered at its feet. Eren felt his bile rising along with his fear.

Today wasn't his lucky day.

Soon enough, the Titan's hunched back began to squirm, and perhaps sensing Eren and Mikasa's presence, the monster turned around. It stood thirty feet tall, and when its eyes fell upon Eren and Mikasa, it swallowed what it had been holding—some unfortunate victim's severed lower half—and took a heavy step toward them. In place of crumbs, blood covered its chin. The corners of its mouth, angled up, hinted at a smile.

"R-Run, Mikasa!"

They rushed back the way they came. Crashing into other people who were also trying to escape, they chose the narrowest alley they could find in the hopes that the Titan wouldn't be able to follow. While its steps were powerful and loud, they weren't very fast. Yet, no doubt because they'd been running the whole time, Mikasa's pace began to slow. Eren gripped her hand and pulled her along. *Keep going, hurry,* he encouraged her.

"I-I'm done. Go without me."

"…Never say anything so stupid again."

They kept running. Before long, they saw a brick dining hall down the road. The spacious restaurant served bland potato dishes, and Eren had eaten there once before. He usually ignored the place because its fare was so poor, but today was different. Monzen was mostly filled with wooden buildings, so the brick edifice was a viable refuge. The Titan probably wouldn't be able to get to them if they went into that building.

When Eren turned around, he saw that the Titan was much farther behind than he expected. It had become distracted by all the people and slowed down to eat them. At this rate, it wouldn't reach them if they dashed to the building. Heartened, Eren squeezed Mikasa's hand and stepped up their pace.

As they closed in on the dining hall, they saw that dozens of people were already inside. Apparently, everyone had had the same thought. Even as Eren and Mikasa sprinted, more people were running towards the brick building, and in no time the crowd formed a rapid of bodies. Soon the surge engulfed them, and Eren almost lost his grip on Mikasa's hand.

"Don't let go!" Eren yelled. "We have to keep going until we slide in there!"

He heard Mikasa say something.

"What?!"

"A child."

Sure enough, at the end of Mikasa's gaze, just a few yards away from the flow of people, a girl of about four or five stood alone. Though she was so still it seemed as if her soul had already left her, she was certainly alive. If the girl stayed where she was, she would definitely end up devoured by the Titan. Eren wavered for a moment but couldn't ignore Mikasa's concern.

Without letting go of their hands, Eren and Mikasa struggled against the torrent of people and somehow reached the spot where the girl stood. Mikasa put an arm around the shoulder of the exhausted young girl, who drifted towards the dining hall with them like a ghost. Eren breathed a sigh of relief just as the earth-shaking rumble of footsteps started again from behind—it was the Titan.

"Hurry! We have to get in!" Gripping Mikasa's hand, Eren dove into the flood and pushed anew towards the dining hall. Far more people were hiding in the building than before. Easily over a hundred were crammed in there. Jostled by the crowd, Eren prayed that there would be space left for them somehow.

Then it happened.

Eren felt intense pressure from his right and lost his grip on Mikasa's hand.

"M-Mikasa!"

"Here!"

Through the din, he could faintly hear Mikasa's voice. He couldn't see her, though. He looked for her in a panic, but the people behind him mercilessly pushed forward. There was more pressure from the right, and pushback from the left. He searched, whirling around, for Mikasa, but couldn't find her. Again he was pushed forward. He heard something collapse. Then the building's entrance was right in front of him.

"Mikasa!"

There was no answer. Eren tried to stay in the doorway but couldn't hold up against the swelling waves. The Titan's footsteps grew louder. Then, what sounded like a powerful explosion came from behind Eren, and he lost his balance. He pitched forward, his vision swiveled to the ground, and he fell. He did so on his knees, and the sharp pain ran all the way up to his shoulders. He closed his eyes and clenched his teeth through the torment.

He heard a dry sound—*klack*. Eren popped his eyes open. He was already inside of the dining room, right in the middle.

Holding his knees, Eren slowly got to his feet and surveyed his surroundings. While the spacious hall contained twenty or so tables, people were crammed in so tightly that they couldn't even raise their arms. Eren had fallen into a small pocket near the entrance and was apparently one of the last to get inside. On the large door was an equally large latch, and it was already firmly barred shut.

"We can fit more people if we squeeze!" somebody shouted from the back.

"It's too late! Don't you dare open that door," someone else said.

"I don't want to die, I don't want to die," another person murmured.

"Mikasa!"

There was no answer.

"Mikasa!"

Still, no answer. Instead came the Titan's earth-shaking footsteps. Eren shouted at the top of his lungs.

"Mikasa!"

It couldn't be. With a horrible feeling in his gut, he peered out through a tiny crack in the door planks. Just outside, several people who hadn't made it in lay on the street. The Titan was right behind them. Eren could only see its legs through the crack. Some of the people were praying, some had fainted, and some sat quietly as if they had accepted their fate. And amongst them—

"Please, no…"

He saw Mikasa. She was crouched as if she'd injured her leg. She looked dead tired, and her shoulders moved heavily as she breathed. It looked as if she, too, had resigned herself to her impending doom. Her expression was dry, almost stoic.

"Mikasa! Stand! Stand up!"

Their eyes met, but Mikasa made no motion to get to her feet. The Titan took another step towards her.

"O-Okay! I'm coming!" Eren hastily tried to dislodge the bar but was held back by a man right behind him.

"Hey, what are you doing, you idiot?!"

"P-Please!" Eren shouted, desperately attempting to break free. "M-Mikasa is still there! Please! Once I bring her in, I'll shut the door right away!"

"H-Hey, calm down! The Titan is right outside! It's too late!"

"You've got to be joking! Please! Let me go!"

Before long, others who saw Eren as a threat grouped together to hold him down. He managed to stay on his feet and twisted to try to shake off their grips. Through the crack, he saw the Titan's legs coming to a halt right beside Mikasa.

"Stop! Stop! Mikasa!"

A few seconds later, indifferently, as if picking up a piece of trash, the Titan plucked Mikasa's paralyzed body. Its hand and her body disappeared from Eren's view.

He screamed.

He screamed as if to sunder his own throat. He screamed so many things he couldn't even understand what he was saying. But it didn't matter what he said; his words fell on deaf ears, failed to touch anyone's heart, and merely rattled the walls of the hall. Eventually, the other evacuees threw him on the floor and held him there.

Pinned down, Eren heard a huge crash. He winced as vibrations spread up through the floorboards.

What happened after that felt like events in a faraway world. Everything seemed bleached of reality, as if he were floating through another dimension. After the sound faded, the people holding him down slowly removed their hands and began to gaze through the windows and the cracks in the door to search for its source. It seemed the Titan was gone. They couldn't hear its footsteps.

Noticing that his fellow evacuees had quieted down, Eren lifted the bar from the door and stumbled outside. He heard it being frantically refastened behind him. As if some invisible force were tugging at him, Eren tottered to where Mikasa had been squatting until just a moment ago.

There was no sign of Mikasa, or her clothes or her scarf. Only a large pool of bright red blood remained. Eren felt all the strength leaving his body. One by one, every cell in his muscles withered away, his blood went cold, and his breathing ceased, everything thawing into nothing, or so he felt.

Then, from behind him came a deafening noise and screams. He turned around to see—without even the energy to be surprised—a new Titan.

It had ripped the roof from the dining hall where Eren had been hiding and was vigorously shoveling the crammed humans into its mouth. Blood and body parts splattered all over. Unable even to scream, Eren began to stagger away.

Souda's words replayed in his head—*Make your way to Monzen and then towards the Second Wall, with all you've got!*

Run. Run.

As if he were trying to forget something, and to forsake everything, Eren began to run.

Two Years Later

II. THE GATES OF HELL

The soldiers, ninety-seven in all, stood in a line.

The blazing sun reflected aggressively against their faces as if to spear them. It was a windless, clear day.

They couldn't ask for better weather for their departure.

A man ambled towards the podium at the center of the stage. He wore the black uniform and leather boots of the Public Order Administration (commonly referred to as "the Military Police"). As he climbed the stairs, his firm footsteps echoed amongst the soldiers. When he reached the podium, he cleared his throat once as if to test the crowd. Then he opened his mouth. As his appearance suggested, he had a deep and impressive voice.

"We paid for our long peace with a calamity."

A stern expression sat upon his already deeply etched face, and he exuded an aura of absolute vigilance. Though his head was covered in closely cropped white hair, he gave no impression of being advanced in age or past his prime. Rather, "experienced" was the more fitting description.

"As you all know, after the invasion of the 'Colossal Titan,' we lost our agricultural 'First Wall District.' Our crisis management back then was utterly incapable of coping with an unexpected Titan, and the monsters did as they pleased. As a result, refugees from the First Wall District, deprived of their homes, migrated here to the commercial Second Wall District. The First Wall District was a major breadbasket responsible for seven tenths of humanity's food supply. The shortage only continues to worsen today, and the emergency stores in the final Third Wall District will soon be exhausted."

Public Order Administration Supervisor Kubal paused for a moment before continuing. "Taking back the First Wall District that was stolen from us is not only our greatest wish, but also our duty. Hence this Outer Wall Restoration Operation… Unfortunately, all of the plans attempted in the past have ended in failure."

He sounded terribly bitter.

Eren glanced to his side to find a uniformed Armin clenching his jaw and locking his eyes onto Kubal in what was almost a glare. Eren understood Armin's pain well, so without saying anything, without disturbing the formation, he quietly faced forward again.

Eren thought about the journey to this day—the path he'd walked with Armin after losing Mikasa.

Miraculously, Eren and Armin had survived the tragedy in Monzen two years earlier. An evacuation vehicle from the Garrison base scooped Eren up, and Armin and his grandfather were picked up by another one from the Second Wall District. They managed to cheat death.

The population of Monzen had been about fifty thousand, but

the survivors, including Eren and Armin, numbered only a few hundred. The main force of the Survey Corps, who were the only ones capable of taking on the Titans, had been out on a westward expedition, and in their absence the dead multiplied rapidly. The victims of the Titans were officially filed as missing persons, but most of them would never return.

During the Titans' assault, the government decided to abandon the First Wall District, pulling back human territory to the Second Wall. A staggering five hundred thousand refugees from the First Wall District relocated to the Second Wall District, already host to a roughly comparable number of people. Having lost its prime agricultural region, humanity was short on food reserves.

The emergency stores in the innermost Third Wall District were being distributed, but they were not enough. And so, the government made its decision. Two hundred thousand of the refugees from the First Wall District were drafted, starting with older men whose future prospect as laborers was limited. As part of what was named the First Wall Reclamation Operation, they were sent towards the First Wall District where the Titans still swarmed. Though the operation had a grand name, everybody understood that it was nothing more than a way to cut down on mouths to feed. They weren't entrusted with any strategy to speak of, let alone decent gear. Nobody, however, could stop it. The reality was that without such a sacrifice, all of mankind would be wiped out by the food shortage. Everybody just watched, taciturn and close-lipped, as the two hundred thousand marched away towards certain death. Armin's grandfather was among them.

Armin's parents hadn't survived the Titans' onslaught, and his grandfather had been his only remaining family. Leaving just his favorite green tulip hat to his grandson, he disappeared off to the First Wall District that had been his home. Armin had watched in silence, tears spilling from his eyes. Afterward, the government forced most of the suitably aged refugees like him and Eren to cultivate the Second Wall District's mountainous region in the west. The western reaches supposedly had arable land, albeit a small amount. Upon arriving, however, they saw that the area was no more than a sparse forest.

The cultivation work was extremely difficult. Every day, Eren and Armin had to perform hellish manual labor, but in some ways, work felt almost like good fortune to the two of them, who were still reeling from despair and sorrow. They didn't have to think too much. Still, sometimes Eren became hopelessly lost in his head. He thought about his own powerlessness when he'd lost Mikasa, about how he hadn't been able to do anything, and about the cause of it all: the Titans. His various thoughts bred targets for his resentment and rocked him.

Meanwhile, the government began to put together a repair and recovery operation for the First Wall in earnest, unlike with the previous operation. Based on reports brought back by the precious few remnants of the Reclamation Operation, they planned a 1st Outer Wall Restoration Operation. About a thousand people were selected, mainly from the elite Survey Corps, to rebuild the barrier using explosives. The attempt, however, failed before it got going. Attacked by far more Titans than expected on the way to Monzen, the forces were decimated. Only a few dozen soldiers, led by the Survey Corps Second Unit Captain, Haku, returned. The operation was deemed a complete disaster. News of the failure spread throughout humanity's territory overnight, plunging it into deep disappointment and hopelessness.

In response to losing more soldiers than expected to the 1st Outer Wall Restoration Operation, the government ordered an emergency recruitment. News of it reached even the Hodo District where Eren and Armin were engaged in their cultivation project, and they applied to join almost immediately. There were many reasons, but the main one was that they hated the Titans from the bottom of their hearts. Another was that the work assigned to them felt utterly meaningless. Even if they completed it as instructed, it would only produce a trivial amount of food. No matter how they looked at it, it wouldn't be enough for the entire human population, and Eren and Armin understood that well.

Eren didn't think that Armin, hardly athletic or resilient, was cut out to be a soldier, and tried fervently to stop him from enlisting. But Armin didn't buckle. For his parents, and for his grandfather, he felt he needed to step up. Sensing his friend's fierce determination, Eren formally submitted his own enlistment papers as well.

Perhaps because there were more applicants than the government expected, a simple exam was administered. It signaled a strong will on the government's part to seek only superior soldiers for the reliable recapture of the wall, but also an impression that they lacked the means to retain so many troops. For the human race, it was only a matter of time before equipment and food stores ran out.

Armin somehow passed the enlistment test despite his subpar physique, probably thanks to his daily hard labor. In the end, there were 111 recruits in Eren and Armin's class, mainly refugees who had escaped the First Wall District.

The training was extremely harsh. The days that followed vividly impressed upon them that their hellish cultivation work had been undemanding in comparison. Supply runs, close combat, strategy lectures, mechanical skills, and vertical maneuvering techniques—all ways of fighting the Titans were thoroughly drilled into the recruits. Though as soldiers they were given a limitless supply of food, it wasn't rare for a day to go by where only water passed through their throats.

As their training neared the half-year point, the government planned a 2nd Outer Wall Restoration Operation. In order to enhance their anti-Titan capabilities based on lessons from the first expedition, they assembled a troop of five hundred including some recruits who had mastered the Vertical Maneuvering Equipment. Twenty people from the new class who showed aptitude would be participating as logistics personnel, but not Eren or Armin.

The operation failed again.

Though the force reached the hole in Monzen, it was routed, unable to hold off the Titans while it attempted to restore the wall. The explosives were lost too. All of the recruits from Eren's year were killed, of course, and the only survivors were the de facto commander of the Survey Corps at the time, Shikishima, and a mere five of his subordinates. Eren and the others grieved for the loss of their classmates but also took their own mission to heart. The deaths needed to be avenged, by themselves. The training sessions only grew more solemn.

By the time they reached the prescribed one-year mark, in addition to the twenty who had lost their lives in the operation, sixteen had either quit or died in accidents during training. Eren's class size had dwindled to seventy-five. Though almost everybody excelled in some field—Jean at vertical maneuvering, Lil at close combat, Sannagi at brute strength, and Armin at strategy—Eren managed to score well in all of them.

And today, almost a month after their graduation—

"This *3rd* Outer Wall Restoration Operation will be carried out by a troop of 102 soldiers including the advance detachment," Kubal continued with a spirited voice. "I hear that some of you have only just completed your training, but you are already proper soldiers. We are expecting a valiant effort that will honor the spirits of the fallen."

Originally, soldiers had been divided into three groups: the Military Police Brigade (the Public Order Administration) that maintained peace within the wall, the Garrison Regiment (the Security Department) that protected the wall itself from the Titans' intrusion, and the Survey Corps (the Extramural Investigation Department) that made repeated research forays into the world beyond the wall.

The Survey Corps, however, had lost many of its numbers to past operations and was virtually defunct. These days, all Outer Wall Restoration Operation personnel were considered "survey corpsmen" as a matter of convenience. On the backs and shoulders of Eren and his classmates' uniforms were embroidered the Wings of Liberty signifying their affiliation with the corps. A pair of wings, bright white and dark blue, spread wide—the symbol of freedom.

"I will go over the substance of this operation."

The voice belonged to Hange, a squad leader with the arms development section who stood on the left side of the stage. Lifting to her forehead the goggles that she always wore, she placed a pointer rod on the large map that was pinned up behind her. The soldiers' gazes focused on it.

"This expedition is basically similar to the past two." Hange indicated the town of Monzen located at the southern edge of the map. "Here, we will close up the hole, about forty feet in diameter, in Monzen's outer wall. In order to do that, we will use explosives to blow up the portion of the wall above the hole. The part we explode will slide down and close the gap like a gate. That section of the wall will be lower, of course, but still be about forty yards high. The Titans should not be able to come through. Of course, it will be a different story if we are attacked again by the Colossal Titan…" She cleared her throat. "Excuse me. Cracks have already been created at even intervals on the wall to ensure that an appropriate portion comes down during the explosion, an achievement of the 2nd Outer Wall Restoration Operation. Therefore there's no need to bore them in the wall during this operation. However…"

Hange tapped her rod at a spot slightly north of Monzen.

"For this expedition, you will need to acquire explosives at a relay point between the Second Wall's southern gate and Monzen, at a place called Omotemachi. A defense facility exists there from the Old Government Era, and we've obtained intelligence that a modest store of explosives sleeps in its basement. The Omotemachi route was, as you know, used by the past two expeditions and has relatively few Titans. Furthermore, this time, five elite soldiers led by Captain Shikishima will sortie first, deploy vertical maneuvers, and clear out any bogeys. There shouldn't be a single Titan left by the time the rest of us depart. Of course, it is better to be safe than sorry. Take the utmost caution while traveling."

The soldiers quietly agreed.

Collapsing the pointer, Hange turned away from the map to face her audience. Her long hair, gathered in the back, fluttered in the wind. "The departure will take place at sunset when Titan activity dwindles to a minimum. Until then, each of you should get some proper rest. Supervisor Kubal."

Kubal gave a slight nod when Hange turned toward him.

"I'm sure you all understand very clearly the current state of the human race," Kubal resumed with even more vigor than before. "In the First Wall Reclamation Operation, we lost 198,604 people; for the 1st Outer Wall Restoration Operation, a thousand and sixteen; for the 2nd Outer Wall Restoration Operation, four hundred and ninety-one. Until now, we have lost so many yet entirely failed in our mission. I don't like to sugarcoat. We will undoubtedly lose a significant number of lives on this upcoming expedition as well. Many of your comrades will fall prey to the Titans. However, you must go on. We are going to secure mankind's future, as well as true peace. Ladies and gentlemen!"

Kubal clenched his right hand into a fist and hit it firmly on the left side of his chest.

"Commit your hearts!"

The soldiers, too, thumped their fists over their hearts with evident conviction.

"Aye!"

Their valiant reply echoed far and wide.

"Make sure to come back, okay?"

"Don't worry. It will go well."

Through the chain-link border of the camp, soldiers exchanged their goodbyes, some with family, some with lovers, some with friends. Believing it wasn't the last time they would see each other, but preparing for the worst somewhere deep in their hearts, they haltingly and tenderly chose their words.

While Eren walked on the path towards the dining room he couldn't help but watch. He saw many of his classmates. Jean was conversing with somebody who looked like his father. Perhaps embarrassed, or perhaps because they simply didn't get along, Jean's attitude seemed cold. His father spoke words of encouragement almost like he was jeering while banging on the chain-link.

Sasha, too, exchanged words with her parents. A while back, she'd said something to the effect that she hadn't been raised by her real parents, but Eren couldn't remember for certain. Sasha bowed deeply and wiped the tears from her eyes.

Eren looked down for a moment before continuing to walk.

Sannagi, the biggest guy from their class, was saying goodbye to his five brothers and sisters. The kids looked to be much younger than him. Perhaps they weren't his real siblings. When the youngest sister passed a hand-made doll through the chain-link fence, Sannagi gave a carefree laugh and stared at the doll. It must have been made to look like Sannagi because it was fairly fat. It grasped his features well.

Eren sighed.

He saw Hiana too. With a poignant expression, she was holding the hand of what looked like a newborn baby—her daughter. A woman who looked as if she might be from a nursing facility held the infant and nodded deeply at the mother without saying a word. Hiana returned the gesture.

Eren screwed his eyes shut before looking out at an area beyond the fence where there should have been no one.

He found Mikasa.

Looking just as she had that day, she stood watching Eren's departure with a solemn expression. He silently imparted some words to the unchanged Mikasa on the other side of the fence.

Finally, it's time. The weak boy who couldn't protect you is gone. I'm strong now. I don't pretend to be avenging you, but I'll be fighting for you too. Please believe in me. We'll make this operation a success. Then, together, we can go home to Monzen.

With a faint nod, Mikasa disappeared from the other side of the chain-link fence. Eren sighed once more and slowly began to walk.

Six transport trucks were parked for their final tune-up right next to the dining hall. Eren saw Armin beside one of the vehicles.

"What are you doing here?"

"Ah, Eren." Armin looked up. "Since I don't have anyone to say goodbye to anyway, I thought I might as well check the fuel for the trucks."

"Fuel?"

"Yeah." Nodding, Armin opened the tank on the truck. "The expiration date of canola oil, a.k.a. biodiesel fuel, is approximately three months from when it's pressed. Any longer than that and it's not usable. So it's a little weird... Canola crops were only grown in the abandoned First Wall District, so it shouldn't be possible to harvest any now. But this truck's fuel tank is completely full."

How like Armin to be suspicious about it, Eren thought. "There was probably an emergency supply of canola in the Third Wall District."

"Right." Armin nodded reluctantly. "But…rubber is soluble in canola oil, so any time you use any, the rubber should begin to deteriorate. The rubber on this truck hasn't deteriorated at all. And rubber is such a high-demand item and hard to replace…" Armin stopped speaking and glanced around as if to check his surroundings. "Eren… Honestly, what do you think of this operation?"

"What do I think?"

"As for me, Eren," Armin dropped his voice, "I honestly think this operation is a little *weird*." As if he felt someone watching him, he began to walk. "I'll explain in the dining room. Let's go."

Eren tilted his head doubtfully but followed his friend.

Though it was called a dining room, in reality, it was a makeshift structure constructed for the camp, and no more than a tent.

After Eren and Armin received helpings of mashed potatoes and a simple soup, they sat in an area that was dominated by their own classmates.

"So for this operation, we're set to pick up a supply of explosives from Omotemachi, just midway between Monzen and our point of departure, the southern gate," Armin spoke in a hushed voice as he ate. "That means that there are *no explosives whatsoever* within the Second Wall, and that we humans are *not able* to manufacture more explosives. Otherwise, there would be no reason to go through the trouble of restocking explosives in the Titans' habitat."

Eren nodded.

"Which means," Armin continued, his expression darkened with anxiety, "this 3rd Outer Wall Restoration Operation is basically the Final Operation. There are no more explosives. We can't make more.

So if we fail, that's the end for humans. No 4th Outer Wall Restoration Operation will ever be planned."

Eren gulped silently so Armin wouldn't notice. *If we fail, that's the end for humans.*

Armin went on. "This expedition, compared to the last two, has too few soldiers. Of course, I understand that we lost a lot of personnel previously. But—and this is just my own estimate—we should still have proficient combatants, three hundred with the Garrison, and close to a thousand in the Military Police. Why are just one hundred, mainly fresh recruits, being tasked with this? It's kind of a sad number to take on a final operation.

"I can't help but think it's a little strange, too, that we're being accompanied by Squad Leader Hange from Arms Development and Supervisor Kubal from the Military Police. Hange is purely a researcher, and Supervisor Kubal actually leads the Military Police. Both should be very important to humanity, and yet they're tagging along on such a dangerous expedition? Also, considering that we're based on the Survey Corps, why should the Military Police, a separate organization, be butting in? I doubt that Supervisor Kubal has front-line fighting skills. As for Squad Leader Hange's vertical maneuvering, from what we've seen, she just won't cut it in combat. Why this absurd assignment of—"

"Maybe you're just thinking about it too much."

Armin and Eren looked up towards the voice that came from right beside them. Hiana was chowing down placidly. With a calm expression on her face, she lifted a spoon to her mouth and slowly sipped her soup.

"I didn't mean to eavesdrop, sorry," she said coolly. "Since this might be your last meal, why don't you have a little more fun? Of course…"

Hiana's eyes settled upon Sasha, who was shoveling her heaped mashed potatoes into her mouth. Noticing three pairs of eyes on her, Sasha laughed in embarrassment and said, "What food shortage? I can have as many helpings as I want, ha ha."

"I wouldn't go that far," Hiana smiled bitterly, sipping another spoonful of soup. "But it's our privilege as soldiers. Why not eat as much as you can?"

Eren stared at his own plate for a few moments and shook his head. "No, I'm okay. We're finally about to fight the Titans… I wouldn't want to be unable to move because my stomach is too full."

"You're already full of yourself!"

Eren's eyebrows twitched at the familiar, sarcastic voice. "Did you say something?" he asked.

"Yeah, I'm saying you're full of yourself." Turning around in his seat to face Eren, the speaker, Jean, crossed his legs defiantly. "Our job is to *plug up the hole*, and you're just skipping right to *fighting the Titans*. Don't get ahead of yourself."

"Even if we do plug up the hole, the Titans inside the First Wall will have to be cleared out. Maybe I got the sequence wrong, but it's the same thing. We'll need to fight Titans."

"That sequence is important, okay? The problem is that you're too eager to die. If you're going to kick the bucket, go ahead and do it, you idiot. Just don't get in our way. Your vertical maneuvering scores are way lower than mine, all you've got is enthusiasm."

Eren's irritation slowly made him rise to his feet. Armin and Hiana tried to stop him, but everyone in their class already knew that it was too late. "If vertical maneuvers are all about going on and on about the equipment's composition, then I can't compete with you, Jean. So survive with just the clothes on your back and hope the Military Police recruits you. Little inlander, never seen a Titan before in your life…"

"Okay, okay, I'm sorry," Jean said, getting to his feet and slowly closing in on Eren. "I've gotta prize your words, man." He smiled sardonically, flashing his teeth. "The words of a survivor, who escaped the Titans by abandoning a girl!"

Eren and Jean swung their good fists at each other's faces simultaneously. Both punches landed, and they quickly went for the second shot. They grabbed each other's collars—

"That's enough!"

"Hey! What are you doing?!"

Sannagi grabbed Jean's body and effortlessly pulled him from the fight, while Fukushi pinned Eren's arms behind his back.

"Eren, you calm down too."

"Let me go, Fukushi!"

His anger refusing to settle, Eren twisted and turned frantically to try to escape the hold. His right hand swung into the face of his restrainer, who gave a tiny groan. Eren had hit his right eye.

Eren regained his composure when he heard the whimper. Fukushi touched the area around his eye and then checked his hand to make sure he wasn't bleeding.

"I'm sorry, Fukushi."

Fukushi laughed gently and waved no. "It's okay. You just hit me lightly. Just, let it go now."

"It's always like this when it comes to you guys." Sannagi was also laughing. "Friendly fire before we set out is no joke." He smiled good-naturedly out at all the soldiers, who'd begun to stare at them. "It's over now and everything's okay. Sorry to alarm you."

The reproachful gazes began to fall away. Luckily, no one ranking higher than Private First Class was there, though they weren't all greenhorns. A superior officer would have harshly reprimanded the two. Eren took a deep breath to calm himself and started to return to his seat.

"Hey, Eren."

When he turned around he saw a cute, petite girl standing behind him—his classmate, Lil.

"What?"

"Fukushi got hurt because you had to go making a scene."

"Yes…I'm sorry."

"Well, I'm sure it's fine. Will you come here for a second?"

"Huh?"

"Just come on."

Confused, Eren took one step towards Lil, and then—

Her right hand shot out at his face and grabbed his mouth. At the same time, she yanked his right arm and threw off his center of gravity. *What's happening?* Before Eren could say, Lil lunged in at him. A blow shook his chin. Lil must have hit him with the base of her palm. *Uh, I'm going to fall.* The moment he thought that, Lil's left foot flashed over him, and Eren flew through the air. His body spun around and landed face up on the ground. His entire body felt the impact.

"Don't bring Fukushi into your stupid fights!" Lil hovered over Eren as she spoke. "If you and Jean want to act tough, why don't you wait until you're a little stronger than me?"

Accepting Armin's hand, Eren got to his feet and straightened his disheveled uniform as if to brush away his shame. Lil was already innocently sitting with her boyfriend, Fukushi, and talking about something. Though Lil seemed elegant and refined, when it came to Fukushi she turned into another person. Eren sighed and returned to his seat. *I just can't beat her. Someday I'm going to learn how she does that,* he swore as he sipped a spoonful of soup.

The cook brought over the pot. "Seconds?"

"I don't need any," Eren answered curtly.

"Come on now, none of that." The cook's voice was far too familiar. "Eat! Eat!" Uneasily, Eren looked up.

"It can't be…" He was astonished. "S-Souda!"

"Hey."

Even clad in a white cook's uniform, there was no mistaking him. It was none other than Souda. "You're alive!"

"I don't go down easy." Souda smiled smugly. "As you can see, I switched to the chow crew, but they somehow let me sign up for this operation. I did want to fly around in that Vertical Maneuvering Equipment like you guys… But they don't provide special gear to a feeble old fortysomething like me. It's age discrimination, I say."

Souda joyfully exchanged greetings with Armin as well, who joined in on the reunion.

"I heard about Mikasa," Souda said drily, probably in an attempt not to sound gloomy. "It was unfortunate… I'm glad the two of you survived, though."

Both Eren and Armin looked down soberly.

"And also…" Souda suddenly gave off a tense air. "This has to stay between us." His eyes shifted from right to left before he leaned in and whispered into their ears, "You really need *to be careful.*"

Armin and Eren immediately looked up at the man. However, he offered no further explanation and donned his previous smile.

"That's all I can say for now. Sorry."

Souda heaped a helping of mashed potatoes onto Sasha's plate and returned to his post at the kitchen. As if to dispel the dark mood, Sasha raised a shout of joy and began to gulp down her potatoes with extraordinary vigor.

The sun set.

The soldiers bustled about the transport trucks, each hurriedly preparing for departure. The medics, who doubled as cooks, checked on the medical supplies. The VME personnel made final adjustments to their gear and filled their tanks with gas. The leader of each vehicle verified their command structure and operation route.

As the soldiers made ready, their souls gradually grew numb as if they had been shot with anesthesia. Only a few dozen had made it back from the previous two expeditions, and it wasn't even worth calculating the survival rate. *And now, it might be our turn…* Night obscured the sky, and as if in agreement, a similar darkness clouded their hearts.

Eren fervently cheered himself on.

There's no reason to be nervous or to despair. I endured a tragedy from hell two years ago, and a training regimen from hell for an entire year to come to this day. Now is the time. We'll do our very best, make this operation a success, and exterminate the unholy Titans.

Done loading, he climbed into the bed of the sixth truck, his assigned post. A total of six transports were being used for the operation. The first and second would take the lead, the third and fourth would make up the second row, and the fifth and sixth would take the rear. Sixteen rode in each vehicle, and fresh meat like Eren and Armin were assigned to the sixth.

"It's a homecoming, isn't it?" Sannagi, having finished with his preparations, sat down beside Eren. The truck shook faintly under the weight of his heavy body. "You and Armin are from Monzen, right?"

Eren nodded.

"I want to go back to my hometown too," Sannagi said half to himself. "Go back, and work the land with my little brothers and sisters again."

"It looks like you."

"Hmm?"

"That doll." Eren glanced at the doll latched to Sannagi's waist. "Your little sister made it for you, yeah?"

"Ha ha," Sannagi laughed awkwardly. "Am I this fat?"

"Actually, you're fatter."

"Harsh."

As Sannagi gave a bitter smile, Souda, having finished preparing as well, approached their truck. Each vehicle was assigned a medic/cook, and he was Eren and Armin's. Proceeding into the narrow cargo bed to where Eren and Sannagi sat, Souda held something out at them with a grin. Squinting through the darkness, Eren saw two cigarettes.

He shook his head. "I don't need one."

"Oh, relax," Souda insisted and offered it again. "Here, big guy, you too."

"Ha, I'm trying to live long," Sannagi said, taking one and smiling. "Fine, maybe I'll smoke it when I'm ready to give up."

Once they were ready, Private First Class Yunohira, the leader of the sixth truck, stood to make an announcement. He was a tall man with handsome features, and a beard around his mouth lent him the dignity of a superior. All the soldiers in the truck bed took notice of him.

"Just as Hange from Arms Development said, Titan activity dies down at night. Apparently, even if they do wake up, it takes a while for their eyes to regain function. Thus, we need to arrive at Omotemachi while it is still night. The elite Shikishima gang that survived the second operation has already gone to clear the road of the Titans. We've basically organized it so that you guys can space out on your way to Omotemachi. The relay facility there is surrounded by a barricade—you could call it a mini-wall—to keep the Titans out, so it should be secure. Therefore our initial ovjective is to reach Omotemachi safely. I don't imagine we'll have any accidents on our way there, but exercise caution and try to pay attention. Inside the transport, there's only one thing you guys need to worry about: *Don't make a sound.* The Titans are exceptionally well attuned to the human voice. No matter how lethargic they are during the night, they'll begin attacking the moment they hear a human's voice. Better to bite your tongue off than scream."

Eren slowly let out his breath and gave a small nod. The other soldiers nodded as well.

Yunohira went on.

"If for whatever reason you need to communicate, utilize the hand signs you learned in training. If something comes up that you cannot convey with hand signs, correspond in writing. Pen and paper will be available at the center of the truck bed."

Yunohira finished speaking and looked around at the other vehicles. When he realized that there was still a little time left, he opened his mouth again.

"Truck Six, along with Truck Five, will bring up the rear. Because it is in the back, our chances of sudden contact with the Titans are relatively low. At the same time, if we have to rely on mobility to shake them off, there's a good chance that we'll be left behind." Yunohira paused briefly. "Unfortunately, as soldiers, our goal is not to 'survive.' It is to 'restore the wall.' If all of us make it back but the wall isn't closed up, we've failed. On the other hand, if all of us bite the dust but have managed to repair the wall, then the operation will have been successful. Compared to the great cause of accomplishing our mission, the life of a single soldier is worth less than a piece of garbage, in other words. If you understand this and still want to survive, then you better save your own ass. Don't rely on anybody else to protect you... That is about all I have to say."

A white signal flag rose up from the first transport out front. It was a sign from a staff officer who was also part of Kubal's personal guard.

Yunohira fell silent and brought his fist to his chest, and all the soldiers in Truck Six quietly responded with the same gesture.

The engine came to life with a low rumble, signaling anew that the operation was beginning. The Second Wall's huge gate slid open painfully slowly as if to tease the nervous soldiers. A dark land stretched endlessly on the other side of the raised portal, with not a single spark of light in sight.

The flag on Truck One changed to red. Gently, the vehicles began to move.

Eren and the others advanced out into the world outside the gate.

III. CITY OF DIS

One lonely point of light from the icy blue moon.

They crossed a world that was just two shades brighter than absolute darkness. The air wasn't particularly cold, but it was piercing. Through an eerie silence, the engine of the truck echoed uneasily. They could feel it in their skin that they were foreign things to this world. It felt as if even the sound of breathing might provoke some kind of wrath.

Seated in the cargo bed, Armin scanned his surroundings. The path was wide enough for two columns of trucks to easily run parallel. The largest town in the First Wall District had been located right outside the Second Wall's southern gate, but it was near impossible to feel its presence. As far as the eye could see, ruins, ruins, ruins. The skeletons of some buildings miraculously remained standing, while others had their roofs ripped off. One of the structures was practically gone with the exception of a single brick wall. Traces of human civilization hung in the air like a leftover scent. Abandoned carts, turret trucks that had lost their wheels, and broken farming implements lay scattered along the road.

Armin felt a tingle run up his spine. The town had only been evacuated two years ago, and it shouldn't be looking this dilapidated. The destruction was due to the Titans. His hands grew sticky with sweat.

A Titan could show up at any moment. Though the Shikishima detachment had already cleared the road, the chances of an unexpected attack were not zero. *If a Titan arrived, just like two years ago, we would be torn to pieces, eaten.* The fear was paralyzing.

Sensing that his thoughts were spiraling downwards, Armin stopped looking out at the landscape and instead gazed at his classmates who sat with him in the cargo bed. All of them were equipped with small lanterns, but their pale candlelight wasn't enough to fully illuminate themselves. The softly flickering flames cast an ominous glow on their faces.

Armin almost let out a groan without thinking. All he needed to do was remain quiet, but that somehow seemed like an insurmountable challenge. He felt as if his fear, his hopelessness, and his anxiety were going to find a voice and spill out of him.

Dammit, I'm getting swallowed up.

If he could at least utter the words "It's okay"—"It's fine, we'll be okay"!

No. Not even that.

What am I thinking? The Titans, the Titans that devoured my father and mother, could be right nearby, and yet I want to talk. What am I thinking? But…I'm scared, scared, scared.

Suddenly Sasha began to wave her hands. Startled, Armin watched her where she sat next to him. She was making hand signs.

Did she see a Titan? Her face floated in the lanterns' dim light, not an ounce of calm in her expression. Clearly, something was wrong. Armin began to tremble violently. He had no idea what Sasha's repeated hand signs meant, and he became all the more panicked. He'd practiced them over and over again, so why wasn't any information entering his head? *No…still no good. What do I do, what happened?*

Cautiously, Armin tried to read his comrades' expressions. Unexpectedly, it seemed like the others couldn't decipher her signs, either. They tensely watched Sasha's violent gestures, but nobody could send a clear response. The soldiers' faces grew grave, and they began to exchange glances with one another. Soon, losing her patience, with sweat dripping from her forehead, Sasha grabbed the pen and paper that was placed in the center. She began to scribble furiously.

What? What happened? It's not a Titan, is it?

Under the gaze of everybody in the truck, Sasha frantically held up the note. There, in crooked letters written in a swaying truck, was her message:

I'm hungry. Does anybody have any spare food?

Armin saw Jean's fists harden. Sasha clasped her hands together and deeply bowed her head many times. Relaxing his shoulders a bit, Armin pulled a steamed potato from his shoulder bag that he was using as his tool carrier. When he handed the tuber to Sasha, she motioned her thanks, removed the cloth wrap from the potato, and began to eat as silently as possible.

The mood in the truck brightened just a little. Even Armin felt his heart grow lighter than before. It wasn't as if Sasha was trying to cheer everyone up, but her presence sometimes worked perfectly to put people at ease. When she finished eating her potato, she dipped

her head to thank Armin again. Then she began to fiddle with her
bow and arrows, precious tools of the trade for Sasha, who hunted
for a living.

Armin let out his breath, carefully so as not to make the slightest
sound. It was no use worrying. He could only try his best, and all he
had to do was stay silent until Omotemachi.

Then it happened.

It was some time after they had left South Gate. The truck suddenly came to a stop. Armin's body lurched, and for a second he lost
his balance.

They'd arrived in—no, it couldn't be Omotemachi yet. There was
no sign of a town around them. The soldiers tensed up.

Private First Class Yunohira jumped to his feet and quickly exchanged signals with the other trucks. All six had stopped. Unlike
earlier with Sasha, this was no joke. The tension was as taut as a wire
and tightly bound Armin and the others. When Yunohira finished
exchanging signals, he began to relay them to everyone in Truck Six.
This time, Armin understood.

*Left, up front... Unidentified noise... Squad Six only, disembark...
Investigate.*

A cruel, cold wind slipped between the soldiers, but they had
neither the time nor the right to protest. Leaving behind the driver
and Souda, thirteen soldiers got off Truck Six with their Vertical Maneuvering Equipment, Armin and Eren among them. Immediately,
with Yunohira in the lead, they got into a formation that allowed
them to see in every direction. Upon Yunohira's signal, they began
to walk. Relying on their feeble lantern lights, they cautiously veered
off of the path to the left. Dirt ceded to damp weeds below their feet.

The leather boots they'd been issued sank slightly in the soft earth.

To the left lay the ruins of a building where the sound had come from. If there indeed was anything, it had to be lurking in the shadows of the two-story concrete structure floating in the moonlight. There was a large hole in the wall. Though it was consumed in darkness, if Yunohira exposed it to his lantern, they would certainly see what was inside. Squad Six cautiously closed in on the abandoned building.

They took their time advancing. When they came before the gap in the wall, they all quieted their breaths. Having paused for a moment, as if waiting for something to pass by, Yunohira lifted his lantern.

Everybody let out a sigh.

Two cows.

Faced by Armin and the others, the two cows backed away distrustfully with subdued moos. Their steps were shaky, perhaps because they hadn't been fed well. Ropes hung from the rings in their noses.

Yunohira made the hand sign to call off danger, then sliced his hand horizontally. It was the signal to return to the truck.

Armin exhaled the wariness that had poisoned his body. The other squad members stood down as well. The worst scenario hadn't come to pass. They began to file away—

But Yunohira wasn't moving.

Suspicious, his squad watched their leader.

As if he had noticed something, he grimly shifted his lantern. He faced it past the two cows, to the right and into the room's corner. The darkness coloring it melted away in the glow.

What they saw pierced them in the heart like a nail. Armin clamped his mouth shut tightly, tightly, tightly, to keep from making a sound.

Over ten severed human heads were lined up in a row.

"Ah…hh."

A moan leaked out. It stopped at first, but the dam broke.

"Ahhhhhhh!!"

The voice rang out so magnificently, it seemed to spread to the ends of the earth. The cows bellowed in response, a flock of birds erupted up from somewhere all at once, and even the plants seemed to wake. Armin had his mouth tightly shut. He wasn't the one who had screamed. Nor had it been Eren, or Jean, or Sannagi.

The owner of the voice finally stopped screaming and muttered to himself, "Dammit, that surprised me…" He bit his lip when he took in the faces of his subordinates and realized what he had done. "Um, sorry," PFC Yunohira said with an awkward smile.

As all of the soldiers faintly accepted Yunohira's apology, a dreadful sound began to resonate from off in the distance. Like an earthquake, it rocked the ground and shook their spines. Armin knew very well that it wasn't an earthquake. Two years ago, he'd heard that same sound over, and over, and over again. The tremors were stamped into his core, and there was no mistaking it.

The Titans' footfall.

The soldiers went pale as their eyes darted around in the darkness. Though they couldn't see the monsters, from the footsteps they could tell that more than two were approaching.

"This is bad," Jean murmured. Since the Titans were already approaching, there was no longer any reason to keep their mouths shut.

"That idiot leader…"

"And he was trying to play it so cool before we left." Sasha's jaw was trembling.

Deep in his heart, however, Armin couldn't blame Yunohira. Even a superior would cry out at that ghastly sight. Armin couldn't help but wonder why *severed heads had been lined up so neatly in such a place*. They hadn't yet begun to decompose, and the blood was bright red. It was unimaginable that they were from two years ago. Someone or something had clearly arranged those heads to scare them. If so, it made sense to think that the two cows had been used as bait to draw their attention. Who would do such a thing…*not a Titan?*

As if to cut off Armin's thoughts, the six transports began to move all at once. From the bed of Truck Five, its leader shouted at the confused Squad Six personnel.

"A message from the staff officer on Truck One! For the sake of the operation, we will stick to our plan and continue towards Omotemachi! Squad Six will shake off the Titans, avoiding combat as much as possible, before meeting us at Omotemachi!"

Jean bit his lip. "It's completely messed up, what they're saying."

"It pains me to say it, but it's the right call," Hiana conceded, sweat dripping down her cheeks. "Making us the decoy is the best option for the operation's success."

Somebody peered out from Truck Two as it drove away. Turning towards Armin and the others, she yelled, "Omotemachi is actually really close! It's basically right up there!" Her goggle lenses glinted through the darkness—it was Hange. "If you keep running, there will be lots more tall buildings! Just run until you get there!"

"Let's go!" Sannagi urged, and one after another the soldiers started after the trucks. The Vertical Maneuvering Equipment would allow for quicker movement, but unfortunately, there were few buildings around them, so the unwieldy gear was nothing more than dead weight attached to their hips.

Armin ran too. The convoy that had gone on without them was nearly out of view. The Titans' footsteps had grown louder, and they were clearly very close. The darkness prevented them from being seen, which was all the more terrifying. Armin was not a fast runner. Gradually he fell behind the others, and an uncontrollable panic began to consume him.

If the Titans came up from behind, the first person to get eaten… would be me. It would definitely be me. Me, me, me.

He fearfully glanced over his shoulder. He was astonished at what he saw.

"E-Eren?"

Eren was standing still, alone. Moreover, his back was turned to Armin. He was facing away from the direction they were running.

"N-No! Eren! What are you doing? Hurry up and run!"

Eren's back gave no indication of flight or fear. He stared down the road with what seemed like complete conviction.

"H-Hey, guys!" Armin called to the others hurrying forward. "Eren stopped running!"

They slowed their paces and looked back at Eren. Dumbfounded, they gawked at his back.

Jean clicked his tongue. "What is he thinking, the idiot?"

Armin felt the same way. *What is he doing? Why won't he run? At this rate, the Titan will…it will—*

It came.

From where Eren was gazing, a Titan emerged, swaying crookedly as it ran. *Thunk, thunk,* its heavy footsteps resonated. It ran overwhelmingly faster than the fleeing soldiers.

Armin's blood froze.

Eren. He couldn't be...

Eren took in a deep breath as he glared at the Titan.

Much like the ones he'd seen two years earlier, it had a sickly complexion, and a grotesque, distorted face. Its appearance was almost of a gaunt man. Its mouth hung open, and the expression on its face was hard to classify as joy or sorrow or anger. Pigeon-toed and with its arms pinned down at its side, it seemed to sneer at Eren.

He heard Armin shouting behind him, but it didn't shake his determination. Taking in one more deep breath, he dug his feet fiercely into the earth. He dashed at the Titan to attack, accelerating, his gaze fixed right onto its unfocused pupils. Eren's fight coursed through his body and set every cell of his muscles boiling. He bared his gritted teeth menacingly and pulled both VME triggers from the holsters on either side of him.

I put up with all that training for this very moment, today. Bearing Mikasa's shadow in his heart, he repeated to himself silently, over and over again. *I'm taking you down. I'm taking you all the way down. The person I am today is different from who I was back then. I know now that Titans—*

"—Titans aren't immortal."

As Hange's voice resonated in the lecture hall, the soldiers in training gasped. With quiet excitement, Eren took in Hange's words like a flash of hope. *Titans aren't immortal.* He repeated the words to himself over and over again. Armin, who sat next to him, was also engrossed.

Hange continued, "You can't defeat a Titan by destroying its limbs, or even its head. Within one to two minutes, the damaged part restores itself. However, this part…"

She pointed to the nape of the neck on a dummy, and her voice rose.

"Under the back of the head, around the nape—you might call it the back neck—apply enough damage here and the Titan dies without being able to regrow itself. Strangely, its body begins to emit steam and disappears in a matter of moments. Thus, we can't bring it back home, much less perform a dissection. Maybe this doesn't matter so much to you guys, but to me this is a major problem. No matter how much we try to perform detailed investigations on the Titans, there's no way for us to do it…so, yes. You got it. We need you to capture a Titan for us alive. That is your most important mission."

…*Huh?*

"Hange!" The instructor watching from the side gave a stern look. "Don't go giving out your own orders."

Hange rubbed her eyes, which had begun to cloud over, and let out her breath sharply.

"I'm sorry, all of you. It's a private matter, but just the other day something terrible happened to my pets Sonny and Bean...and that has me a little riled up. I'm sorry. Forget what I said about capturing them alive. Everything apart from that, however, is the truth. If you can seriously damage the nape of their necks, you can take down a Titan."

Hange cleared her throat and pointed at the nape on the dummy.

"Unfortunately, it is exceedingly difficult to strike this area with firearms. But now, there is a more effective, more mobile, art of fighting the Titans, and what makes this possible is..." She set on the lectern an apparatus like a small iron barrel and patted it almost lovingly. "The Vertical Maneuvering Equipment. Or so the theory goes. By fastening this to our hips, we can quickly move through the air."

Quickly move through the air. A question mark rose up in Eren's head. *Is that really possible?*

As if sensing the skepticism floating in the room, Hange grinned broadly. "Ha! You all doubt me? Why don't I give you a demonstration, then."

Hange told the recruits to go outside and then rushed out of the lecture hall as well. She and her students ended up on the training grounds. Before them, a thirty-foot wall had been prepared.

"I've kept you waiting," Hange said as she removed her jacket and showed her own gear to the soldiers. "As you can see, in order to wield the VME, you have to wrap leather belts around your whole body, fairly tightly. You can't see it because I'm wearing shoes, but a belt is wrapped even around my soles. In the air, you need to calibrate with your hips and your feet. You should start studying how to apply your weight to extract the desired output."

Sure enough, several leather belts crisscrossed Hange's body, from her shoulder to her chest, to her lower back, around her thighs, and to the bottom of her feet. The barrel-shaped apparatus they'd seen earlier was installed at her waist and jutted out behind her.

"This part that runs back from the thigh is the sheath for the blade and the gas tank. All controls are operated by this pair of trigger units." Hange pulled these from the holsters on either side of her. "Based on how you pull each trigger, you can control the anchor's emission, the winding tension, the gas propulsion, and the anchor's release. A complex combination of those factors allows you to move through the air in an arc. Your fingertips will have to perform extremely precise movements even as you're gliding through the air at a high speed. In other words, you need to be both delicate and bold to master this gear. And now…" Hange pointed a finger at the training wall. "Let me try flying up to the top with my VME."

The recruits held their breath as she slowly assumed a running pose.

"Hey, Hange…" the instructor tried to speak to her, but she didn't heed him.

A trigger gripped in each hand, she turned toward the wall and dashed. Gradually she accelerated, and when she reached top speed, she crouched for a split second and released both anchors at the same time. Wires unspooled from the device attached to her waist at an explosive velocity, and the pointed tips of the anchors darted into the top of the wall. She instantly tensed her back again and kicked off the ground. At the same time, she fired copious amounts of gas from the tanks on either side and reeled in the wires.

Hange's body floated into the air—but didn't soar.

Just licking the ground, her supine form shot forth.

The friction sent up massive clouds of dust. Hange swept the earth in a most brutal manner.

Then she fell.

Eren and the others were at a loss for words.

"I told you," the instructor muttered, cradling his head.

Hange slowly picked her battered body off the ground.

"So…" she said, lifting up her goggles, "I, myself, can't!"

…*Whaaat?*

"Sorry to get your hopes up! For some reason, I thought it might go well today, but I couldn't do it after all."

She sighed as she dusted off her clothes and turned to the instructor to take her place. He was already wearing the equipment, and employing a similar process as Hange but with greater skill, he gracefully alighted on top of the wall. Noting the instructor's performance, Hange nodded.

"That was an easy jump, but once you get used to it, you'll be adjusting the wire action to perform far more complex moves. Or rather, they'll be necessary to attack a Titan from behind. Well, you probably don't want to hear that from me…"

Hange sighed wistfully. In another world, her counterpart was flying around just fine, she seemed to want to say.

"I'll stick to explaining things," she reprised with more composure. "If you want to kill a Titan, it's not enough to just fly around. You also need to attack. For that, you use this blade."

Hange pulled one from the sheath at her thigh.

"Even if it breaks, the edge is designed to be replaceable. When you need to use it, it's installed above the trigger unit. Thus, you can operate the anchor while wielding your weapon. It's intentionally made to bend a little since it has to slice through the thick skin of the Titans. At the moment of attack, wield one in each hand and—as if slicing a pie—cut off the Titan's nape in a triangle. There's a chance the blow won't be fatal if it's shallow. You want to gouge deep, as deep as you can."

Cut off the nape, Eren turned the words over in his heart as if to carve them there.

"No matter the size of the Titan, this rule holds. Slice off the weak point that exists at the nape of the neck, three feet tall and four inches wide. Unable to regenerate, right there and then, the Titan will—"

⸻

⸻

—The Titan will die instantly.

Tensing his entire body, Eren continued to glare at the Titan.

As the distance between them shrank, the reality of its size struck home. The thing was probably twenty feet tall. Though they had used a comparably large dummy during training, an actual Titan was different. The real deal had *something* that exceeded its numerical dimensions and was overwhelmingly huge and intimidating.

At that moment, nobody's voice, no sound of any kind, could reach Eren's ears. He was so anxious that his triggers were slick with sweat, but he had to do it. And he was going to do it.

There were nearly no buildings in the area, so he couldn't use a structure to fly through the air. That meant the only anchor point that Eren could use was *the Titan's body*. He'd never driven an anchor into a moving target during training, but he was aware that the technique existed.

I can do it, Eren told himself. *Sure, Jean posts the best overall score for vertical maneuvers, but just exclude the academic side, and I beat him in terms of pure skill.*

The distance between Eren and the Titan shrank further. At this point the way they viewed each other overlapped perfectly. Eren saw the Titan as something to be hunted, and the Titan saw Eren as its edible prey. Eren measured his timing as the Titan's footfalls washed over him.

Three, two, one—*now.*

Defying death, Eren shot out his left anchor. The wire burst out at such an explosive rate it could have been a cannon ball. A direct hit, it pierced the monster's left flank.

—The Titan eyed the anchor curiously—

Yes. Eren crouched and kicked against the ground, simultaneously reeling in the wire. Turning his wrist to control the gas stream, he rose into the air. *I'm up!* Guided by the anchor, his body soared in a gentle arc towards the monster's waist. *I did it.* He was engulfed in the roar of his body cutting through the air.

—The Titan stared at Eren as he flew—

Confirming that his trajectory was secure, Eren released the pierced anchor, and for a second he was weightless. His clothes and his hair rippled in the wind. He took a breath and shot out his right anchor. Another direct hit, it pierced the Titan's left shoulder true to his aim. Eren reeled in the wire, and burning gas to give him more elevation, he leapt up above the Titan's head. He calculated his trajectory to reach its nape.

—The Titan raised its left arm—

The monster was preparing to attack, but too late. Eren would decide this first. Shoving both triggers into their holsters, he yanked out his blades, which shone blue-white in the moonlight. Eren released his anchor. If he simply went into free fall now, he'd arrive at the nape. He raised his blades...overconfident.

—The Titan swung its left arm at Eren—

The arm was faster than expected. Eren had estimated wrong. The arm churned up a fierce wind as it moved. Suddenly, before his eyes, was the Titan's hand, its grubby fingers a sickly color. Eren braced himself. Game...

—The Titan almost gripped Eren in its hand—but suddenly knelt down as if it had lost its balance.

What happened? Wondering, Eren plummeted. *No, I only eluded its grasp for a date with the ground. The anchor, I have to shoot the anchor.* But he didn't see any suitable target. The earth came rising up from underneath. He was crashing...

Something flashed before his eyes and grabbed him like the wind.

"Why so rash?" Fukushi had come flying in his VME to snatch Eren. Once they were a safe distance away from the Titan, Eren's comrade lowered him onto the ground and chided, "I've never had to use an anchor at such a low altitude before, you hear me?"

"I'm sorry..."

"Apologize later. First, we have to run."

Eren saw that the other soldiers were close. The Titan that Eren had confronted was on its knees, its ankle apparently cut. Sannagi, who had sliced its Achilles tendon, broke off his chipped blade, his shoulders heaving.

"We're escaping, Eren!" he shouted.

As the Titan tried to get to its feet, Sasha's arrow flew through the air and pierced the monster right in its eyeball. Of course, the damage wasn't fatal to a Titan, but hitting it right in the eye wasn't pointless. For a moment its visual field would narrow. An eerie groan rose from the Titan as it covered its eye with both hands.

"Hurry, run!" beckoned Sasha, waving her arms over her head. "Straight to Omotemachi!"

Fukushi grabbed Eren's hand before he could apologize again, and they began to run. Seeing that, the other soldiers disengaged as well. Armin, Fukushi, Lil, Hiana, Sannagi, Sasha, and even Jean had stayed behind. Jean's face looked stern as he ran cursing Eren.

"And the others?"

"They went ahead towards Omotemachi," Fukushi replied to Eren without looking back. "Let's hurry up and meet them at the relay point."

From behind them, a new Titan's footsteps began to reverberate. However, it seemed to be too far back to overtake them. The wounded Titan showed no sign of giving chase, either. When Eren and the others had gone about a few hundred yards, as promised the number of buildings began to increase. Structures four to five stories high stood in rows and gave a strong sense of the remains of a civilization. It had to be—

"It's Omotemachi from here on," Armin said to Eren, nodding. "We're almost at our building. Let's keep going."

Eren nodded back at Armin, who was running alongside him, when—

They all stopped.

From the shadow of a building peeked a huge form.

No, two.

On the right, a plump, thirty-foot Titan. Behind a building to the left was another plump Titan twenty feet tall. Both had their backs turned as they crept around like suspicious lurkers, but before long they faced toward the soldiers.

"Eek…" Sasha let out a shrinking gasp. Eren, too, couldn't speak.

The two Titans held pieces of people. The right Titan, its mouth stained red, had its hand clenched around the upper body of a person. The left Titan, which must have eaten from the top down, clasped just the lower half of a body. Dark blood dripped and fell to the earth.

It didn't take long for Eren and the others to determine whose bodies the Titans held. The upper body belonged to Yakumo from their year. The guy's face was noticeable from between the Titan's fingers, and even drenched in red as if he'd been dipped in sauce, there was no mistaking it. That was Yakumo. His neck broken, his head hanging loosely at an impossible angle, life had completely left his body. The bright smile that had stayed on his face even during training was gone. On the other body, they could see a pair of long boots. Only one person had been wearing them today—PFC Yunohira. Apparently unconcerned with boots or clothes, the Titan easily swallowed the lower half of their squad leader whole and wriggled its mouth as if it were enjoying the aftertaste.

Their audience was speechless.

The soldiers stood petrified, their eyes glued to the mastication of the two men. One they had trained with, the other had led them on this mission; both were cruelly devoured as they watched. Men who had just moments ago been speaking, wearing expressions, conversing, were brutally finished.

Remains of several other bodies littered the earth at the Titans' feet. The scraps lay scattered about—a foot, a hand. Loose lengths of wire and blades also dotted the ground. They had fought, and been defeated.

The soldiers stood as if paralyzed. While they'd been rescuing Eren, they'd been lost in their own world. Fukushi and Sannagi had been able to fight just like in training, or even better. But now nobody could move. Witnessing the deaths of their comrades, their hearts sank, and they couldn't take a step.

"This sucks," Jean spat. "We're done for. Not even that stupid superior Yunohira could win against them. The end…"

Eren wanted to say something but couldn't find any words. Instead, he decided on one thing. He'd attacked that first Titan on his own and thrown the squad out of order. So he was the one who had to do something about this.

He let out a long breath to expel the fear from his body. He began to dash, glancing at both Titans in turn. Dwelling on the difficulties of the scenario would only weigh him down. He would mount a frontal assault, fully prepared to perish in the process. Unlike earlier, there were plenty of buildings around. If he could get behind his foes, the chance of success was substantial. Eren was about to fire his first anchor at a leftward wall, when—

Something came flying.

Eren stopped in his tracks.

What could it be?

The mysterious entity speeding in from beyond the Titan flashed in the moonlight as it danced through the sky. Swiveling quickly from right to left, it made a loud noise, twice, that sounded like something ripping through the air. Eren dropped his body to steady himself against any incoming gust.

Along with a gale came the flying thing itself.

Landing beside Eren, it opened its mouth.

"For goodness' sake…"

Eren stared at *it* in confusion. It was definitely a person. It was even wearing the Vertical Maneuvering Equipment. *Who is it?* he wondered, but only for a moment before quickly regaining his mind. Two Titans still stood before him, and this was no time to get distracted.

But there was a large rumble.

When Eren looked up, both Titans had fallen to their knees. Almost as soon, they collapsed to the ground. Eren shielded his face from the dust that they churned up. Rising up along with it from the earth was—steam. Something had cleanly sliced away their napes. The carcasses spat hot vapors as though they were boiling.

Finally, he understood. A man had come flying and taken down both Titans with those flashing strikes. Eren couldn't believe it, but it was the truth.

The man slowly stood up straight and sheathed his blades. "You were late so I came to check on you, and it was just as I thought."

He was taller than Eren, over six feet tall. Over his regular uniform, he wore a deep, rust-colored topcoat, almost like a cape. An elegant white scarf was tied at the base of his neck. He had refined features, and while his sharp gaze was that of a grizzled veteran, it was by no means savage.

"Y-You are?" inquired Armin.

The man returned his triggers to their holsters and answered,

"Captain of the Shikishima Advance Detachment, 3rd Outer Wall Restoration Operation—Shikishima."

A shock ran through them. It was almost moving.

This man was Shikishima: the captain of the 2nd Outer Wall Restoration Operation's only surviving unit, the strongest man in the world, the Titans' nemesis.

"Looks like you're a bunch of recruits," Shikishima said with a tender look. "Can you all still run? The meeting place is surprisingly close."

Just as Armin sighed with relief, there was a thunderous sound. The building behind Shikishima crumbled and a new Titan sprang from it.

"C-Captain Shikishima!" stammered Armin, pointing. "B-Behind you, a Titan!"

While the greenhorns panicked, Shikishima retained his cool.

"It's okay." He didn't even turn around.

A moment later, a blue-white flash ran across the sky like a shooting star. As the light glinted, the Titan gave a dying cry and lost its balance. The Squad Six stragglers caught a glimpse of its nape, sliced off no less perfectly than before.

"To be on the safe side," Shikishima smiled proudly, "I brought *one of my close aides.*"

The Titan crumpled into the ruins of the building, sending up plumes of dust and steam. Eren and the others looked away to protect their faces. In no time, the soldier described as Shikishima's "aide" performed two wire actions and swooped down next to the captain. A metallic smell drifted through the air, perhaps from the overheated wires. The aide landed successfully and slowly looked up.

That face—Eren's vision wavered. He doubted his own eyes. He couldn't believe it offhand.

Words of denial and disbelief bubbled up and popped in his mind, and frothed again. The more he stared, however, the more the aide's appearance strongly, *strongly* agreed with his recollection. The soldier referred to as Shikisima's "aide" was rooted deep in the center of his memory. She could be none other.

Eren couldn't speak.

Armin did instead, in a trembling voice.

"M…" He had to squeeze out the words. "Mikasa, is it you?"

Meeting the two youths' gazes, Mikasa looked shaken for just a moment. But she quickly calmed her expression, murmured something to Shikishima, and soared away with a vertical maneuver.

Dumbfounded, Eren and Armin followed the traces of her wires with their eyes.

IV. THE LATE REPENTANT

The building that was said to hold the supply of explosives was located in about the center of Omotemachi. During the Old Government Era, it had been used as a defense facility. However, until two years earlier (before the Titans attacked), under national control, it had been operating as a public institution that could be used for various purposes. It was made up of a large, circular hall and a six-story building and surrounded by a thirty-foot wall, a remainder of its era as a defense facility. Though a fifty-foot Titan could possibly get past the wall, it would still buy the soldiers ample time. The facility was more or less considered a "secure location" within the habitat of the Titans.

The gates of the institution slid open for the six transports, which quickly drove into the grounds. With the exception of the Squad Six members who had been left behind, all the personnel and trucks succeeded in proceeding on course without encountering any Titans.

Upon arriving at the facility, two designated squads kept watch over the wall, while the commanders led the rest of the soldiers to the building.

Once the soldiers arrived at their assigned waiting rooms, they opened mouths that had been tightly shut and let out their sighs of relief. So long as they didn't speak too loudly, they were allowed to have conversations. Happy to have survived, they quietly congratulated one another on their bravery.

Kubal and his three guards, who had been riding in Truck One, went to check on the status of the explosives as soon as they disembarked. They didn't proceed towards the six-story building like the other soldiers, but to a round hall. The walls of the hall consisted of unfinished concrete, cold and inorganic. A single soldier was waiting for Kubal and his guards at the entrance. Recognizing the supervisor, the soldier promptly saluted.

"Kanaya of the Shikishima Advance Detachment, reporting. Supervisor Kubal, we've been waiting for you."

Kubal reciprocated with a nod. "It's been a hard road. So you're Kanaya. You took down six, assisted on twelve. You're young but I hear you're quite the fighter. It's certainly very impressive."

"Please, it's nothing."

"And Captain Shikishima?"

"Since the main force was later than we expected, he and another soldier went out to check on you."

"I see. It would be great if they could bring back the soldiers from Squad Six that were delayed."

As Kubal spoke he walked into the hall with Kanaya. Avoiding the center of the hall, they went directly to the staircase at the edge of the room and descended towards the basement.

"To tell you the truth," Kanaya began, climbing down the stairs, "just recently we tried searching for the explosives with Captain Shikishima but were not able to find any—"

"Searching?" Kubal cut Kanaya off. "That was inappropriate. Shikishima went looking on his own?"

"Y-Yes…" Kanaya confirmed hesitantly. "He said that waiting to look for them until the rest of the force arrived was a waste of time and that the advance detachment should just find them."

Kubal stopped in the middle of the stairwell, and for a little while looked as if he was lost in thought, a bitter expression clouding his face. His eyes wavered as he considered the matter for several seconds, but he merely said, "I see," and continued walking.

A large metal door was waiting at the bottom of the staircase. The guards ignited their lanterns to illuminate the dark. Perhaps because it had been so long since humans had inhabited the room, or thanks to the peaceful appearance of the concrete walls, the basement felt vacant, and a hint of death floated in the air.

"The door wasn't locked…" Kanaya said, opening it. Because it was a little rusted, it took a lot of strength to slide the door open. "But as you can see…"

The guards pointed their lanterns beyond the doorway, revealing a wide space, almost like a warehouse. It had a round shape, as if the hall above had been copied below, and was quite large. There was not a single object to be seen, much less any explosives, and more room than anybody would know what to do with.

"After the incident two years ago, perhaps somebody used this room…or perhaps the information that the explosives were stored here was false…" Kanaya looked fairly desperate.

Kubal stepped into the warehouse with his guards. Then he began to speak to Kanaya, who followed behind him. "Are you aware of the Designated Knowledge Confidentiality Law?"

Kanaya smiled bitterly. "Funny. There isn't a single human within the walls who isn't."

Kubal flashed a wry smile of his own. "It comes under a fair share of criticism, but that law protects the order of this world and is an important part of the system. We're not hiding anything from the public. Rather, we're keeping them far away from dangerous information. We're protecting the people from issues that they do not need to know about. That's what I mean."

Kanaya nodded.

"This building…" Kubal walked to the center of the room and stopped. He turned around to look at Kanaya. "Up until two years ago, this building was lent out by the government as a public facility. By request, any citizen could use it. In the past, I heard there were even little dances held here. Isn't that lovely?"

Not knowing where the story was going, Kanaya nodded.

Kubal suddenly shrank down and touched the concrete floor almost tenderly. The guards shone light on his hands. Kubal brushed away the dust that had collected on the floor.

"It's here." When Kubal pointed to a section on the floor, his guards immediately brought out a hooked-shaped piece of metal and pried at the spot.

"Could you please move back a little?"

As Kanaya took a step back, the guards twisted the hook. There was a hard click as if a lock had opened. A narrow crack appeared on the floor where Kanaya had been standing. It was about ten feet long and just wide enough for the palm of a hand. Unconcerned with Kanaya's astonishment, the guards stretched their hands into the crack and pulled upwards. The concrete that had been part of the floor lifted up, revealing a hidden staircase underneath.

"This is...amazing."

The guards pushed the section all the way up and over. The concrete cover that had been the lid to the hidden staircase swung on its hinge and hit the floor. Cold dust whirled through the air.

"Light," Kubal said.

One of the guards pointed his light down into the staircase. At the bottom lay some kind of black packaging that looked like explosives.

"Incredible," marveled Kubal.

"I can't believe it!"

"It's like this," Supervisor Kubal said, facing Kanaya. "There was no need for the public to know that this trap door existed." Getting to his feet, Kubal gazed down the stairs with distant eyes. "There was no need for anybody to know that there were explosives in the basement during a ball. Otherwise, the wonderful time would be ruined. When you dance, you might as well dance. There's no need to think about what's below your feet. If you knew there were explosives under your feet, it would disturb your steps."

"So you dance on top of explosives."

"Ironic." Kubal exhaled through his nose. "Just like the Paradox of the Disarmament Treaty."

One of the supervisor's guards shook his head disapprovingly. "That kind of talk—"

"How rude of me," Kubal riposted before addressing all the

guards. "Summon Squad One and Squad Three immediately and begin loading out the explosives. All the explosives go in Truck One."

The guards bowed and left the room to give the order.

"Hey, Kanaya." Kubal narrowed his eyes. "I like this world. If I'm to be completely honest, I love this world."

"…Yes."

"So if something threatens its peace, I'm not about to tolerate that. Such a thing must be completely eliminated."

"You mean the hated Titans?"

Kubal gave a suggestive smile. "Kanaya," his voice echoed through the huge warehouse. "What do you *see*?"

He was grabbed by the collar.

He could see the clenched fist, but no fight welled up in him. As expected, a solid blow came at his face. Eren just took it and slid down onto the concrete. He saw not just Jean, who had struck him, but also the others who'd come to break it up. But it was as if the scene belonged to a distant world. Saved by Captain Shikishima, they had arrived at the Omotemachi Relay Point. Once they reached their assigned room and removed their equipment, Jean began to harass Eren vehemently.

Yup, think about this rationally, it's because you had to go acting on your own authority that this happened. If we hadn't been jerked around by your actions, we would have been able to head for the relay point with that stupid superior. If we had fought with them, that superior, Yakumo, and the others might not have had to die. It's all your fault…

In general it was along those lines. The details, however, had not stuck in Eren's mind. It appeared that Sannagi, Fukushi, and Hiana were defending him, but he could see them only vaguely.

Jean, that's just what you think. Our orders had been to rendezvous at Omotemachi after shaking off the Titans. You could say that Eren took the proper course of action while we feared for our lives and panicked. Besides, we don't know if our added strength would have made any difference for Yakumo and the others. Calm down a little. We're not supposed to shout...

Eren remained strewn on the floor. He stared at the ceiling, where the scene that he'd witnessed replayed itself. Captain Shikishima, and Mikasa. The Mikasa that he thought he'd lost that day two years ago. *What—what in the world is going on?*

"Mikasa!"

At the sound of Armin's voice, Eren sat up frantically. Her spitting image crossed the hallway. Ignoring Jean's continuing abuse, Eren scrambled to his feet and dashed out with Armin.

As they entered the gray corridor, they indeed saw someone who looked very much like Mikasa from behind. She seemed to notice their presence, and after hesitating for a moment, slowly turned around. Black hair, a deep glint in her sinking eyes. Pale skin, a slender frame—there was no mistaking her. No matter how they looked at her, she was Mikasa.

"Y-You are Mikasa, right?"

She looked down in response to Armin's question. Uncertainty and indecision floated in her eyes. She pursed her small lips, giving herself up to the flow of time.

"Mikasa," Eren murmured as if to confirm it was her.

"I…" she finally opened her mouth and tilted her face up as if she'd made up her mind. "I am Mikasa, true. I lived with both of you in Monzen. But…" Mikasa took a breath before finishing, "I might not be the same Mikasa that I was before." Her words resonated in the concrete hallway.

I might not be the same Mikasa that I was before.

"You mean—"

"So this is where Squad Six is assembled?" a deep, booming voice interrupted Armin's words.

When Eren turned around, he saw a man clad in a black uniform. He was Military Police and one of Kubal's guards. Addressing the waiting room for Squad Six, he had them confirm that he was in the right place before continuing.

"Following the death of Squad Six leader PFC Yunohira, and in accordance with military regulations, you will fall under the command of Squad Five leader PFC Hotogi. When he arrives, refresh your battle formations for the operation. And—" The guard glanced down for a moment at the document he was holding and then looked up again. "Is there a recruit named Armin here? If you're here, please answer."

Next to Eren, Armin began to tremble.

"Th-That's me."

The guard turned away from the waiting room to face the hall where Armin stood. "So you're Private Third Class Armin?"

"Y-Yes."

"Come," the guard commanded, approaching Armin without waiting for a reply. "Supervisor Kubal wants to see you."

Armin went pale and numbly followed the guard.

Eren was also confused.

Why would Supervisor Kubal call for Armin? What could...

Before Eren could think any more about it, he remembered Mikasa. When he turned around to where she'd been standing, he saw that she was already gone.

I have to go after her.

He started to run and turned the corner only to bump into someone. Though it was a minor collision, he looked up to apologize to none other than—

"Hey." It was Shikishima. "Well, well, if it isn't the greenhorn from earlier."

"Captain Shikishima..."

"I was watching you," Shikishima grinned a little too widely. "Out of all the terrified recruits, you were the only one who tried to fight the Titans. Your spirit is commendable."

Not knowing how to answer, Eren nodded lightly. He had planned to excuse himself and go after Mikasa but changed his mind. "Um..." he broached hesitantly. "About Mikasa..."

Shikishima gave a forced smile. "Hmm? Do you have any business with the squad leader?"

Squad Leader.

Mikasa was a Squad Leader.

Eren swept away the uneasy thoughts that ran through his mind and continued with his question. "Why is Mikasa with you, Captain Shikishima?"

"The way you talk about her, I presume you two are acquainted with each other?"

Eren nodded vaguely.

Again Shikishima flashed his fake grin, the kind that made it seem like down deep he actually wasn't laughing at all. Perhaps it was the sort of smile you wore to humor a child, superficial, polite. Eren couldn't tell if it was Shikishima's usual expression or if there was some special meaning to it. Either way, Eren didn't get a good feeling from it.

"Let's move. There's an open room over there. I'd rather sit while we talk," Shikishima suggested and headed two doors down. It was much smaller than the waiting room, but as the captain said, it was empty. It had a small window, a small table, two wooden chairs, and nothing else—a simple room. Shikishima offered Eren a chair and then sat down himself.

"Two years ago, during the attack on Monzen," Shikishima began speaking once Eren took his seat, "I saved her from that tragedy, though just barely. Somehow, she survived."

As he spoke, Shikishima kept his eyes trained on Eren, as if to test him. Unable to bear the captain's gaze, Eren dropped his eyes to the table. A tiny breath escaped Shikishima's mouth like a chuckle.

"However, she had suffered considerable injuries. She gave no signs of regaining consciousness, much less of being able to walk. She was a regular 'Sleeping Beauty.' I brought her to the Second Wall East District where I was raised and gave her medical treatment. Not only is that area quiet, it has relatively good security. After half a year of that, she finally recovered and regained consciousness."

Eren's hands tightly gripped his knees.

Shikishima went on. "Although her physical injuries had healed, her soul still needed care. She needed some kind of putty to fill the gaping injury that had opened in her heart...and that was when I began to drill her on how to fight the Titans. Intensely, so she didn't have the time to think about anything else. I don't know whether that was bad, or inhumane, or thoughtless. But it was the only thing that I could do. To cut into Titan flesh and shave it off. To teach the immortal Titans how to die. Unfortunately, that was the only valuable thing I could offer.

"To tell you the truth," the man dubbed the strongest in the world continued, "the girl has outstanding talent. Vertical maneuvers are, to begin with, an art of fighting better suited for women, who are nimble and capable of withstanding a lot of G's, but she is extraordinary. Her flexibility and strength, quick judgment, breadth of vision, all of it is exceptional. I must say that she is superior to any soldier I've encountered so far, including myself. Perhaps it's in her blood, but immediately she began to display explosive power... In any case, she is a certified prodigy."

The longer Eren listened, the further away Mikasa seemed. He fell silent in his lonely thoughts.

"I decided to bring her along on the 2nd Outer Wall Restoration Operation. Quite impressively, she succeeded in single-handedly bringing down twelve Titans and assisted on twenty-one. It's unthinkable, considering how difficult it is simply to survive out here."

Shikishima's expression was somehow proud. For a moment, Eren felt an uneasy feeling take over. *Why are you taking pride in her achievements as if they're your own?*

Shikishima wouldn't stop smiling. "Soon thereafter, I designated her as my aide de camp. You see, her existence was, to me, supremely exciting. Until then, no human could match my fighting skills. As a soldier, and as an individual, I began to embrace her with a fierce passion. We came to work together and also to live together. I've been given this goofy title of 'strongest man in the world,' but these days, without her, I would be nothing more than a wooden doll that could not go on living. The way I see it, it's not an exaggeration to say that she has become a part of me. Everything about her is my driving force… You're a friend from before the attack, so you don't know this, but the injuries she suffered were so, so grave. Even now, underneath the left side of her chest to around her lower back, she bears a Titan's tooth-marks, bright and clear. Every time I see her naked, I think—"

"Okay!" Eren sprang up from his chair. Though it didn't fall over, it rocked from side to side before slowly settling back onto its four legs.

I might not be the same Mikasa that I was before.

A brief silence.

"I went a little…" Shikishima gave a relaxed smile. "Too far there. I'm sorry."

"Thank you, sir. I'm fine now," Eren said and tried to rush out of the room.

"Hey," Shikishima stopped him. "I haven't even heard your name yet."

Eren hesitated for a moment, but in the end, he had to answer. "It's Eren."

"Eren?" Shikishima's expression changed drastically. "The Eren who grew up in Monzen?"

Eren wondered if he should be cautious of Shikishima, but his unpleasant feelings regarding the man took over and he nod-ded, feeling somehow reckless. In contrast, the captain's visage had unmistakably clouded over with consternation. It was almost the same expression that Eren had shown Mikasa: a chaotic mixture of surprise, denial, and doubt.

"This is amazing." Shikishima let out a resigned sigh. Then, looking into the hall to confirm that nobody was around, he asked in a hushed voice, "How much do you know?"

Eren didn't understand what he meant, and from his expression, Shikishima seemed to realize as much.

"Excuse me. Let me reword that." The captain looked his most serious self. "Under whose instruction are you here? You don't have to hide anything. I have no intention of doing you any harm."

"Instruction?" Eren shook his head. "I came here of my own will. I came here for my own sake."

Hearing the reply, Shikishima sank into thought. He bobbed his head softly for a few moments before shaking his head.

"Thank you." His gaze was more sincere than it had been throughout their entire conversation. "I look forward to working with you, *Eren*."

"I see..." Souda said, exhaling cigarette smoke. It floated slowly to the concrete ceiling. "I'm sorry I couldn't be of help." His expression was sober as he took in what Squad Six had gone through after getting off the truck. "I didn't think the transport would just go on driving like that...though I don't know how much use I would have been, not even being able to use the Vertical Maneuvering Equipment."

Sannagi, who had explained the details, shook his head with a smile. "It couldn't be helped. Nobody could have done anything."

"And how is that?" Jean snapped, clicking his tongue. "The one who alerted the Titans may have been that idiot superior, but actually the guy who did the most harm was that asshole with a death wish. If he hadn't thrown us out of formation—"

"Jean," Sannagi said sternly. "I told you, didn't I? You're shifting the blame."

"Well," Souda dropped his cigarette on the floor and crushed it with the heel of his boot. "Thanks for saying that at least. The kid— Eren—is dealing with a lot of difficult stuff. Go a little easy on him, okay?"

Jean looked the other way unhappily. "And what's up with that anyways?"

"That?"

"The Mikasa girl. The moment he saw her, that asshole started acting all weird."

As if to toy with the extinguished cigarette, Souda brought his toe down on the butt and twisted it from side to side. Dried leaves spilled out of it. "She's the girl that Eren thought he'd left to die two years ago."

Jean looked back at Souda in surprise. Sannagi's eyes were round as well. Souda let out a long breath and cracked his neck right to left.

"To think that she was alive... I was surprised too."

"She was ferociously fast with her VME. She even kept up with Captain Shikishima."

"Hmm." Souda stared at the tobacco that lay scattered on the floor. "I can't really get into specifics, but..." His eyes remained focused on the leaves. "Don't trust Shikishima. That guy might be as strong as a demon, but to the same extent, he's less human. Don't seek anything from him besides his strength." Souda kept staring at the cigarette as if he were deliberately avoiding eye contact. He kept pushing the butt around, lost in thought.

Mikasa was alive and picked up by Shikishima of all people... What a strange, fated relationship. Such a curious thing. To think that the world would fashion itself in such a way.

Souda sighed.

Oh well. I just hope that nothing gets in the way of my mission.

From the fourth floor, down to the second floor.

His heart beating violently, Armin followed the guard. Like the waves of people flowing through the downtown streets where he was raised, his various thoughts crashed relentlessly against each other and confused him.

Why did Supervisor Kubal call me? Between the Public Order Administration Supervisor and a Private Third Class in the Outer Wall Restoration Operation, there was a difference in social status as great as that between a god and a slave. *Why was I chosen?*

A possibility occurred to Armin.

New Technology Suppression Violation. Banned technology use by a civilian, which would include handmade timers. He'd committed several potentially inflammatory deeds. Perhaps they had found out about his activities in Monzen; since he'd become a soldier he had taken meticulous care not to do anything suspicious around other people. Still, if someone found out about his timers, there was plenty of reason for him to be summoned. The core purpose of the Public Order Administration (the Military Police) was to crack down on scofflaws. It was the explanation that made the most sense.

Suddenly, in a panic, Armin realized he was still carrying his shoulder bag. It contained a handmade timer, as well as several tools that he had brought in case they might come in handy during the expedition. Now they were working against him. Armin wondered whether he could drop his bag off somewhere, but while he was considering it, they arrived at their destination.

"It's this room," the guard indicated in an oppressive voice. "Get in."

When he saw that Armin was shaking, the guard gave a disgusted look and knocked on the door. He opened it without waiting for a response.

"Excuse me."

"Thanks for your trouble."

Armin could see Kubal: deep, weathered wrinkles; cavernous eyes that harbored a certain strength; a healthy complexion; shortly cropped white hair. There was no mistaking that he was the same Supervisor Kubal who had given the pre-departure speech.

The room was small. It held the chair that Kubal sat in, a large table, and nothing else worth mentioning. Just as with every chamber in the building, concrete walls stood on every side, and unstable candlelight was the sole illumination. No doubt due to the authority that emanated from Kubal, however, the room seemed more like the bureau of a high government official to Armin.

Controlling the shaking of his body, Armin saluted. "E-Excuse me, sir. Private Third Class Armin, sir."

Kubal shook his right hand to dismiss the formalities. "I'm sorry," Kubal said to the guard, "would you please give us some space? I want to speak to him alone."

It was not only Armin but also the guard who looked surprised. Not about to disobey orders, the guard bowed and promptly left the room. The click of the door shutting sounded to Armin like the lock on a prison cell.

"Now, don't be so stiff." Kubal smiled as though to try to unravel Armin's anxiety. "Sit here."

"N-No!" Armin replied shrilly. "I-I'm fine standing!"

Kubal laughed and began flipping through some documents on the table. "Armin, Private Third Class," he read out loud. "A native of the town of Monzen that came under attack two years ago. Uncomfortable with physical activity. Field skills just below average. But you overwhelmingly exceed your contemporaries in classroom learning. The report from your instructor states that your 'powers of observation and insight are beyond that of an ordinary person and exemplary.' Well, aren't you amazing."

"I-It's nothing, sir."

"Your home was a canola oil store… Biodiesel fuel, yes? And your parents?"

"They both passed away during the invasion two years ago."

"How unfortunate." Kubal sighed, closed the file, and slid it to the side. Then he placed his elbows on the table and clasped his hands. "I'm going to speak candidly." He dropped his voice. "I received a report from an MP who happened to be in the vicinity that you made a rather profound statement at the dining hall before departure."

The air became tense.

Armin tried to remember the conversation from the dining hall, but for some reason, he couldn't recall anything. *I'm sure I was talking about messing around with my tools that day. Maybe I even pulled some of them out? No, I wouldn't have. Wait… No. My mind is a mess.*

"Private Third Class Armin. I want to ask you something."

"Y-Yes," Armin answered immediately.

"What do you see?"

"Pardon me?" Armin croaked.

Kubal's face was exceedingly serious. His gaze was like some kind of black magic that tried to wring out all the dormant things that lay buried within Armin's soul. Armin gulped.

"I'm sure that you are able to see it." Kubal's voice was full of confidence. "It hasn't been long since you started this mission, but it seems you already harbor many doubts regarding this operation. I want to ask you about that. *What do you see?*" he repeated.

Finally, Armin understood the supervisor's intention and nodded slightly. Relieved that Kubal hadn't called him to take him to task, Armin's brain suddenly began to operate normally, and sharply. He remembered what he'd said to Eren in the dining room. Though he hesitated for a bit, under Kubal's burning gaze, Armin decided to reveal all of his thoughts. Slowly, he opened his mouth.

"I-I'm sorry." He took a deep breath. "The first thing that made me uncomfortable when we were told about the mission details was that the number of participants was too small. Previously the operation required a thousand, or five hundred people, while this expedition involves a mere hundred. I had my doubts, and I wondered about the reasoning. Furthermore, I thought that there was no reason for you and Squad Leader Hange to participate in this dangerous mission and felt uneasy about that too."

Armin examined Kubal's expression. Kubal nodded deeply to urge him to continue. Armin nodded back and did so.

"On our way to Omotemachi, Squad Leader Yunohira cried out, and as a result, we were attacked by Titans, but this was strange too. Because, as if somebody was trying to scare us, numerous human heads were lined up neatly in a row. Also, it's a mystery as to how two cows, herbivores, survived for two years tied to a rope. I can only assume that they were placed there as a kind of trap to lure in humans. And as I got to thinking about that, I began to wonder if there might be several more such 'traps' set for us. For example, though Shikishima's detachment had supposedly already done a sweep of the area, the Titans attacked surprisingly quickly after hearing the PFC's voice. As if…" Armin thought about stopping, but forced himself to blurt it out. "As if somebody were controlling the Titans."

Kubal closed his eyes and nodded.

"I-In all honesty," Armin concluded, "I feel that from the shadows, some human is pulling the strings to make sure this operation fails."

The concrete absorbed the echo. Kubal crossed his arms and sat back in his chair. Time passed heavily through the room as though the air had hardened. Eventually, the supervisor placed his elbows on the table again and looked directly at Armin.

"Well, that's more than I expected, isn't it?" Kubal rubbed the top of his head with his right hand and nodded several times, collecting his thoughts. "I'm going to tell you everything. As for your hypothesis, I feel nearly the same way."

With his mouth clenched shut, Armin nodded.

"In fact, we encountered similar sabotage the last two times as well." Ignoring Armin's surprise, Kubal continued. "Of course, it cannot be denied that the operation posed a high degree of difficulty to begin with. Even without the sabotage, it may have failed. *However*. However, that is not the issue. The important thing is that someone undeniably disrupted us, and we lost almost all of our soldiers. This is the unwavering truth. That is to say, *somebody who wishes to hold us back and keep human territory within the limits of the Second Wall has infiltrated our operation.*"

Kubal shifted in his chair.

"I need to expose the traitor that is hidden within our ranks, or rather, within 'mankind.' In order to do that, I limited the participants of this expedition. I figured it would be difficult for the traitor to operate among such a small number of people and carry out any large actions. In addition, from our perspective, there are fewer 'suspects' to choose from, so it's easier for us to take a guess as to who the traitor is. I'm convinced that, if only out of pride, the traitor decided to accompany us again. Even among such a small force, and knowing the risk, I'm sure the traitor will try to hinder us. We are betting on this. Of course, we also cannot fail to accomplish our mission proper. It's a gamble."

"A gamble…"

"The traitor could be mixed in amongst the veterans." Kubal's eyes glinted with a ferocious vigilance. "Thus, I decided to participate in this expedition myself and to form it out of innocent recruits as much as possible. There are exceedingly few people who can be trusted. With fresh faces who haven't participated in any operation in the past, the risk is low... And with that, I have something to ask of you."

Armin let Kubal's words sink in.

"I want you to cooperate with me," the supervisor said. "There is definitely a traitor wrapped up in this operation. I won't go as far as to ask you to *find the traitor*. I only ask you to *keep an eye out*. That is all. I want you to doubt everybody aside from myself, and to question everything. And if there is any shadow of betrayal, if you notice even the slightest hint of it, please report it to me post-haste. Do not go through my guard. Come directly to me. This is very important, so the traitor doesn't catch on."

Armin finally realized that he was opening a door that he wasn't supposed to. A new and mysterious world was encroaching upon him. Yet he could only heed the order.

"I understand."

"Thank you."

Armin saluted gravely, accepting the burden.

"I was actually planning on calling each new recruit one by one to find the most suitable candidate. I didn't think that I'd be able to find such an excellent, talented person on my first try... We'll call it my good fortune."

"I-It's an honor, sir."

"By the way." Kubal pointed at Armin's back. "About that bag."

Armin stopped breathing. The relaxed atmosphere suddenly became tense again.

"May I see the contents?"

Armin stiffened for a moment. He broke out in a cold sweat.

He racked his brain ten times over for a way to get out of it, but no brilliant ideas came to mind. He wasn't dealing with a soldier from his year, or just any superior. This was the head of the Military Police, Supervisor Kubal, and not someone who fell for amateur trickery.

He needed to stay cool. It wasn't as if Supervisor Kubal had noticed the backpack out of the blue.

I'm already in his grip. Resigned, Armin slowly took his shoulder bag off and set it down on the table. Carefully, as if handling fragile objects, he began emptying the contents of the pack. His prized tools and the timer he had used in his oil shop days emerged onto the table as Kubal watched with cold eyes.

"If I'm not mistaken, these are your personal effects?" inquired the supervisor.

After processing the words, Armin uttered a brief "yes."

Nodding, Kubal gently picked up the timer and began to examine it with great interest. "Is this something you made on your own?"

"I'm so sorry."

"From scratch?"

"Yes…" Armin waited, as if on the gallows. He no longer tried to hide anything. "I made it to measure the extraction time for canola oil. Based on how much you wind the mainspring it can measure up to twenty minutes."

When Kubal finished his meticulous and lengthy examination, he placed the timer onto the table so gently that it didn't make a sound. He nodded a few times, and his expression softened.

"How amazing."

"Sir?"

Kubal motioned to the shoulder bag with his eyes. "You should put it away. Right now it's just the two of us, but if a guard finds it, I'll have no choice but to punish you."

Armin was so shocked he couldn't move for a moment. After Kubal prompted him once more with a look, Armin began to return his things to the shoulder bag. This time frantically, as if hiding stolen goods.

"Do you," Kubal asked as he watched Armin in that state, "like this world?"

"Y-Yes," Armin replied as he continued putting away his things.

"Well, that's good." Kubal smiled. "I like this world too. It is by no means rich, but in the spirit of love and selflessness, everyone helps one another. This world, in which people bravely go on living aware of the preciousness of life and the difficulty of surviving—I love it tremendously. Just as you do, Private Third Class Armin."

When Armin finished packing his timer and his tools, he bobbed his head without fully taking Kubal's meaning.

"The thing that we fear is not the advance of technology. It is the advance of 'misguided' technology. Or to put it more accurately, the advance of technology in the hands of 'misguided people.' In that respect, Private Third Class Armin, should what you have"—Kubal pointed at the shoulder bag—"be strictly punished? I think not. Though in terms of these rules we call laws, we cannot afford to perform detailed investigations on these kinds of matters. This is purely my personal opinion."

Armin bowed deeply in gratitude.

"Are you interested in the inland area?"

"The inland area?"

"Life within the Third Wall. If you seek it, and if you can prove that you hold the right ideas, I can recommend you…"

The offer came so suddenly, Armin couldn't reply.

"Well, just give it some thought." Kubal got to his feet and held out his right hand. "In any case, first we must make this operation a success. I trust you in this collaboration."

Wiping his sweaty palm on the hem of his uniform, Armin quickly held out his hand. They exchanged a firm handshake. Kubal's hand gripped Armin's with far more strength than expected. Tightly, firmly, as if to seal a pact.

"Together, let's protect this world to the end."

Armin did nod then.

When Eren left Shikishima, he didn't know where to go. Armin had been taken by a guard, and returning to Jean in the Squad Six waiting room wasn't exactly enticing. It seemed there was still time before they'd finish loading the explosives.

Where am I supposed to go?

As he started walking down the hall helplessly and without a destination, his head became filled with the same stagnant thoughts. Mikasa was alive. That fact should have made him happy. He ought to be shedding tears of happiness, no doubt. Yet Eren was in a state of extreme denial so consuming he couldn't even find a place to rest his gaze.

Eren remembered the image of Mikasa he had seen at the wire fence before departing. She'd gazed boldly, and affectionately, at him. Of course, Eren understood that she hadn't been the real Mikasa. It had been an illusion of his making. A delusion, nothing more than a wish. Still, Eren couldn't give up. *That* Mikasa had to exist somewhere. Inside Eren, perhaps, she needed to be that person.

So who was that? he wondered. Then he wanted to cry out with shame. *What was I thinking? Battle of Revenge for Mikasa. Vengeance for Mikasa. Take down the Titans for Mikasa. How pathetic.*

Eren remembered Shikishima's words, which seemed to have been fine-tuned to hurt him. There was no telling how much of it was fiction. The more he remembered, the further he fell into his dark mood.

—I might not be the same Mikasa that I was before.

A stream of information stirred aimlessly around in Eren's head. In his current state, he hardly knew what to believe. He had neither the will nor the courage to search for Mikasa, who was somewhere inside of the building, to ask her.

He realized he was standing before the stairs. As he contemplated whether to descend, climb, or turn around and trace back his steps, he saw the shadows of two people at the bottom. Candlelight illuminated the halls, but in general, it was difficult to see very far within the building. Eren strained his eyes and tried to identify the shadows. When he realized who it was, he hastily turned on his heels. Pronto, but taking care not to let his footsteps ring, he slunk away.

It had been Fukushi and Lil, caught in an embrace. Though Eren hadn't tried to confirm, it looked as if they were kissing. Their murmurs and sweet sighs clung to his ears like an echo. Though it was common knowledge among the recruits that Fukushi and Lil were close, Eren had never actually seen proof that they'd reached that stage. Driven by the awkwardness of witnessing his classmates' romantic moment, other images began creeping into his mind. Fukushi and Lil's form overlapped with another couple. Eren took a deep breath to calm himself down.

"So you're just going to run away."

Startled, Eren halted and turned to look towards the voice. He saw yet another person in one of the dark rooms facing the hall. When his eyes adjusted, he recognized who it was.

"You're such a prude." It was Hiana, alone in an empty room. She smiled teasingly.

"What are you talking about?" Eren shot back, his voice prickly.

"You saw, didn't you? The two of them."

As Hiana spoke, she beckoned a bewildered Eren into the room, patting the floor next to her. He thought about ignoring her and going somewhere else, but he had nowhere else to go. He also feared that if he ran again, he'd be admitting some kind of defeat. Perhaps Hiana had been sitting quietly in that room for a while. If so, there was a good chance she had seen him walk towards the stairs and hurry back. There was no denying it. Eren crumpled down at Hiana's side.

"Do you have a past with that person?"

"Who are you talking about?"

"That person," Hiana said. "Captain Shikishima's woman."

Eren felt like gravity had reversed itself, but he gulped and fought the sensation. Once Hiana's words had melted into the silence, he gave a simple reply. "Shut up."

Hiana sighed. "You're such a child."

"Only compared to you."

"How rude." Hiana chuckled, then looked at Eren knowingly.

"You're making fun of me just because I have a baby?"

Her voice was sweet and breathy, and she brought her hands smoothly to her chest. Then, one by one, with her slender fingertips she undid the buttons of her uniform, revealing the soft valley of her chest.

"I'm still plenty attractive, don't you think?"

"W-Wait."

Hiana took Eren's trembling hand. His shoulder twitched. Her hand was much warmer than he imagined, so alive. She caressed Eren's skin.

"Do you want to touch me?"

Eren couldn't speak. Slowly Hiana brought her face close to his, and as if she couldn't hold back any longer—she burst out laughing.

"Hahahaha!" Letting go of Eren's hand and clutching her stomach, she doubled over with laughter. After chortling for a while, she said, struggling to catch her breath, "You're so cute, you actually believed me."

"Don't…" Eren tried to cool his bright red face. "Don't you ever do that again."

"I'm sorry." Hiana finally returned to normal and exhaled. "I'm probably acting strange too. The state of affairs being what it is." She jumped up and stretched her arms towards the ceiling. She dropped her arms with a sigh. "Ah, I wonder why it's like this."

"It's because you volunteered."

"Haha, I guess that's right," admitted Hiana. She ambled towards the window, glanced outside, and facing Eren, relaxed down on the windowsill.

"You shouldn't get close to the windows," he warned. "The Titans might see you."

"It's okay. The lookouts are keeping tight watch from the top of the wall. If something comes up, they'll immediately raise a signal." The dim moonlight that shone from behind her made her look somehow magical. "If you volunteer you get child support," she said almost as if to herself. "That was the only reason. There was no big sense of purpose or duty. That was the only reason that I enlisted."

Eren watched Hiana wordlessly. He had never heard her talk so much.

"I understood that giving birth to a child, and raising a child, would be a very hard road. There's the heavy tax on anyone who has a child, and it's not easy to get an exemption. Nor is there any groundbreaking new solution to the problem. I should have known all of that. Everything that has happened has brought me to this place, to circumstances where I don't have a choice. It's as if...I'm only living for my child. It's not that I hate my kid or that she isn't dear to me. In fact, I just love my daughter, Riko. If I didn't have her, I would hardly have any reason to be alive. But on that note, sometimes I have to seriously wonder: Am I able to go on living because I have my daughter, or am I being made to live so my daughter can go on living? Hey, Eren..." Hiana looked at Eren with her calm eyes. "Why did you enlist?"

"Well..." Eren realized only after he opened his mouth that he had no reply. *Why did I enlist?* he asked himself. *For this, for that, or for something else...or maybe for Mikasa.*

Hiana shook her head to tell Eren not to bother with an answer. "Thank you." Her face slackened as if she were very tired. "There are a lot of things that can't be put into words."

After a pause, Eren changed the subject. "I've been wondering for a while, but...where did your husband go?"

Hiana shook her head coolly. "Who knows."

"Who knows?"

"He disappeared suddenly one day." Hiana sounded less sad than appalled. "I thought he went out, and that was all. He never came back."

"Where did he go?"

Hiana smiled. "Well, if I only knew. I asked at his workplace, I asked his friends, and nobody knew where my husband went. I had no idea what was going on. Then when I searched through his office for some kind of clue, the only thing that was left was this..." She put her hand into the pocket of her uniform and pulled out a frayed piece of cloth. "This was the only thing on the desk."

"What's that?"

"Who knows?" Hiana tilted her head. "Perhaps a badge."

Eren examined the object that Hiana held in her hand. It did seem to be some kind of badge: a round piece of cloth the size of a palm, tattered threads hanging from all sides as if it had been torn off. Some kind of bird was painted on the surface. Unfortunately, Eren didn't know enough about birds to immediately identify it. He had a strange feeling, however, that he had seen the image of the white bird before.

"What kind of bird is that?"

"I don't know. I don't know anything. I kept it as a charm, but I don't know anything specific about it."

Eren stared intently at it until Hiana returned it to her pocket. He was sure he'd seen it somewhere—the design of a white bird spreading its wings, circling the sky. *Where?* Eren frantically fumbled through his memory, but in the end, he couldn't remember.

"Oh, yeah," Hiana said. "Actually, I think a friend told me before. This was the bird—"

Suddenly, the moonlight that had been shining through the window faded and disappeared. Only the light of the candles remained. Perhaps a cloud had covered the moon. Eren thought so for a moment, but instantly changed his mind. Behind Hiana, it moved, rippling through the night. Eerily. Smoothly. They were on the fourth floor. Which meant…

"Get away, Hiana!"

The glass broke as if the night was being smashed to pieces. Before Eren's shout could trail off, something burst into the room and wrapped around Hiana's body. With no time to resist, she was dragged out into the darkness. Eren rushed towards the shattered window. He could feel the wind; there was a blank space in the wall. As the wind whipped around him, Eren was unable to turn away from the ghastly scene. In the right hand of the Titan, Hiana didn't move an inch.

It wasn't because she was resigned to her fate and ready to die.

Hiana was simply already dead.

The Titan had grabbed her so violently that her body, whipped back and forth, was broken. Her legs hung at an impossible angle from its right hand, which gripped her like a clamp.

Eren couldn't do anything.

The Titan clumsily lifted Hiana's body to its sleepy face. Just like a baby eating with its hands, with no grace, no sense of refinement, it shoved her into its mouth. Bent in half, Hiana was sucked into its maw and chomped to bits. Only her left leg, which didn't make it in, plopped down to the ground.

Unable to speak, Eren dashed as though to escape the sight.

V. COCYTUS

By the time the tremor had run through the entire building, close to ten Titans surrounded the perimeter. With no warning from the lookouts about the sudden attack, the soldiers were in a state of intense panic. In an instant, fear spread throughout the building, and opposing feelings of duty and terror blended together and ran through the air. The soldiers who had been resting jumped up, put on their equipment with shaking hands, and rushed down to the first floor. Armin, who had only just returned to the fourth-floor waiting room after his talk with Kubal, tumbled down to the first floor with the other soldiers. Right around the second floor, he ran into Eren.

On the ground floor, the soldiers collided into one another in a tangle as they each tried to find their station. Forgetting that it would draw attention from the Titans, they shouted and cursed. It was like a scene from hell. The earth rumbled, and with each tremor concrete rained down from the ceiling like powdered snow. The light from the candles flickered as if to accentuate the soldiers' trembling. When Armin and the others finally reached their new superior Hotogi, they received their instructions.

"Squad Six, along with the non-combatants, will guard the explosives in Truck One, which has—" With a large rumble, everybody lost their balance. "—Which has traveled," Hotogi went on, "half a mile south with Truck Two to escape the Titans' assault. Currently, two of Shikishima's people are guarding the explosives, but we don't know how long they can hold. Proceed with urgency. VME personnel are to depart from the rooftop in a scattered formation to avoid catching the Titans' attention. The rest will depart from the ground."

"Why did Truck One leave the safety of the wall?" Sannagi asked with a stern face.

"Because the front entrance was opened, and the Titans came pouring in. The courtyard ceased to be safe. Understood?"

"E-Excuse me!" Armin brushed Sannagi aside to ask his own question. "What happened to the lookouts? Why didn't they signal that the Titans were coming?"

"The lookouts…" Running a final check on his equipment, Hotogi spoke tersely as if to remind them that there was not much time. "They were all killed. That is all."

Hotogi ran off as Armin and the others frantically continued to put on their gear. As Armin made his preparations, he chewed over Hotogi's words in his head. The squad leader had said that the soldiers were "killed," not "eaten." Maybe it was just his word choice, but it seemed very significant. Armin feared it was as Kubal said: the culprit was not the Titans, but a human, the traitor. Harried by his fear both of the monstrosities and of the other thing that did not yet have a shape, he adjusted his equipment. Sannagi, Jean, and Sasha also finished putting on their gear. Lil and Fukushi, who had come late with flushed faces, were done as well. There was no sign of Hiana, though. Eren's extreme trembling didn't seem normal, either.

"Eren..." Armin said. "What's wrong?"

"I couldn't do anything."

"You couldn't do anything?"

"Hiana..." Eren sounded like he was stifling a sob. "Hiana was eaten, and I couldn't do anything."

Not only Armin, but the rest of Squad Six froze upon hearing Eren's words.

Another one of them had died.

The building shook, and beginning with Squad One, the VME personnel began to climb up to the roof.

"Let's go," Sannagi said. "We can think and mourn after we accomplish the mission and survive."

The Squad Six members forced themselves to stomach that reality and followed Squad Five up the stairs. Even as they climbed, the footfalls of the Titans—perhaps they were assailing the walls of the building itself—did not relent, sometimes nearly sending Armin falling down the stairs. Somehow he regained his balance and made for the roof.

Fourth floor, fifth floor, sixth floor.

The rooftop.

Slipping through the door, Armin noticed that the sky was beginning to brighten, the darkness thinning as if white paint had been mixed into the viscous night. But he only had a moment to make such observations. The scene that stretched before him and the others was one of utter hopelessness.

"What is this..." Jean murmured, his voice barely audible.

Absolute fear consumed Armin now. He recalled the first time he had beheld a Titan, two years earlier. An exceedingly similar scene unfolded before his eyes. Squad Six had been ordered to "guard Truck One." The command issued to the rest of the force was to "exterminate the Titans around the perimeter and safeguard the building." The soldiers from Squads One to Five who climbed to the roof first were taking the battle to the Titans to secure the base as ordered.

It was a task that was utterly fruitless.

From where Armin stood he could see easily over twenty Titans: from larger fifty-foot Titans to smaller fifteen-foot Titans—Titans, Titans, Titans.

The soldiers were fighting hard. From the right and from the left, they flew magnificently with their Vertical Maneuvering Equipment and launched their attacks. Nearly all of the soldiers were Armin's seniors. Their bodies' movements through the air, so sophisticated he couldn't even compare himself to them, reflected their arduous training. From the rooftop, however, the human soldiers looked so small, so helpless. It was a sad thought, but they appeared like nothing more than flies buzzing through the air, tiny and stupid. No matter how skilled, to the Titans they were slow bugs. They were struck, squashed, chomped, and eaten. Some were chewed thoroughly, some swallowed whole.

Before Armin's eyes, they fell and passed like meteors in a shower. One, and then another. Steam rose to his right. A Titan had been defeated, but it was the only one as far as he could see. The images that flooded his vision were of wires drooping sadly from the wall where they'd been anchored and of grunts sapped of their fighting spirit, petrified with fear.

From somewhere he heard a scream, as the rumble in the ground continued.

The Titans would not stop.

They could not be stopped.

A Titan standing right in front grabbed another soldier, who frantically tried to resist, slashing at the Titan's fingers, but was eventually squeezed so tightly he could no longer move. Gradually, like a wind-up timer coming to a stop, he weakened, and at a certain point he ceased to be. His comrades who had flown up into the air to save him were smacked down and crushed. Red forms were painted across the wall.

People were dying.

All too easily, they were being killed.

They each had a name.

They each had a life.

They all had friends, family, and lovers, no doubt; verbal tics, virtues and vices, favorite foods. Before coming here, every one of them had surmounted countless walls and experienced joy and sorrow and led irreplaceable lives. These were being plucked, without feeling, condolences, or even any logic. Snatched indifferently.

Armin clutched his stomach. His insides ached as if they were being wrung, as if they were rotting. Fear had taken over not only his heart but also his body.

"Armin!"

He blinked.

"You need to fly!"

Sasha was right in front of him. Doubtless, she too was overcome with fear. Her face was pale, and cold sweat soaked her forehead.

Still, with a firm voice, she called to Armin to give him courage.

"Our task is to guard the transport. It's okay, we don't need to fight!"

As her words sank in, Armin let out a long breath. To expel his terror, he let out as much air as he could. "Right…" He gripped his triggers and gave a small nod. "We just need to protect the truck."

"Now let's go."

"Th-Thank you."

"Compared to when you shared your food with me, it's absolutely nothing," Sasha forced a smile and spoke the brave words.

Armin returned an awkward grin, prepared for death, and jumped from the roof with Sasha. They shot their anchors toward their destination. They headed south to where the transport trucks were parked.

Eren didn't head for the roof.

When he reached the fifth floor, his legs halted as if all life had been sucked out of him. Watching his buddies' backs as they climbed the stairs, he moved to a random room on the floor. Unable to sit or even lean against the wall, he stood still.

The reason was simple.

On the fourth floor, he had seen Shikishima and Mikasa putting on their gear at the end of the hall. They'd appeared to be confirming operation tactics, facing each other. Eren had seen them for only a moment. He hadn't stared at them or overheard a single bit of their conversation. Still, the tiny glimpse of Mikasa's expression had robbed him of all strength.

Her gaze spoke of a trust and respect that she had never shown him. It was the sort of gaze that proved that she had given some deep part of her soul to her partner.

The moment Eren saw that expression on her face, something inside of him began to shrivel, leaking air. It wasn't as simple as jealousy or envy. Nor was it the heartbreak of unrequited love.

Taking measured breaths through his mouth, he goaded himself: *Why won't my legs move? We're in Titan territory, and they're swarming around the building right now.*

From outside he heard anchors firing, Titans stomping, and soldiers yelling, incessantly. The ground rumbled. The building creaked, and pieces of concrete fell from the ceiling. There was no reason not to fight. There was no excuse whatsoever not to fight.

Still, his legs wouldn't move. His heart wasn't letting him face the right direction and step forth. Hiana's voice echoed in his heart.

Why did you enlist?

Eren bit his lip. Mikasa's words flashed through his mind, too.

I might not be the same Mikasa that I was before.

Even in his confused state, there were two things Eren knew. The first was that he couldn't stay where he was. To fulfill their objective, he had to fly outside, and of course fleeing combat was unforgivable. There was nowhere to run to even if he wished to. He had to slip past the Titans and head for Truck One. He had no other choice.

The second thing he knew was that if he flew out into the open in his current state, he would certainly die.

Eren wrestled with his own heart. Standing still, he did battle with what lurked inside of him.

An intense force pressed on him as he cut through the wind. When he reeled in the wire, the leather belt that wrapped around his body tightened instantly, choking him all over. After rigorous training sessions, it wasn't rare to get bruised and scratched under the straps. If you tried to move at too high of a speed, the gravitational force could cause you to pass out. Vertical maneuvers looked like a graceful technology that allowed you to glide through the air, but the physical component placed extreme demands on anyone executing the tactic.

Armin tensed his lower back mid-flight and reeled in the wire. At the same time, he fired the gas. He arrived at the roof of a new building. When he landed, he could barely catch his breath. In the air he needed to brace his entire body, and a heavy fatigue consumed him.

Fortunately, he hadn't seen any Titans on the way. Ordered to take separate routes, Armin had split up from Sasha and the others. If he was okay, surely they were too. Cheering himself up, he confirmed the direction of the transports and stepped to the roof's edge. Then, below, he saw someone sitting on the ground.

Though she was only a speck, Armin could tell that it was Lil.

Why isn't she trying to fly? Is she out of gas? Either way, I have to help her.

He leapt from the roof and shot his anchor. Passing between three buildings, he dropped down near Lil. Though he hadn't been able to tell from above, when he got closer he saw that she was frantically pumping her arms up and down.

Noticing him, her face relaxed slightly. "Armin! Thank you…

Please, help me."

He didn't reply. He just stood there.

In front of Lil lay Fukushi. His body was limp, and it didn't look like he was breathing. She was pushing down on his chest with both hands over and over again in order to revive him.

"He's not breathing," she remarked gravely.

Armin shook his head.

"Let's go, Lil."

"You're joking," she scoffed without resting her hands. "There's no way I'd leave Fukushi."

"Lil…" Armin bit his lip and stared at Fukushi, whose body lay motionless. From the waist down—

He was missing.

As if it had been torn at the abdomen, or swallowed, his lower half was gone. Armin couldn't bear to look at the area. The smell of iron drifted in the air, and Lil's hands were already soaked a vivid red.

"Please, Fukushi… Please."

"Lil."

"Fukushi… Fukushi…"

"Lil!" Armin set his hand on her shoulder. "Lil, you have to survive."

She finally pulled her hands from Fukushi's body, clenched her eyes shut, and gritted her teeth. Then, to make sure not to alert the Titans, she killed the voice in her throat and began to weep ever so quietly.

"Let's go, Lil."

Armin helped her to her feet and guided her towards the transports. Luckily, they could already see the two trucks and were able to reach their destination on foot. Sannagi and Sasha were standing guard there. When they saw Lil's tears, they looked away solemnly, not having to be told what had happened.

"Eren and Jean aren't here yet," Sannagi noted as though to change the subject. "Did you see them?"

Armin shook his head. The transports were parked in an open area. Truck One's bed was packed tight with explosives, and on the other rode the non-combatants including the medic/cooks. Armin looked for Souda but couldn't find him. Where was the man?

"Is this everyone from Squad Six?"

It was Hange who looked out of the passenger seat of Truck Two. With her goggles resting on her head, she was addressing Armin.

"No," he answered. "There should be more coming. I'm sure of it."

Hange nodded. "As of now, there's no sign of the Titans around here. Because they have a habit of flocking to places with the most humans, we shouldn't be in danger while the VME troops are taking them on. However, we should keep our voices hushed. It's better to be safe than sorry."

"I heard that two members of Shikishima Detachment have been posted here."

"They were probably assigned to the convoy taking Supervisor Kubal to safety. Although it's doubtful there's any kind of safe spot around here. I seem to have been placed in command here for whatever reason. I've only just barely gotten a taste of running strategy, so I'm a bit confused as to what to do."

Hange cracked a resigned smile, but she looked nowhere near confident.

At the moment, only the scant few Squad Six members there were capable of vertical maneuvers, and it was doubtful whether Lil counted. Just the thought of being attacked by a Titan made Armin's blood run cold.

Then suddenly a motor began to rumble. As Armin jumped in surprise, the truck with the explosives began to roar as if someone were gunning the engine. There was no change to Truck Two, which was still parked.

"What? What happened?" Hange leapt from the passenger seat of Truck Two. Even as she spoke, Truck One rolled out and quickly gained speed, raising clouds of dust. "I didn't give any orders to head out! Are the Titans coming? What is the driver thinking?"

"I'm here..."

They turned to face the voice and a male soldier collapsed on the ground where the truck had been. Holding his right arm, he groaned at Hange.

"I'm sorry... Somebody elbowed into my seat and chucked me."

A possibility flashed through Armin's mind. "The traitor..."

"Wh-What?" Flustered, Hange pointed at the receding Truck One. "S-Stop them! All the explosives—they're on that transport! If they get stolen, this operation is over!"

The driver, still on the ground, pulled his firearm from his hip and aimed at the vehicle's tires.

"Wait, wait, don't shoot! What if you hit the explosives?"

"We have to go after it." Sannagi clutched his trigger, fired his wire, and flew over Armin's head.

"I'll go!"

This was Lil, who fired an anchor and rapidly began to close the distance to Truck One at a speed no one had ever witnessed. White smoke rose from the intense friction of the wire as she burned her gas. The other soldiers, who for a moment stood fascinated by the sight, also hastily engaged in vertical maneuvers. They could not afford to lose the explosives.

Throwing all caution to the wind, Lil pursued Truck One. She shot both her right and left anchors and reeled them in simultaneously with all she had. Glaring at the cargo bed, seeing Fukushi's shadow there, she desperately gave chase.

He had been a kind man, the most compassionate among their class. His breadth of perspective had made him a very considerate man as well. He'd understood Lil well and could murmur such sweet words to her that she would actually blush. Aside from his being "weaker" than her, he'd been "perfect" for Lil.

Her father had drilled her in a martial art since her earliest years. Day after day, he had taught her how to use her body until she knew it in her bones. His one dream had been for this martial art of his own creation to gain wide acceptance. Not for material gain, not out of some desire to bring peace to the world—rather, he'd simply hoped that his style would spread. Perhaps he'd seen an opportunity in his own daughter, Lil.

While eccentric, he had certainly been passionate. A farmer, he'd spent nearly all his time outside of work on his art, perfecting it. Without holding back, without any view to profits, all in.

But he had died in an instant.

A clumsy, stiff-bodied Titan with not an ounce of martial arts tutelage had devoured him.

The monster had grabbed him and brought him to its mouth and swallowed him.

The end.

Her father's techniques had been laughably useless.

After losing him, Lil almost doubted herself. Was all the rigorous training she had undergone completely meaningless, merely exhausting, nothing more than a self-satisfied way to make up for a lack of fulfillment? As she began to think that way, Lil's mind became dominated by pessimistic thoughts. Her prowess was supposed to protect humanity, but no matter how strong she was, she couldn't take down a Titan. *If so, what kind of value does my existence have? I'm just scared of myself now.*

The person who had found Lil in such a state was—

"Fukushi…" she murmured through gritted teeth as she shot out her anchor. It flew far. She burned her gas to avoid hitting a pillar in front of her and twisted ninety degrees to the right. Then she regained her balance and soared to the left. She released the anchor and glided. Though her body had spun around, she hadn't lost sight of her target. Dodging obstacles, she headed straight for the transport.

This time is different, Lil told herself. *This time, I'm not a soft little girl who's just going to get eaten. The art that Father taught me is perfect for vertical maneuvers. How to move my body, how to maintain my balance, how to keep the enemy in sight—I need all of it to fight the Titans. My father's teachings weren't useless. They're being used right now to save the world. Just like Fukushi said.*

Lil shot a last anchor into the cargo bed. As she began to reel it in, she avoided the explosives and landed on the roof above the driver's seat. She clung to the top of the fast-moving vehicle. Maintaining her balance so as not to get thrown off, she inched towards the door to the driver's seat. For her father, for Fukushi, she couldn't allow the operation to fail.

I don't know who you are, but I can't let you steal these explosives.

When Lil finally reached the edge, she stretched her arm and opened the door. Then, holding onto the roof, she swung her legs down. She felt herself kicking someone's face with the tip of her boot and smoothly slid into the truck, pushing the driver to the passenger seat at the same time.

"It's over…" Lil said, immediately straddling the driver. A black mask hid the so-called traitor's identity. All she could see were the eyes. Judging by the person's physique, it wasn't a woman. Controlling her breath, Lil pulled off the black mask.

"No…" Lil didn't believe her eyes. "Why you?"

"You might want to face forward."

At the male voice's warning, she turned to face thick, pale pillars—no.

A Titan's legs.

The truck was still advancing out of momentum. Lil frantically pulled the break, but she was too late.

Shoving her aside, the man jumped from the still-open door and rolled to safety.

Lil bit her lip and murmured to herself.

I'm sorry, Dad.

I'm sorry, Fukushi.

It looks like this is it for me.

She closed her eyes.

The truck collided with the Titan.

Clinging to a wall with his wire, Armin twirled to face away from the blast. In the end, neither Armin nor Sannagi nor Sasha could reach Lil.

Confirming that the transport was about to ram a Titan, they had aborted and scrambled for cover. Just as expected, the collision engulfed them in the blast.

A deafening sound, the smell of gunpowder.

Armin pasted himself helplessly against the wall. His body swung like a pendulum by the anchor. Steadying himself, he scraped his forehead against the surface—to blame himself, to carve his despair into his brow. Another one of them had died. The explosives were gone.

Frustration and a premonition that the end was near welled up from the pit of his stomach. As the blast died down, he looked over to where the transport had collided with the Titan. Nothing remained of the truck. The Titan was hunched forward, and luckily, its head and nape had been destroyed, and it was dying. White steam rose gently from scattered pieces of it.

There had been an explosion, no doubt.

But Armin had to wonder. The blast was far smaller than expected given the amount of gunpowder loaded onto the bed. Perhaps the explosives had lost some of their potency from lying unused for so many years in the basement. In other words, even if the traitor hadn't gotten in the way, all of their gunpowder wouldn't have closed up the hole in the First Wall. Success had never been possible.

Armin sighed.

It was over.

He didn't move from the wall until Sasha and Sannagi came calling to him. There was nothing to be done.

Eren tried and climbed up to the roof, but his heart didn't follow. As if consumed by some invisible decay, he couldn't jump. He began to feel utterly pathetic. He squeezed his fists tightly, and his fingernails ate into his hands.

"Are you just going to let fear take over?"

He whirled around at the voice that came from behind. The person who had spoken landed on the roof and stepped toward Eren.

"Captain Shikishima…"

No doubt because he had been fighting Titans, the strongest man himself was panting a little. But he seemed extraordinarily calm and in no way fatigued. There was not a trace of unease in his eyes.

"Your legs are shaking and won't move?"

"It's not that. It's just…" Swallowing his complicated feelings about Shikishima, Eren answered honestly. "I'm confused."

"Hmm."

Shikishima adjusted his disheveled scarf. The Titans' rumbling didn't cease, and fewer and fewer soldiers were visible in the air.

"We just lost the explosives on Truck One," the captain stated plainly. "It's not likely we'll be doing any more explosive-related outer wall restorations."

"What?"

"It's hopeless," Shikishima said coolly, not sounding hopeless in the least. "At this point, what does a soldier fight for? I wouldn't know if you asked me. There's only one thing I can say for sure."

He didn't look at Eren and remained facing forward.

"There are two ways to live," the captain declared. "The first is to live to *live* and die trying. The second is to live idly, killing time until you die. I'm not talking about which life is the more lovely, more desirable for society. I for one truly, overwhelmingly, aspire towards the former."

Shikishima's words sank into Eren's heart.

"It seems similar circumstances have brought us both to this place."

"What do you mean by that?"

"What do I mean?" Shikishima smiled sarcastically. "Nothing important, I just felt that way now. I didn't mean anything by it."

Another soldier's scream came from somewhere.

"In this world, there are actually very few choices. That is why, bearing the Wings of Liberty, we leapt outside for more options. Perhaps there was no real meaning to our expeditions. Perhaps our labors were fruitless. Perhaps we never created another option. Still, I have to commend myself, because I *went outside*. I took the best path for living to *live*. No matter who denies it, this truth is unwavering. Listen, Eren."

Shikishima turned to stare intently at Eren as though to etch him deep into his eyes.

"You need to live to *live*. Even if you are handed a die with a six on all its faces, cast it hoping to roll a one. Warp it with all your strength to obtain the outcome you desire. Haven't you ever yearned to see the outside world?"

"I have, yes."

"Then fly. Don't you feel cramped, trapped inside these walls? Think about it carefully. It's not as if the Titans shut us in here. We humans shut ourselves up out of fear of the Titans. From there, whether you leap over the wall or stay cooped up is all your choice. Break your bars."

"I…" Eren spoke as if to himself. "I'm not livestock."

Shikishima smiled. "Interesting expression. Why did you want to go outside?"

"Because…"

Eren felt the light that definitely shone in him. In the blink of an eye, his doubts, his misgivings, and his anxiety vanished. He wasn't one for abstruse reasoning, but an answer had existed all along.

"Because I was born into this world!"

Shikishima nodded firmly. "I teased you too hard earlier. I'm sorry," he apologized with a sigh. "But that's the spirit. You want to go outside because you were born into this world. You want to break free of the bonds that tie you down. To do that, you need to kill the Titans. For now, that is enough. As for what comes later, you will understand in time. Go on, destroy everything that threatens you."

Shikishima pulled out his triggers and smoothly installed his blades. And then quickly surveyed the area. "I'll take the two on the left. You take the one on the right."

Eren looked to his right, where one gaunt Titan was stumbling around.

Its chin jutted severely, and its mouth stretched to its ears, giving it the air of an able predator, but Eren wasn't intimidated.

I'm going to do it.

"Once you've gathered your resolve, the rest is just technique." Shikishima set his right foot on the roof's edge. "I'm sure it will be frightening at first, but be brave and slip within their reach. Their motions are powerful but relatively simple. Get into close range, and kill before you're killed. To do that you need to take the shortest, quickest routes possible. If you stretch out your wire and move in a large arc, it will be easier on your body, but they will see you. Always seek a path that will surprise the Titan, and make many tight movements. Of course, if you pass out, you're done for. Defeat gravity. Otherwise, you can't defeat the Titans."

Eren gripped his triggers and nodded firmly.

"Good luck out there."

"Yes, sir."

Eren ran. When he reached full speed, he jumped. He flew down from the roof, and his uniform fluttered in the wind as he fell. After descending a bit, he fired his left anchor, which stuck fast on a wall surface. The pressure tightened around his hips, and his body creaked as gravity attacked it. He gritted his teeth and shot his right anchor forward—a hit. At the same time, he released his left anchor. He rode his arc and closed in on the Titan.

It had been roaming aimlessly, but when it caught sight of Eren it slowly changed course and gazed at him head-on.

Very good.

Eren continued to accelerate. He shot anchors into the walls on either side and rapidly closed the gap between himself and the Titan.

His vision shook violently as his consciousness threatened to cede to the centrifugal force. He wasn't succumbing to it, though. He snapped his eyes wide open and planned his route for the Titan's nape—as Shikishima had advised, one that would surprise it.

When he was only thirty feet away, Eren decided to leap over its head.

—The Titan swung its right arm wide to swat him down—

It was too slow. Eren shot his anchors simultaneously at the walls to the right and left, and both found purchase. As if on a swing, he swept up right in front of the creature.

—The Titan brought down its right hand—

It missed, striking the ground instead. Eren had released both his anchors and now soared far above its head. For a moment he was weightless, and for that moment, everything went silent. As his momentum carried him toward the Titan's dorsal side, he flipped his body over in midair and got behind it.

—The Titan looked around toward him—

It was still moving too slowly, its motions powerful but also simple as Shikishima had said. Eren fired his anchor. *I'm going to bury it in its side while it's turning its head.* A hit. The Titan's flesh rippled and shook. The wire twisted due to its movement, but that too had been planned. Eren pulled his trigger hands back and began to wind the wire. He rapidly closed the distance between himself and the Titan.

—The Titan swung its arm up at Eren again—

He wasn't going to attack just yet. As his speed increased, he released the anchor and fired anew, this time aiming for the top of the Titan's shoulder. A hit. Eren was swiftly changing course at a close range as Shikishima had instructed.

—The Titan, unable to acquire the target, failed to bring down its arm—

Gravity like Eren had never experienced before enveloped his body. He tensed his abdominal muscles and flew in a path that orbited the Titan. As if slicing the air, he finely alternated between shooting and releasing his anchors and didn't allow for the creature's gaze to settle.

—The Titan slowly swiveled its head, attempting to acquire the target—

But it couldn't. Confirming this, Eren patiently waited for his opportunity despite his dimming consciousness.

—The Titan, vexed, slammed its right fist into the ground with all its might—

Now was the time. Eren jumped over the Titan via a wall. The monster's back was completely exposed. Its arm still slammed down on the ground, it was basking in the afterglow of its own strike. Perhaps it was under the illusion that it had squashed Eren. Either way, it was now or never. Releasing both his anchors, Eren reeled in the wire. Aiming at the Titan's nape, he ensured that he would free-fall onto it. He pushed his triggers into their sheaths and extracted the blades. He could do this.

After that, all he thought about was slicing Titan flesh. Deeply, deeply, deeply. He'd gouge it out. He adjusted the angle of his right arm, his left arm. With all his strength, he lifted his blades.

—The Titan did not turn around—

I've got this. With all the force he could muster, he slashed.

—The Titan gave a short yell—

The impact reverberated up into both of Eren's hands. He shot an anchor to gain altitude and looked behind him. There he saw the Titan, its nape removed with surgical precision. It slowly dropped to its knees, knocked its head against the wall, and fell all the way to the ground. Steam rose from its body and rose up to the heavens, echoing Eren's triumph.

I killed it. Eren felt a powerful sense of accomplishment. *I killed a Titan.*

After watching its carcass gradually bubble and vanish, he faced forward again, unable to hide his smile—

And his heart stopped.

Shock, and calm.

Before his eyes, a gaping maw. A giant mouth big enough to swallow him whole, waiting.

He had been careless. *When did another Titan...*

Eren madly pressed down his trigger and shot out an anchor at the left wall. He reeled it in the moment it hit its target and propelled gas at full throttle.

The Titan's mouth snapped shut. The hard clamping of its teeth and a sound like grinding cutlery shook Eren to his core.

A severe shock ran up his left leg.

Eren grunted and gritted his teeth but failed to shoot his right anchor. He fell backward towards the ground. He curled into a defensive position to protect himself from the impact, but the cruel crash racked his body and a groan left his lips. The ground smelled like defeat. Eren pushed against it with his sore palms and tried to stand up but couldn't muster any strength under his waist. He groaned again. When he glanced at his left leg, which wouldn't listen to him, he was speechless. Despair crept through his entire body.

It's a lie. It has to be a lie.

His right leg was clean gone from the knee down.

Blood oozed from the stump. When he saw the wound, intense pain overtook him. He screwed his eyes shut and tried to drag his body using his arms. He had to escape from the Titan.

Through his pain, Eren looked up. He realized that the Titan wasn't paying attention to him. Instead, it was squeezing something tightly in its right hand.

That's—

After seeing Truck One explode, Armin returned to Truck Two where Hange waited with Sannagi and Sasha. Perhaps the squad leader already grasped the outlines and didn't seem surprised as Sannagi briefed her. Still, unable to hide her immense disappointment, she let out a sigh.

They could see Souda, who hadn't been around until that moment, near Truck Two. His breath was ragged as if he'd been running.

"Souda. Where were you?"

"I was looking for Eren."

That reminded Armin that his friend was nowhere to be seen. Nor did he spot Jean. *Where did the two of them go? Are they okay?*

"Hey." The voice was Sannagi's. "There."

He pointed out a pair of Titans. Because they were so far away, they hadn't noticed Armin and company. Instead the creatures were reaching for the roof of a building and drawing their hands back, repeatedly. It seemed somebody was still there. Armin recognized the figure scampering around on the roof.

"It's Jean," he muttered.

"He was stranded there all this time?" Sannagi said bitterly. "I though he aced vertical maneuvers."

Armin bit his lip. The Titans catching on to the presence of Truck Two meant more casualties. To begin with, most of the personnel there didn't even have VMEs. They would likely suffer a crushing defeat if they took on two monsters. Still, Jean was a dear classmate. They couldn't lose any more of their own.

"Let's go," urged Sannagi.

Armin told him to wait for a second. An idea was beginning to form in his head, and he quickly relayed it to Sannagi and Sasha. It wasn't a full-blown "plan" but stood a better chance of success than attacking the Titans head-on. When the others heard it, they nodded in agreement.

"We have to bet on Jean," Sannagi sighed.

Armin and Sasha dashed across the ground to a point about fifty yards from the Titans. Then, grabbing the signal flares they each had at their hips, they aimed for the Titans and fired. With a high-pitched sound, thin white streams of smoke drew a beeline to their targets. The creatures sluggishly turned around to see what had hit them. They noticed Armin and Sasha.

"Jean! Jean!" they shouted, trembling under the Titans' gaze. "Look over here, Jean!"

Jean gingerly emerged atop the roof and looked down at them, his face pale.

"Please!" cried Armin.

The Titans, also reacting to their yells, shifted their full attention to Armin and Sasha and began to sidle towards their new prey.

"It doesn't matter which," called out Armin, "can you just kill one? Their napes should be completely accessible now! Please, Jean!"

Jean looked lost and, as if to reject Armin's plea, disappeared from view.

"It's okay, Jean! I know you can do it!"

Sasha, who stood beside Armin, swiftly lifted her bow. In seconds, she was shooting. Her consecutive arrow strikes accurately pierced the Titans' eyes. She beautifully succeeded in taking away their vision.

"Yes!" Armin heard her exclaim next to him. The two Titans held their eyes and shook their heads in agony.

"Fly, Jean! If you don't hurry their vision will return! Please!"

"You need to fly!" Sasha shouted too.

"It's okay, Jean, you're good at this!"

Suddenly they spotted him again. He seemed to take a deep breath. Even from far away, they could see his shoulders heave. Then, as if he'd finally made up his mind, he pulled his blades from their sheaths.

He flew.

Shooting his anchor into a nearby wall, he descended smoothly. With the perfect movements they had witnessed so many times during training, he homed in on the Titan on the left. Swinging his wrists, he glared at his mark. He even let out a war cry.

A flash.

The Titan halted, and slowly, as if being swallowed by the ground, it fell. A clear and deep gash was left in its nape. Seeing that the Titan had fallen, Jean flew to the roof of the opposite building.

"Yes." Armin found himself clenching his fist. "Good job, Jean."

"Now just one more," Sasha said.

Armin was no longer worried. From the building on his right, like some meteorite or a bullet, a large meaty bundle came flying. Thanks to its mass, even the iron wire screamed. It was Sannagi, who had been waiting on the roof of another building. Waving his two blades, he pounced on the remaining Titan's nape. Then, with all his strength, he sliced it off.

Sannagi landed on the ground. Belatedly, as if remembering to die, the Titan twitched and fell backwards. Clouds of dust swirled, and steam rose from its body.

"I'm glad I could do it."

Relieved, Sannagi walked over to the Titan to examine its nape. The cut wasn't very sharp, but due to his strength, it was very deep: Sannagi style. He wasn't nearly the best at vertical maneuvers thanks to his weight.

Armin said, "Let's go to Jean."

The three of them flew to the roof of the building where their squadmate had landed. Perhaps still tense from the battle, he was on all fours, and his back was moving up and down. When he heard their footsteps, he curled up and hid his head, ashamed.

"I'm sorry," Jean muttered as if he were confessing.

"Don't worry," Sannagi consoled him cheerfully, "if you're safe, that's enough."

"It's not that. I just watched it happen. Just stood there like an idiot. I just watched."

At his words, a chill ran through the group. Before the silence became too heavy, Armin asked, "What are you talking about?"

Jean's raspy voice barely made it from his throat. "When it got Eren…"

Time stopped for Armin. His throat ran dry, and his vision flickered. Something snapped inside of him and rang violently as if to signal an end of sorts. Yet he managed to speak.

"Did a Titan…" he timidly broached the worst possibility, "eat him?"

"It was just one leg, but he was definitely eaten. It only happened just now. He might still be lying around somewhere."

"Lying around somewhere…"

"Armin!"

As Sasha's voice rang out, something heavy slammed into Armin's back. If somebody told him that a truck had run into him, he might have believed it. The impact was that great. The blow shook his entire body, and his jolted mind lost all sense of reality for a moment. When he came to, his body was wrapped in something. It didn't take him long to understand what it was.

A Titan's hand.

"Armin!" bellowed Sannagi.

A Titan had snuck up on them. Sweat gushed out of Armin's every pore, and he struggled like a drowning man. Sadly, his body didn't budge an inch, and in the Titan's stiff grip it began to crack all over. The pain was too much that he couldn't even cry out.

Gradually, his companions' voices grew distant. Sasha was firing her arrows, but her aim was poor. Maybe her hands were shaking. When the pain reached its limit, Armin's body was finally freed.

But it was no cause for celebration. The only thing awaiting him was a pitch-black world.

He couldn't see anything. A stinging odor hung heavily in the air. Just smelling it was almost enough to make him vomit.

His hands were wet. A sticky, slimy layer of liquid clung to them. It was obvious.

I'm in a Titan's mouth.

I was grabbed by a Titan and thrown into its mouth.

Realizing the truth, Armin writhed blindly. It seemed he was still on what would be the tongue. As proof he saw several faint slits of light in front of him. They had to be the teeth. If he could somehow get out, he might still be saved. The more he wriggled, however, the more he was pulled back towards the throat. He couldn't brace himself because of the mucus. He tried to get a blade out, but his slippery hand couldn't grab the trigger.

No, no. I'm going to die if I don't get out. Armin wasn't ready. He was simply and purely scared. He desperately tried to shake off the black curtain of despair. *I absolutely don't want to die. I absolutely refuse to get swallowed by a Titan. I don't want to think about the afterlife or to come up with parting words.*

Armin wasn't accepting any of this.

Somebody, somebody save me. Somebody...

At that moment, something strange happened. Everything opened up before his eyes. Slowly, forcibly, the Titan's mouth had been wrenched open.

"Armin!"

There, holding the upper jaw with both hands, and the lower jaw with just a right leg—

"Eren..."

It was Eren. He was missing a leg just as Jean had said. Naturally, the wound hadn't closed yet and dripped fresh blood like a leaky faucet.

Steeling his entire body against the Titan's crushing jaw, Eren extended his left hand towards Armin.

"Don't you die in this shit hole, Armin."

Gazing at Eren, Armin's heart grew full. Stretching his arm pleadingly in turn, fighting against the membrane, he finally grabbed Eren's left hand.

Taking firm hold, Eren took advantage of the slime and tugged at his friend. Armin felt his body slipping into freedom, gliding smoothly over the mucus and out of the maw.

Yes. I'm saved.

Guided toward the ground by gravity, Armin looked up at Eren. Words of gratitude certainly seemed to be in order. What should he say to Eren, who had fired his wire for the Titan's mouth to come save a friend even after losing a leg?

Still yanking the mouth open, Eren flashed Armin a tiny smile.

At that very moment—

As if some spell was broken, the mouth snapped shut.

Silence.

As if to show off its rows of teeth, the Titan looked at Armin and bared them to its gums. There was no sign of Eren, who had been there just now.

Something fell at Armin's feet.

Upon realizing that it was Eren's right arm, which until seconds earlier was propping open the Titan's jaws, Armin tumbled down into the pits of despair.

Even as Sasha scooped him up with her VME, his soul continued to sink.

Eren was dead.

Armin's heart, too, was dying—melting into pitch-dark hopelessness, and dying.

VI. GIUDECCA

It was a freezing winter day, and Mikasa was still six or seven.

Though she couldn't really remember the reason, on that day she was angry at her parents. Because she couldn't remember why, she was sure it wasn't about anything very important. It was, without a doubt, not something that caused any lasting rift between her and her family; it left no aftertaste. Still, at the time it was more important than anything to her, and she thought she would never forgive her parents. She'd been a little child.

Mikasa had left her house.

With her eyebrows knit together in fury, she faced north and began to walk. It wasn't as if she had a destination. If she could get away from her house, it didn't matter where she went. She just walked. She left the town of Monzen, passed the fields, headed for the path where the trees grew thick, and when the path disappeared completely and her surroundings began to resemble a forest, finally sat down. At that moment, she already couldn't feel anything resembling anger inside of her.

She sighed. *Time to go home.*

She sniffled. She realized that the air was far colder than she thought. Perhaps her fury had offset the cold. However, the moment she became aware of the cold, the air turned into sharp teeth and began to attack her. Because she had let her emotions carry her impulsively from her house, she was dressed lightly and wasn't even wearing an overcoat.

Filled with regret, Mikasa began to walk back on the path she had taken through the trees. She walked, and walked, and walked, but she couldn't see any way out of the forest. While she thought she was simply walking back the way she came, she saw no indications of the familiar path. Gradually, she grew unhappy, and soon she couldn't stop trembling. The tips of her toes and her fingers began to grow numb. It wasn't even snowing, but still it was freezing.

Her body continued to shake.

No matter how much she walked, she couldn't seem to get anywhere. Soon, she reached the limits of her stamina and decided to lean against a tree trunk.

A short rest.

She pressed her back against the trunk. Then as she quivered against the faint warmth of the tree, she realized that she couldn't stand back up. It felt as if her nerves had been broken off from the waist down, and she was unable to move.

She considered her situation. Right then, she would be having dinner at her house. She would be passing the time as she always did. Tears began to spill from her eyes. She didn't have the strength, however, to wipe her tears or to blow her nose. And then, when everything inside of her was nearly completely exhausted, Eren arrived.

He was breathing heavily, exhaling white breath like a boiling kettle. He seemed to be speaking to Mikasa, but she couldn't hear him. Eren wrapped the red scarf that he was wearing tightly around her and picked her up.

Like that, his sights set on Monzen, he began to walk. Though Eren was very young, he lived alone. The shabby hut that stood right beside Mikasa's home was Eren's house. Sometimes Souda would come around to care for him, but other than that Eren didn't have anything resembling parents. Mikasa's often worried for him and cared for him. Naturally, Mikasa and Eren saw each other frequently. They were practically like family. Yes, they'd become family.

Her consciousness fading, Mikasa desperately clung to Eren's shoulders.

They reached Monzen safely, and after weathering the repercussions of her trip, Mikasa went to return the scarf to Eren. But he wouldn't take it back.

I'll let you have it. I don't want you to freeze to death if you run away from home again.

Mikasa nodded. She kept the scarf.

Eren in those days. Mikasa in those days.

Mikasa——

——

——swung down her blades.

When she made her beautiful cuts, she hardly felt any impact on her hands, only a smooth, faint sensation that quickly dissipated. She passed through the steam wafting up into the air and landed on a roof. With a sigh she looked up at the sky, which was getting considerably brighter. Night was ending.

Why would I remember that at a time like this? she asked herself. She also thought about the cold attitude she had adopted around Eren and wondered, *How much have I changed since that day? Or rather, how much of me has been left unchanged? My parents were eaten by Titans and killed. I've lost my dear family. I lost my birthplace and a home to return to. I've lost so many other things. Am I still really capable of being around Eren? Am I really somebody whom Eren still needs? I knew that he had survived and didn't once visit him. I didn't even tell him that I was alive. What does that make me...*

Stop. I have to concentrate.

Mikasa saw a new Titan, made three jumps, and slashed at it. It wasn't hard. Shikishima had told her to count how many she killed, but she honestly didn't care. Titans were merely to be killed as far as she was concerned. They only mattered while they were being killed and meaningless afterwards. They existed to be forgotten or to be cut down.

She alighted on a building and revved the engine to test the gas. The trigger felt weak. She was low on fuel. She looked around, and when she spotted Truck Two, where she could resupply, she flew towards it. From above she noticed many soldiers gathered around it for some reason. She landed and approached the truck. About ten non-combatants were awaiting orders. She started to ask for fuel, but when she saw Armin, she stopped.

He was slumped on the ground. His face was pale with misery. Though Mikasa thought he'd perhaps suffered a terrible injury, it seemed he was unharmed. Hange from Arms Development and the fresh-faced soldiers Mikasa had seen earlier surrounded him. Their numbers had dwindled.

She could only count four including Armin.

And there was no sign of Eren.

Shaking off her unease, Mikasa slowly turned and strode towards Armin. No matter how long she put it off, the answer would be the same.

When Armin saw her approaching, he covered his face. "Mikasa..." His voice was as feeble as a mosquito's hum.

Unable to ask anything, she just stood before him.

"Eren, he..." Armin managed to speak through his sobs. "He was eaten."

A soft wind blew. Mikasa's world receded slightly from reality as if shifting out of phase.

"It was my fault."

Armin's grief-stricken confession tickled, like cotton, something deep inside her.

"I'm sorry, Mikasa... Eren took my place... I couldn't do anything. I'm sorry."

Looking closely, Mikasa realized that Armin gripped a white cloth bundle. Eren's severed arm poked out of it. It was just an arm, but she could tell. The arm was Eren's. Though they had been apart for only two years, even after ten she would have known.

It was Eren's arm.

And that was why Mikasa had no choice but to accept Armin's words.

Eren was dead. Devoured by a Titan, killed.

From somewhere in the distance, she could hear the familiar rumble. She traced it to a Titan crouched in the shadow of a building that stood a hundred yards away.

"Armin," she said, with only her face, her mouth, her throat, and not her heart. "Now is not the time to get sentimental."

He looked up in shock. Perhaps he resented her callousness, her calmness, her heartlessness. It didn't matter what he thought. She didn't care, and she continued evenly.

"Our task hasn't changed. I'll take down that Titan over there and open an avenue for escape. Until further instructions, just focus on surviving."

Mikasa turned and ran towards the Titan. Once she gathered enough speed, she transitioned to vertical maneuvers. Armin seemed to be screaming something, but his words didn't reach her ears. She equipped blades in both hands, charged at the Titan at top speed, and narrowed the gap in no time at all. All the emotion that she couldn't process, she converted into velocity and accelerated, her body generating friction in the air and turning into wind.

The Titan was right there. She gripped her blades.

Then, as though the wires had snapped, Mikasa's body hung midair.

She'd lost her power. Enveloped by gravity she dropped straight towards the building below her. She crashed. Pain coursed through her, but she was lucky. The structure was made of wood, and her wounds were not fatal. Mikasa flipped and tumbled down from the roof, thudded onto an abandoned wooden crate, and then onto the ground. The pain gradually faded from her body as she stared up at the sky on her back.

Right, I was running out of gas. I'd completely forgotten and burned it too hard. I'm such an idiot. What was I thinking? "Now is not the time to get sentimental." "I'll take down that Titan over there and open an avenue for escape." What a joke.

The earth rumbled close by and shook her body. Still on the ground, she turned to look. It was the Titan she had marked as hers. Swinging its ample flesh, it steadily approached Mikasa, its dim, narrow pupils locked firmly onto her. She lifted her triggers. Her blades had broken in the fall and were both about the length of daggers now. With a sigh, Mikasa slowly lowered her arms back to the ground.

This again, thought Mikasa. *And so this senseless world robs me of all kinds of things again.* She was losing, in earnest now, her will, her mental fortitude, to resist the cruelty of the world. Turning away from the Titan, she looked back up as if to renounce it all. In the sky above her, she saw three birds.

Where were they going? Without a care for the Titans, the world, and of course, Mikasa, they were flying straight to some other place. Their beautiful wide wings hinted at true freedom.

Then suddenly, from a faraway world, she heard a faint voice.

—I'm going to join the Survey Party and go find the Ocean. And after that, I'm going to take you there too. It's a promise.

A louder rumble than before. The Titan's feet were nearly upon her. As it stared at Mikasa, it raised its left hand high. It probably meant to snatch her up. To snatch, grab, squeeze, and eat her. To prey on her as was its wont.

For a moment, Mikasa imagined a world where she was devoured and gone.

Who is going to grieve for me? Who is going to cry because I'm gone from this world? In fact, might anyone feel joy over it? Might anyone find any gain in it?

Quicker than light, the thoughts rushed through her mind, and she arrived at an answer. She closed her eyes and bit her lip firmly, hard enough for the unmistakable taste of blood to spread through her mouth.

The taste of blood is the taste of death.

The taste of death is the taste of iron.

The taste of iron is the taste of the fight.

The Titan brought down its hand. Mikasa snapped her eyes wide open and rolled out of the way. With a thunderous sound the hand hammered, in vain, where she'd lain supine moments ago. The Titan glanced at Mikasa's new location.

Ignoring her aching body, she slowly got to her feet and pointed her truncated blades at the creature.

I can't just die, Mikasa chanted, swore in her heart, *I absolutely cannot die. I must survive. Survive in this cruel world. That is my only atonement.*

Who stood to gain least by her death? Herself. If she died, she would never be able to influence the world or touch another person again. She wouldn't be able to stand back up again, for Eren.

Mikasa gritted her teeth. *I must survive. And then, and then I...*

Her thoughts were swept away by the wind.

A whirlwind.

The intense gale had come from behind faster than a typhoon. She crouched down a bit to brace against the impact.

She didn't understand the situation at first.

What...is this?

Her hands gripping her triggers, she stood mutely as the scene unfolded.

The Titan that had been looming above her just a moment

earlier—fell from the explosive impact.

Mikasa hadn't done anything.

A Titan's hand had come from behind her and—punched the other Titan.

The new Titan had moved in too quickly for Mikasa to even notice. Clenching its right fist, it had jumped over her, coiled its arm back like a spring, and swung.

The blast of the contact swept over her.

The first Titan, flailing, collapsing, had slid a few dozen feet. The dust that rose obscured Mikasa's vision and deepened her confusion. No hypothesis, no theory, stepped up in her mind to provide a clear answer. It was inexplicable.

The Titan that had struck its own kind let out a loud howl, almost as if to make a point.

This particular one cut a braver, a tougher, a wilder figure in Mikasa's eyes than any Titan she'd ever seen. Its revelatory howl seemed to reverberate through the world, shaking something buried deep in her core.

A Titan striking another Titan—she had never heard of such a thing and had no clear idea as to the reason.

But she felt elated.

She was simply and unabashedly fascinated.

Armin jumped from the roof and shot an anchor. He grabbed Mikasa, who stood unmoving, reeled in the wire, and escaped with her back to the safety of the roof.

"Are you hurt?"

Mikasa nodded vaguely. She was still staring absently at the Titan. Jean, Sasha, and Sannagi, the last of whom carried Hange, soon joined them. Armin could imagine why Hange had taken the trouble to come up to the roof though she couldn't fly. With the others, he turned his attention towards the strange Titan that had arrived so suddenly.

It was howling.

It was about forty feet tall, and its right arm, which had hit the other Titan, was damaged from the powerful blow and gone from the wrist down. Still, steam began to rise from it, and slowly, in the shimmering heat, it repaired itself.

The Titan howled for a while longer before walking up to the brethren it had felled. Astonishingly, just one blow had shattered the other's head into smithereens, hinting at the intensity of the impact.

The Titan glared at the headless carcass and stomped firmly down on the nape without hesitation. Even the building where Armin and the others stood shook, and the ground almost sounded like it was screaming. Steam began to rise; it was dead.

"What the…" The voice came from Hange, who clung to the railing on the rooftop as she studied this Titan. "A Titan attacked a Titan…and killed it, no less. It knew the weak spot." Her mouth agape, she didn't try to conceal her excitement. "What is happening? It's clearly intelligent."

Then, as if to answer its howl, three more Titans arrived on scene: two from the right, one from the left. Armin nervously grabbed his triggers, but there was no need to fight.

The newcomers didn't even cast a glance at the humans and made straight for the mysterious Titan.

"Hey, hey…" Hange removed her goggles and stared. "Do other Titans see it as an enemy?"

It howled again and began to dash far faster than any Titan they'd seen before. Gouging the earth with an agile, even beautiful gait, it charged at the pair of intruders on the right at a speed that put the wind to shame.

Lifting its right fist, and still accelerating, it struck one of them— and blew away its face. An instant later, the Mysterious Titan craned its neck and bit off the defenseless nape, killing its foe. The other Titan chomped down on its shoulder in turn, but with a brief cry, it trapped its adversary's body and wrestled it down to the ground.

The impact was such that Armin lost his balance.

Straddling its foe, the Mysterious Titan slammed down its fist with the force of a blade, tearing the other's neck in one go. The sheer power on display was overwhelming. Steam immediately began to rise, and the giant form stood up to look for its next prey. It glowered at the last Titan and charged again, lifting its left arm and swinging it like a whip this time to destroy the head.

It was a complete wipeout.

"Is it…on our side?" Sannagi muttered to himself.

"I've never seen anything like it!!" cried Hange. "What is this?!"

Though Armin was disturbed that Hange seemed to be losing it, he couldn't help but understand. He, too, was excited by what he'd witnessed. The Mysterious Titan differed from the others not only in behavior but also in physical appearance. Its loose hair gave it a wild look; its toned muscles seemed impeccably exercised; the corners of its wide mouth angled up savagely; its pupils flashed an eerie red. It didn't have the slightest air of stupidity that the others had. It almost appeared to be a "demon of justice" come to bring an iron hammer down upon the Titans. Somehow Armin was also reminded, if only a little, of a friend whom he'd cherished.

Four more Titans arrived, two from the right, two from the left. The Mysterious Titan was already running. It bent its body and struck. Sending shock waves all the way up to the building where Armin and the others stood, it continued to attack with world-destroying force. Freely, it sprinted. The incoming Titans went up in white steam one after another until the last one also vanished.

The humans, their eyes glued to the spectacle, were speechless.

Perhaps the series of battles had exhausted even the Mysterious Titan. It showed faint signs of weariness, exhaling steam and gently raising and lowering its shoulders. It let out another cry as if it were trying to forget something. The air shook.

As its long howl ended, the Mysterious Titan lifted its gaze, very slowly, towards the roof where Armin and the others stood. Its bright red pupils had an uncanny expression.

"What…" Jean muttered. "Why's it looking at us?"

The Titan took a step. Without bothering to calm its breathing, it took another step. Shaking the ground, it approached. Another step.

"Hey, hey, who said it was on our side?"

As it had done earlier with the other Titans, it lifted its right hand up toward the sky. Armin and the others entered its range.

"I-It's going to strike. Run!!"

At Sannagi's voice, Armin made to fly away. But realizing that Mikasa and Hange couldn't, he paused. *What do I do? At this rate…*

The Titan swung its right hand towards the roof—but collapsed as if it had used up all its strength. The tip of its right hand brushed the roof and chipped off pieces of the wall on its way down, and with a heavy thud the giant form itself toppled to the ground amidst the debris.

As the dust began to clear, a silence enveloped the world. Everybody stood perfectly still.

"What do we do?" Sannagi asked Hange, who was in command. "Should we end it just to be safe?"

"H-Huh?" Hange stared wide-eyed at Sannagi and stepped towards him with her head tilted. "What did you just say, hm? Please repeat yourself."

"Uh, I was saying...should we end it?"

"You idiot!!" Hange berated him. "Haven't you been watching? Hmm? That is a valuable research subject! One way or another we have to bring it to a safe place and test the hell out of it! We capture it alive. Alive!!"

"Well…"

Watching their conversation from the corner of his eye, Armin slowly approached the railing. When he looked down over the side, the Mysterious Titan was prone and limp. Suddenly thick steam began to rise up from its body.

What, is it going to die of exhaustion?

Even as he thought this, Armin noticed that the steam was rising most densely from its weak spot—the nape. It looked almost like a volcano was about to erupt. The vapors flowed continuously as if from a boiling source, and a white column of mist ascended like a signal fire.

Armin wondered what was going on. Next to him Mikasa stood watching the Titan, her gaze also transfixed on the nape.

Then, as if to answer their question, the nape slowly began to throb. Though it was from a distance, they could definitely tell that it was twitching. Almost like heartbeats, it bulged intermittently.

A few seconds later, the nape split wide open, spewing up a plume of trapped steam. Armin jumped back even though he was too far away to be caught in it.

Why had the body cracked open right there?

As the steam cleared, what lay there gradually came into view.

It was an unimaginable one.

"Take me down, Armin."

Armin nodded and carried Mikasa to the ground with a vertical maneuver. Hange descended too, held by Sannagi. The other soldiers followed in turn.

Having landed, they stared at the Titan's massive form, and then, at the nape in question. The heat of the vapors enveloped Armin.

He swallowed his breath.

It hadn't been a mistake.

He was entirely bewildered. He had no idea what had happened, why it had happened, or how to process it. He wished somebody would tell him whether to be simply happy or to see this as a prologue to a tragedy.

While Armin turned his thoughts over in his head, Mikasa slowly stepped forth.

She hopped onto the back of the Titan, which was still steaming. It must have been extremely hot, but seemingly unconcerned by the heat, she went straight for the nape. There, she stood still.

She stared at Eren, poking out on his knees.

His shorn limbs had been restored, and at least externally, he seemed uninjured. Instead, however, he was smeared in pink pieces of meat that didn't appear to be human, as if he'd been fused with the Titan. To his cheeks, to his arms, the sticky, slimy flesh clung.

Unable to come up with any explanation, they all stared blankly.

Out of them all, only Mikasa moved. She stretched her hand towards Eren.

He was unconscious, eyes shut and mouth half-open. Shrouded in steam, Mikasa spoke into his ear.

"Eren," she whispered. "Wake up, Eren."

※　　　※　　　※

When one is dreaming, the dream seems far more real and more important than reality. Even the products of a dream that later become faded as if wrapped in a shroud are extremely vivid and delicate down to the tiniest details. Nothing is fake or cryptic. In the dream world, everything is solid *reality.*

He was having the same dream again.

He was a young child, and helplessly, he was being tugged by something to *that place.* That was the only thing he could vaguely understand.

Someone was pulling his hand.

A man who was much taller than him was scanning their surroundings restlessly. Perhaps they were being chased. Night was almost fully upon them, and only the weak light of the stars guided them.

His palm was soaking wet in the man's grip.

Before long, the man approached a single home that was apparently his destination and looked around cautiously once more before knocking. A person who had to be the house's owner emerged with a surprised expression.

"You…why in the world?"

"Excuse me," the man said softly. "Would you let us in?"

The owner of the house let them inside and prepared two glasses of water on the table. Then he offered up two chairs and sat facing them.

"They found us." That was the only thing the visiting man said.

The owner of the house nodded gravely and dropped his gaze to the floor.

"My wife," the man continued. "My wife was caught. I worry that she's already…"

"And you escaped," the owner of the house said. "With that kid. He's your son?"

"My younger, Eren."

Eren.

That's right, I'm Eren.

Eren finally understood what should have been obvious. In the dream, everything was vivid, and at the same time, his own mind was obscured.

"Eren," the host repeated the name as if to memorize it. "Which means, that child—"

"That's right," the guest said. "I'm sure you guessed it the moment I came here. Please, could you listen to my one request?"

"Hmm." The host crossed his arms. Under the dim candlelight, his face wavered warmly.

"I want you to take care of this child," the guest said. "I can no longer be with him. I've already left my older child with someone I can trust. Now I just have this boy. This is all I ask."

Still, for a while, the host remained silent.

"Please, Souda."

Souda.

That's right, that's who the house's owner is, Eren belatedly realized again. *Now that I think of it, it has to be Souda.*

This Souda, much younger than the one Eren knew, had a somewhat different demeanor, but there was no mistaking him. This was a younger version of Souda.

Finally, Souda scratched his head in resignation, and with a grimace, he said, "All right. You know I can't turn you down. You can ask anything."

"Thank you." The visitor humbly bowed his head before pulling several sheets that looked like important documents from the bag he was carrying. He spread them out on the table. "Here are the documents related to Eren. When you've memorized them, burn them all."

Eren innocently glanced at them. He couldn't read the contents but could make out some kind of symbol.

It was at the corner of the document: an image of a white bird, its wings spread wide, flying through the sky. Eren tried to get closer to see more details when the guest grabbed his left arm. He was holding a syringe when Eren turned to look.

"I'm sorry, Eren. You'll feel a little pinch." The man rolled up Eren's sleeve and carefully examined the spot where he would insert the needle. Then quickly, without giving Eren a chance to resist, he plunged the needle. A tiny but certain pain spread up Eren's arm, and he began to feel woozy.

"With this shot, Eren's memory will be altered," the man explained to Souda. "Will you tell him that I died, and raise him yourself? And when the time comes—the timing will be up to you—will you tell him about his *power* and his *fate*?"

"For our convenience?"

"No, for the future of mankind."

Eren's consciousness began to flicker as if a fog were gradually rolling into his mind. As if everything were receding, the truth grew further and further away.

Of course, strictly speaking, it wasn't that he was getting farther away from reality. Rather, Eren was *returning* to reality. After all, everything was happening inside of a dream. If he woke from the dream, the fallen snow on the ground would melt away immediately, and in an instant he would forget all that had happened. Those things would go on existing only within the dream reality, for all eternity. Eren would never be able to leap out of the dream and affect his real self.

It would all become an ever so faint afterimage. An illusion.

"Eren."

Again he heard the man's soft voice.

"Please forgive my selfishness."

Eren.

Eren.

Goodbye, Eren.

※   ※   ※

VII. MINOS' JUDGMENT

"Private Third Class Eren."

Eren's eyes snapped open as if he had been slapped. His innermost core rattled from the powerful voice, and he was suddenly awake as if his body had been shaken by thunder. To dissolve away the white mist that clouded his vision, he blinked his eyes several times. The world's contours came into focus.

What's this place?

Eren trembled at the scene laid out before him and his position therein. He couldn't understand what had transpired, or how.

First of all, where am I? Eren scanned his surroundings. It seemed he was inside. All around him stood concrete walls that curved in an arc. Was this, then, the circular hall next to the structure at the relay point, where the explosives had been stored? Eren would still be in Titan territory in that case.

It was bright there. Sunlight streamed in from the ceiling. When he looked up, he saw several shattered skylights above him. The night had completely ended.

How long was I out? I can't remember anything.

Eren was in the middle of the room. He felt almost as if he was supposed to be the star of some stage. He was kneeling. He tried to move his body, but nothing happened. He wondered if it was his imagination and tried once again to shift his body, but still couldn't move. His hands were behind his back and seemed to be handcuffed; he heard the faint clink of metal against metal behind him. His ankles, too, were in shackles, and the chains were fixed to the ground (or perhaps to some kind of stake), bolting him down.

Either way, unable to budge, Eren couldn't make out any details.

"You're finally awake."

The person who stood before him was the Public Order Administration Supervisor. Pinning a hostile and aggressive gaze on Eren, Kubal slowly paced around the hall. As if immensely wary of something, he didn't look away for even a moment. Unable to endure the scrutiny, Eren looked down. He still couldn't understand what was happening. There were other soldiers assembled in the hall, perhaps about thirty of them. If they were the only survivors of the battle, it meant that many, many lives had been lost.

The soldiers stood along the walls, surrounding Eren. Recruits, squad leaders, and support personnel—they all stared at him. Whatever it was that they feared, they wore VMEs.

What did I do? Why are they all looking at me like that?

To his left, Eren could see Armin and Mikasa. He could also see Sannagi, Jean, Sasha, Hange, and Souda. Their faces were somehow uneasy, or perhaps bewildered, as they also stared at him.

Wait. Where are the rest of them? Could it be… No, I have to think about that later, Eren reordered his thoughts. *Right now, I have to find out why they are staring at me like I did something.*

The military policemen, clad in black uniforms, all pointed the barrels of their rifles at Eren. Their faces were stern, their fingers firmly on their triggers. Their stances suggested that if Eren made the slightest move, bullets would immediately start flying. Of course, he didn't know what kind of action would get him shot, or on the contrary exonerate him.

The door to the hall opened, and another MP entered the room. He saluted Kubal.

"Did Shikishima and his gang leave?" Kubal asked curtly.

"He went back to HQ to report that continuing the operation would be impossible after the loss of our explosives."

Kubal nodded and returned his gaze to Eren. "My goodness, was I surprised." With a cynical smile, the supervisor paced slowly around Eren again. "To think that we had a *Titan* mixed in amongst our recruits."

Eren couldn't speak. He must have heard wrong. *A Titan? What is he saying? What does he think I did? No, my mind is in complete chaos. I can't remember anything right now.*

"If you pull some stupid trick on us, or even make any 'odd' movements, we will fire at you without mercy. We will not hesitate. So answer truthfully."

Eren couldn't even nod. Quicker than the speed of sound, an inconceivable world flitted before his eyes.

"How is it that you became a Titan?" Kubal spat out the words. The moment he did, the air in the room grew heavy as if the atmospheric pressure had skyrocketed. The weight constricted Eren's chest. It was as though the world's fate hinged on how he responded.

"I-I don't…" Eren managed to utter through his confusion. Because it had been a while since he'd spoken, his vocal chords didn't work well. "I don't understand the question."

"I see." Kubal's eyes hardened. "You feign ignorance. You've got some guts."

"I-I really don't! Wh-What happened, and how this…and how I…"

"Well now, what are we to do?" Kubal sighed bitterly. "Several of the people here saw you emerging from a Titan. They witnessed you acting as a Titan. And still, you think you can make excuses."

Eren continued desperately to try to process Kubal's words, to take them in. Still, he couldn't digest any of it.

I came out of a Titan? I acted as a Titan? It's no use. I don't understand.

Suddenly, he felt as if something was bursting inside of his mind. Dim fragments of his memory flashed one after another, announcing their existence. But he couldn't remember well.

Remember. You have to remember.

"I'm going to ask you one more time," Kubal said. "How is it that you became a Titan? How did you gain that power?"

Eren thought about it, thought hard about how to respond. However, no matter how much he scrutinized the meaning of the question, he realized that there was only one answer. He spoke the only truth he knew.

"I…don't know. I-I'm a human!"

Silence swept through the hall, so still and tense that no one even blinked an eye.

"I see…" Kubal said in a rather disappointed voice. "Your severed limbs were restored… You must be an incredible person."

Almost automatically, Eren looked down at his body. He couldn't examine his limbs because he was bound, but it was without a doubt as Kubal said. Not long after he'd parted from Shikishima and leapt from the roof, a Titan had eaten his left leg. After that, another Titan had bitten off his right arm. He could remember it: the hopelessness, the pain, and even the cruel red of his blood. *And yet there are hand-cuffs and shackles on all of my limbs.* He could definitely feel the cold metal against his skin.

Again, something burst open in his mind.

One by one, Eren gathered the pieces of his memory.

I… That's right.

I was eaten by a Titan.

I was eaten by a Titan when I tried to save Armin, and after that, I was swallowed by an even bigger Thing.

Not physically. He had been swallowed up by some kind of current, some force that welled up deep inside of him. And the next moment, a Titan had been standing in front of him. He recalled, however, that he hadn't looked up at it.

No, I was looking down at it. Then I lifted an arm that felt heavier than a truck and slammed it into the Titan's head.

The faint sensation of the blow remained in his right arm. Gradually, he was also able to remember some of the fury that he'd felt.

I punched it. I struck many Titans. And then I killed them. I guess—I essentially became a Titan.

"Let's try a different question." Kubal narrowed his gaze. "What is your affiliation?"

Eren was careful with his answer. "S-Squad Six, sir."

"You have quite the sense of humor." Kubal chuckled viciously. "I'm not asking about that. What I want to know is *which organization you hail from*, Private Third Class Eren."

"Organization…"

"I'm talking about the anti-government organizations seeking to disrupt the order of this world," Kubal said plainly. "We have been aware for quite some time now that rebellious elements have been sabotaging the operation. And in order to uncover them, we made some adjustments for this expedition. As a result, incredibly, *you* have boiled up to the surface… Whether true or false, we had long received reports that your anti-government faction was formulating a terrifying plan to merge humans with Titans. To think, however, that the plan had actually been implemented… Well, I was surprised too."

"Rebellious elements?"

"S-Supervisor Kubal!"

The sudden cry belonged to Armin. He took a step from where he had been standing and, though his body was trembling, managed a crisp salute. Perhaps because he was nervous, he kept his eyes on the ceiling as he spoke.

"I-If I may, Eren is by no means a rebellious element! I have known him since we were little! Eren is innocent!"

Kubal glanced at Armin and shook his head. "Private Third Class Armin. Unfortunately, this is the reality. Your friend has been deceiving you for a long time and secretly been operating in the shadows. I fear he is a Gull, if not a Falcon…and now, we are going to hear in great detail all about this rebellious element's objective and why he sabotaged the mission. Why he tried to hijack the explosives. Why he wants to restrict humanity's territory. Perhaps he even has a base outside of the wall. Perhaps he communicates with the Titans and conspires with them to formulate a plan for our extermination."

"W-Wait a minute!" shouted Eren, unable to hold back any longer. "I really have nothing to do with anything like that! I volunteered to be a soldier *for* humans! Please believe me!"

"If you don't know anything," Kubal stated with an expression devoid of all emotion, "that only means you haven't been informed of anything. Isn't that so? The fact that you are a rebellious element is uncontestable. You are the anti-government faction's final weapon, and they still haven't told you anything. Either way, our operation has failed. We have lost the explosives. We no longer have any means to close up the hole in the wall. We were thoroughly outsmarted by you people."

Kubal raised his right hand and signaled to the MPs armed with rifles.

"If you don't know anything, there's nothing to be done. It seems we cannot get any information out of him." The muzzles aimed anew at Eren. "Kill him."

"W-Wait! Please!"

The person who stopped Kubal was Hange. She shook her head fervently and was breathing so heavily that her goggles were clouding over.

"H-He's a precious test subject. Killing him…would be inexcusable!" she insisted, spreading both her hands out before her. "If we study him, we might begin to be able to uncover the secrets of the Titans! It would be a major first step for humanity! Learning how to effectively use his strength could allow us to plan another operation to restore the wall!"

"Right…" Armin murmured. After deliberating for a few moments, he gave a trembling nod as if in agreement. "The operation… the operation can continue!"

Kubal's cold expression didn't thaw at Armin's words, and the MPs gave no sign of lowering their weapons. Still, Armin continued.

"There are more explosives."

"Private Third Class Armin." Kubal's eyes, glinting dully like lead, pierced Armin. "Unfounded nonsense will only reduce your value."

"I-It's not nonsense." Armin pursed his lips, collected his thoughts, and cautiously opened his mouth again. "I am from Monzen. I lived there for over ten years until the Titans attacked that day two years ago."

Kubal didn't say anything. He listened calmly, and indifferently, but Armin didn't flinch under his gaze.

"Up the hill to the east of town…"

Eren immediately understood, and Mikasa seemed to as well. Out of the corner of his eye, Eren could see her open her mouth.

Right… That's right.

"There's an unexploded missile," Armin concluded.

As his voice rang through the hall, a sudden trembling rippled through the soldiers. They weren't shaking out of fear, though. Rather, it was from excitement at the faint light of hope that Armin's words had cast.

Still Kubal's expression didn't change.

"Two years ago," Armin eagerly explained to prevail on the supervisor, "the unexploded missile was there on the hill. It should still be there. Although I do have some doubts as to whether the gunpowder is still potent, based on the situation back then I believe that only the fuse was defective. If so, the explosive material should still be effective. Because it's a cylindrical bomb, we can't install it along the cracks in the wall, but given its size, we can expect a fairly large blast."

"It could work…" Egged on by her elation, Hange was muttering to herself. "It could actually work!"

Armin made a noise in his throat, then spoke forcefully so his words would reach Kubal's heart. "In order to install it, we will need Eren's Titan strength."

The hall absorbed his firm voice. Before a perfect silence could fall, he turned to Eren.

Armin's eyes seemed to cling desperately to a far-fetched hope, but at the same time contained an undeniable force.

"You can do it, right?"

Taking in the words, Eren let them echo in his body. Looking down, he furiously contemplated the question.

I turned into a Titan—it seems that's the absolute truth. Though they are faint, the fragments of that memory are still left inside of me. Not just Kubal, but even Armin isn't trying to deny it. But as to how I became a Titan, and how to do it again, I have no idea. Besides, even if I could become a Titan again, since I've lost the memory of that moment, it seems unlikely that I'll be able to retain my senses. Installing the missile… Can I complete such a rational and delicate operation as a Titan? It's a…

But Eren hardened his heart. *This isn't the time to be puzzling things out. It's a one-in-a-million chance that Armin created for me. If I don't take it, I'll die. That means it's not the time to say, "I can't do it." I can't say that. I can't bear to die in a place like this, without even knowing what's going on.*

"P-Please let me do it," Eren hurled the words at Kubal. "I don't know myself what's going on, but I'm sure I can master this Titan power. If I can turn into a Titan, I'm sure I can carry that heavy missile. I will prove to you that I'm not some rebellious element. I'm finally…finally starting to see what my purpose is. I've finally been able to shake off…" Without realizing it, Eren glanced at Mikasa. "…the side of me that was just controlled by my anger and by my own selfish quest for revenge. So…"

"So," Kubal turned towards Eren and completed the thought, "please save my life. Is that it?" Kubal snorted. "You put on a good performance to plead for your life…however, I do have my mission." He raised, once again, the right hand he had lowered. "I'm sorry."

When he clenched his fist, the MPs pointing their rifles at Eren stared down their barrels.

Eren felt time stop.

It was the end.

He couldn't persuade Kubal.

To think…to think I'm dying in a place like this. What's more, without understanding anything, without knowing what happened. To be killed not by Titans, but by humans.

Kubal swung down his right arm.

Eren closed his eyes and bit his lips.

Gunshots, several of them.

The deafening sound reverberated and swelled in the hall. It tore at his eardrums, shook his brain, and pummeled him to the core. But as it dissolved into the smell of gunpowder, with the scent of violence lingering in the air, Eren realized something.

Timidly, he opened his eyes.

He wasn't dead.

He was alive.

"Good job."

Before Eren could even understand what had happened, he heard Kubal's voice. For some reason, his gaze was directed behind Eren, up at the second story of the hall, towards the balcony. When Eren turned around to trace the gaze, he saw several more armed MPs standing behind him. It seemed the soldiers had fired at something from the balcony, and white smoke rose quietly from the barrels of their rifles.

What happened?

"M-Mr. Souda!"

Guided by Armin's voice, Eren faced forward and saw Souda lying face up, limp on the floor.

"H-Hey, old man?" At almost the same time that Eren spoke, dark red blood began to seep through Souda's uniform. He had been shot.

"Souda! Souda!"

Armin rushed over and softly shook Souda's shoulder, but there was no response. Souda didn't blink an eye, moan, or move his fingertips even slightly. All the strength had left his body. The life that had made him who he was had passed.

He was already dead.

It can't be.

Why did Souda have to die?

Harboring a doubt akin to fury, Eren realized that Souda wasn't the only one shot. Two more lay on the floor, bleeding in the same way. They, too, were already dead. Eren had seen them several times during the expedition but didn't know their names. One was clad in a cook's uniform just like Souda, and the other soldier wore a VME.

What the hell is happening?

Moreover, upon closer observation, the three slain men were all holding pistols. Of course, pistols were useless against Titans. Thus, other than military policemen, nobody in the operation should have been supplied with more than signal flares. Why did Souda—and the other two men—have pistols? And why had they gotten them out then and there?

"Just three men?" Kubal asked.

The soldiers on the balcony nodded. "No mistake," one of them answered in a clear tone. "The moment we tried to fire at Private Third Class Eren, they were the only people who aimed their weapons at the MPs below to try to disrupt the volley."

Disrupt...the volley? So in other words, they tried to save me? Eren tried to sort his turbulent thoughts in a hurry. *Old man Souda tried to save me... I understand that much. But who were the other two? I'd never even seen them before this expedition.*

"The details."

"Yes." In response to Kubal's order, an MP began to read the details out loud. "Souda, born in Monzen, medic/cook. He had been with the South District Garrison. Next, Ichibuse, born in Kuki, also a medic/cook. East District, again with the Garrison Regiment. Finally, Kunawa, born in Yuki, originally from the North District Garrison. Their pistols are all M36s. The model and count agree with what went missing at a Military Police station the other day."

"Their affiliation?" Kubal asked, and the MPs standing near the three fallen men tore open the shirts of their uniforms.

All three had the same symbol on the linings on the back of their left breast pockets.

Eren had seen it before. It was the symbol of a white bird spreading its wide wings and flying through the sky. Unlike the Survey Corps' Wings of Liberty, the entire bird was drawn in detail. It was the same symbol that Hiana had shown him on her badge.

Kubal stared carefully at the symbol for a moment, then nodded with conviction as if he had come to a profound understanding.

"Good work," he said curtly, to which the MPs returned a salute. With that, Kubal and his soldiers seemed to relax a little.

Naturally, Eren was still utterly perplexed by what had unfolded before his eyes. *Was Souda one of the rebellious elements that Kubal mentioned? Is that why he was killed? And am I, as Kubal said, their "final weapon"? If that's the case, why was Souda on the Titans' side? Why was he trying to bare his fangs at humanity? Why did he have to ruin the operation? Why? Why...*

Before Eren could get lost in his jumbled thoughts, he heard the stiff sound of metal—*click*. He faced the barrel of a gun again. The person who held it was Kubal, and he was smiling.

"I'm sorry that everything has been so hectic. I'll hurry up and allow you to join your friends."

This time, I'll really get shot.

It's over.

I wanted to learn some kind of "truth" at least.

Giving up on subduing the chaos in his brain, Eren clenched his eyes shut.

And then...

A crash.

Armin fell to the floor.

The hall shook violently. Every part of it was ringing. The soldiers looked around anxiously, and in seconds, they all understood.

It was a Titan attack. They had been careless. Because they had only performed a simple repair on the damaged wall that surrounded the facility, it must have been torn open again. The building itself was not very sturdy. Unable to withstand the impact, the cracked glass in the skylights shattered, and countless shards rained down on everyone inside.

Armin covered his head and crouched on the ground and waited for the glass to stop falling. With barely a pause, however, there came an even heavier sound. The concrete wall was crumbling on one side. Crackling like thunder and raising violent gusts of dust, huge debris mercilessly fell amongst the soldiers and robbed everyone of their vision.

Struggling to protect his head, Armin pointed his hazy gaze towards the other side of the decimated wall. There was a large hole, and he could see blue sky. Beyond the wall was a single Titan standing motionless.

"What is that..." Hange's question came wedged in between the sounds of falling debris.

The Titan's appearance was entirely different from the ones Armin was familiar with. It was probably forty feet tall. It didn't have the pale-blue complexion of the regular Titans, nor the bright red muscle tissue of the Colossal Titan. It was covered in hard white skin that looked almost like a coating of slate. Like the scales of a fish, or perhaps like armor, white plates wrapped around its body in several places. Its face, too, was covered in the same white plates. As a result, the Titan's expressions, ordinarily obscure, were completely unreadable. Its body clad entirely in armor, it was a White Titan.

The White Titan's glittering yellow irises gazed into the hall. As if to survey the situation, they ran over the entire interior and alighted deliberately on each of the soldiers' faces as if to take in their every detail.

With the debris settled, Armin frantically grabbed his triggers. While focusing on the Titan, he glanced at the hall's interior out of the corner of his eyes. It was a miserable sight. Rubble and glass from the ceiling had rained on the soldiers at a cruel rate, and many of them had been flattened. From under several pieces of debris poked limbs that had lost all signs of life. They'd been crushed. Fortunately, not much had fallen where Armin and the others stood, or where Eren was shackled, but the damage was extensive. As far as Armin could see, only a dozen or so soldiers had survived unharmed, including Eren. Armin's eyes flickered.

"Ready? Go!" a call to attack came from across the hall. It sounded like the leader of Squad Three.

In response, five soldiers shot their anchors and engaged in vertical maneuvers. Amongst them was Kanaya of the Shikishima Advance Detachment, the elite of the elite, whose lightning-quick movements far outpaced the rest. Though the walls had crumbled, the remaining skeleton of the hall was still suitable for VMEs. The other soldiers also briskly alternated between shooting their anchors and reeling in their wires and quickly closed in on the White Titan after Kanaya. They attacked simultaneously from all directions. It was a beautiful battle formation, enough to inspire awe.

"Let's go, too!" urged Sannagi.

"Wait!" objected Hange. "It's not just its appearance... Something else is off."

They immediately registered Hange's warning. Armin had felt uneasy as well. Compared to previous Titans, the White Titan's movements were incredibly calm. It didn't spring at the sight of humans. It didn't even lift a finger. It just carefully observed the hall's interior.

It was eerie.

The five soldiers including Kanaya soon swooped down on the White Titan. They would have had no problem suppressing a regular Titan, Armin thought. There were no gaps in their formation, and the movements themselves were clever and quick. There was no way Armin could emulate them. Drawing perfect, efficient paths, they targeted the nape.

However, all of their finesse was pathetically meaningless in the end. The White Titan watched the maneuvering soldiers with something similar to boredom before eventually making its move. It didn't simply swat at them with its palm as a normal Titan would. Instead, the White Titan grabbed the three anchors buried in its chest and tore them out.

"Wha..." a cry leaked from Jean's mouth.

With one hand the White Titan grabbed the anchors and wires and, taking advantage of the centrifugal force, swung the bodies of the soldiers—against the wall.

They were dead before they could even scream. In an instant, three soldiers were layered upon each other against the wall in streaks of bright red.

Armin couldn't speak.

"It has intelligence."

By the time Hange did, Squad Three, including its leader, was gone. The Titan hadn't eaten a single soldier. It merely killed them. It was entirely different from an ordinary Titan and was endowed with a human intellect. Armin's heart sank.

Though the only one left in the air, Kanaya continued to put up a valiant fight, landing alone on the nape with blades raised. Without fretting in the least, the White Titan placed its right hand directly on its nape, protecting its vulnerable spot. Failing to penetrate the hard skin on the back of its hand, Kanaya's blades snapped off and spun away uselessly.

Still, unflinchingly and to the bitter end, Kanaya assaulted the White Titan. It was in vain. The White Titan grasped Kanaya, and perhaps out of consideration, or simply weary of the sight of blood, almost tenderly, with both hands, broke its remaining challenger's neck.

It was over.

Armin could hardly endure the dread that devoured him. All he could do was hope that somebody would come up with a brilliant plan to attack the White Titan and take it down.

No matter how much he waited, not a single person tried. It wasn't because they were frozen with fear. It was simply because, apart from Armin and his friends, all the soldiers were down. Nearly all of them had been flattened underneath the rubble.

Armin felt his heart freeze. It was horrible. Close to twenty soldiers had lost their lives during the White Titan's attack. Of course, the military policemen were not exempt. The dust that cloaked the entire hall was thinning, and when he glanced at the place where Kubal had been standing, he was, of course, no longer there. In his place were large pieces of debris. From between the cracks, Armin could see leather boots. They were unmistakably Kubal's.

Armin tensed his abdomen to try to control his trembling. That was when another impact came.

The White Titan suddenly began to move. As if getting into a bath, it stretched its arms and sank its body into the hall. The wall that it gripped with its hands crumbled even further, and Armin and the others were surrounded by dust again. They couldn't see anything.

There was a metallic sound, and a few seconds later, the White Titan slowly returned to where it had been standing. As if it had completely lost interest in the hall, it turned its back on Armin and the others.

What is it up to?

Then, through the dust that the Titan sent up, they caught a glimpse of its hand. When Armin realized what was clenched in its grip, he understood what was happening and cried out, "Eren!"

The moment he did, he had to shield his face against the swirling dust. The Titan definitely had Eren in its hand but didn't seem interested in squashing him, or eating him. As if taking care not to hurt him, it had left plenty of space between its fingers. It apparently wanted to abduct him.

"This is bad! This is bad! We can't lose him! Get him back!"

Before Hange had even finished shouting, Mikasa was in the air. Burning a tremendous amount of gas, she blasted apart the clouds of dust. At such a speed, it seemed she would outrun her own anchors. Leaving only the white smoke of wire friction as her tire tracks, she climbed. Armin and the others tried to follow, but just then, as if the sun had suddenly sunk, everything around them went dark. With the hall's interior thrown into grayness, they couldn't fathom what was what.

Armin looked up. The sky that had been visible through the openings above was covered by something. He strained his eyes.

"Wh-What happened?" Sannagi's voice echoed.

From what they could see, the thing that covered the ceiling was a large piece of wall. It was almost as if the rubble of some other structure had been forced on like a lid. Of course, there was only one thing that could pull off such an extraordinary maneuver. Armin bit his lip.

"It's keeping us from following."

"That's crazy," Jean blurted out. "It picked up such a huge piece of rubble? I can't believe it."

Mikasa landed right beside Armin. Blocked at the last second by the wall, she hadn't been able to chase after the White Titan. With no intention of sheathing her blades, she grimly dashed towards the ground-floor exit.

"M-Mikasa, where are you going?"

"I'm going after it!"

The anger in her voice was palpable, but as she tried to rush outside, she collided with a man who had come running in. His chest was heaving and his forehead was slick with sweat.

"Things couldn't look worse…"

It was Shikishima. He exhaled deeply to calm his jagged breathing and scanned the hall's interior to get a handle on the situation.

"Could you explain to me what's going on? On the way to the Second Wall, we saw smoke rising from this building. I headed back here alone. I'd like as brief an explanation as possible."

"We were attacked by a White Titan…and…" Hange clenched her fists. "He was taken away! That Eren kid, by some strange Titan, he was taken away!"

Shikishima gently dropped his eyes to the ground. For a while, he pursed his lips as if deep in thought, and then, as if something had occurred to him, he nodded twice. He turned around to leave the hall.

"Got it. In that case, I'll go after Eren and that Titan. You guys wait here."

"I'm going too," Mikasa appealed with a ferocious look.

Though she made a definite crack in Shikishima's expression, he firmly shook his head to refuse her company.

"Please trust me. I've got this."

Mikasa's blades shook in her tight grips, and she watched with resentful eyes as Shikishima left. When he had completely disappeared, she thrust her blades back into their sheaths, closed her eyes, and faced down.

Armin and the others made a round of the hall to search for survivors. However, betraying their faint hopes, they couldn't find a single soldier who was breathing. The ones not directly killed by the Titan had been done in by the falling debris. In the end, the only survivors were Armin, Mikasa, Hange, Sannagi, Jean, Sasha, and Eren, who had been taken away—a mere seven. The six excluding Eren got out of the hall and climbed to the roof of the adjacent building where they would be able to keep watch for approaching Titans. Once Sasha and Sannagi had confirmed that there were none in the area, the six of them gathered in a circle.

"It's ironic…" Jean observed with a defiant, wry laugh. "Of all things, only we recruits who were too scared to go at the Titan lived. How so funny."

"Jean," Armin opened his mouth to scold him, but couldn't. It was pretty much exactly as Jean said.

"What the hell is going on? I don't understand anything." Jean sighed, appalled, and not bothering to hide his consternation, he said, "That quick-to-die bastard is a Titan, and a rebellious element? That guy stole the explosives and ruined the operation?"

"Eren didn't do anything wrong," countered Armin. "It looked like he didn't know the first thing about himself. Even if Souda and the others had been rebellious elements, Eren didn't do anything wrong…"

While defending Eren, Armin himself was attempting to sort out the information in his head. Eren had turned into a Titan. That was an incontrovertible truth that Armin had witnessed with his own eyes and did not doubt. But Eren not having been told anything also seemed to be true. He clearly hadn't been lying in proclaiming his innocence, which meant that unbeknownst even to himself, he had possessed the ability to transform into a Titan. Kubal had said as much: *We had long received reports that your anti-government faction was formulating a terrifying plan to merge humans with Titans.*

Setting aside the question of how Eren had come by the ability to harness a Titan's power, Souda was certainly the one person who had cared for Eren from the time he was very young. Thus, it wasn't impossible that Souda might have done some kind of work on Eren's body. In that case, Souda really had been a rebellious element—the "traitor." Armin couldn't think otherwise. In fact, to think otherwise felt unnatural. With Eren in danger, Souda and the other two anti-government faction members had tried to fight with pistols stolen from the Military Police.

You are the anti-government faction's final weapon, and they still haven't told you anything.

They all had the same emblem hidden on the inside of their uniforms. But if they really were part of an anti-government faction, Armin was still immensely confused as to what their motives were. Why would Souda disrupt the Outer Wall Restoration Operation? Humanity had nothing to gain from such a move. Failure meant not recovering the formerly human lands within the First Wall. People would be forced to live a harsh life behind the Second Wall and eventually run out of resources. They'd only be waiting for their downfall. No human, and only the Titans, would reap any benefit.

Were Souda and the others communicating with the Titans and conspiring to exterminate the human race? How stupid that would be.

But if Armin fully accepted that hypothesis, the White Titan taking Eren away made some sense. The White Titan hadn't abducted Eren. It had welcomed him in as one of them and protected him.

Armin closed his eyes and inhaled deeply. *Stop. Calm down. I'm jumping to conclusions.*

"We're wasting time just standing here," Mikasa said impatiently. "We have to go save Eren."

"I understand the sentiment, but it's not very realistic," Hange calmly objected. "We've already lost sight of the White Titan. We don't have any trail to follow... Let's leave Eren to Captain Shikishima."

Mikasa threw Hange an almost recalcitrant gaze. "It will be too late once Eren has been killed by that Titan. We need his power."

"We don't have to worry about that." Hange's expression grew tender and comforting. "If that thing wanted to kill Eren, it could have squeezed him right there. The fact that it didn't means that the Titans see some point in keeping Eren alive. For a while at least, we don't have to worry that they'll take his life."

Though Mikasa still seemed to disagree, perhaps embarrassed by her own fretfulness, she swallowed her words.

"It's okay. 'The strongest man in the world' went to go rescue Eren, right? Let's believe in him for now. You've seen Captain Shikishima's strength up close. If it's up to him, it'll be okay. Right?"

"I don't know anything," Mikasa said in a low murmur as if it were some incantation, "about that man."

For a few moments, Armin couldn't turn away from Mikasa, whose eyes gazed off at something far away. She left an odd sensation in his mind, like a name that he couldn't for the life of him remember. What was Mikasa seeing?

"I-Is there anything we're supposed to be doing?" Sasha reprised their stagnating discussion.

"Right, we don't have many options," replied Hange. "One is to simply retreat back to the Second Wall. Fortunately, Truck Two is undamaged, and there's still plenty of fuel to get back. If we drive at full speed, we might avoid any incoming Titans and return safely."

They all chewed on Hange's proposal.

"The other option is, as you said," she continued, pointing at Armin, "to retrieve the undetonated missile and to restore the wall according to the original plan. Though of course, it will be next to impossible for us to succeed when the mission was supposed to be carried out by over a hundred soldiers."

"It's no use," Jean spat. "I don't care how much of an honor student Armin is. We don't even know if the missile is there in the first place."

"It was certainly there until two years ago," Armin claimed, casting a confirming glance at Mikasa.

Perhaps because she was thinking about something else, a moment passed before she gave a small nod and said, "It was."

"I don't think it's a bad idea," Sannagi spoke up. "We came all this way. We could try returning with or without accomplishing our mission…but I somehow don't think that our chance of survival is all that much higher with the first option. The probability is pretty low anyway. If that's the case, it'll be much better to go recover the missile and bet on meeting up with Captain Shikishima or Eren. If we do everything we can and it's still no use, then we turn back. If we don't try and just hightail it, then everybody who died, died in vain."

"Are you in your right mind?"

"I also think we should do everything we can," Sasha added. "Otherwise, I'll never be able to enjoy my meals even if we return safely. Let's give it everything we've got."

Delivering the final blow on Jean, who was shaking his head in disbelief, Armin nodded as if to convince himself and assented. "I think we need to do it too. Just like Sannagi said, too much blood has been spilled. If we suddenly turn our backs on the hope that's been guiding us...nobody will be able to rest in peace."

"Ahhh..." Jean covered his face and made to cry out. Perhaps recalling that there were Titans around, he instead vigorously scratched his head as though he were washing his hair. "You gotta be kidding... It's not like I can go back alone!"

The sight of Jean in such a state was somehow amusing, and they couldn't help but smile.

"I gotta do it, right? I gotta," Jean said.

"So it's settled," concluded Hange.

Armin looked at the only person who hadn't given her opinion. "You're coming too, aren't you, Mikasa?"

After meeting his eyes with a chaotic gaze, she delivered a concise answer.

"I am."

VIII. THE TRUTH OF EDEN

He awoke suddenly. As he slowly sat up, he realized he was sitting on a soft sofa. It was dark brown leather, and when he touched it, a light layer of dust clung to his fingertips. It seemed it hadn't been used in a long time.

Eren scanned his surroundings. Much like the chambers in the structure at the Omotemachi relay point, the room had concrete walls on all sides and was modest. However, thanks to all the candles, and because it wasn't particularly large, he could see fairly well. Perhaps it was a private residence that was no longer being used.

There were no windows. Compared to the relay point building, it appeared to be in astonishingly good condition. Though it was slightly dusty, nothing appeared to be broken, and nothing was dirty. The sofa that Eren sat on, the coffee table before him, the bookshelf, and the books lined upon it were all still perfectly usable. As far as Eren could tell, he was alone.

Though it was the second time that day that he had awoken in an unknown place, he felt a bit less uneasy this time. He wasn't placed all alone in the center of a large hall, his arms and legs weren't bound, and nobody was interrogating him. Moreover, he had a relatively clear recollection of what had happened.

I was attacked by a Titan while I was tied up and taken away. And then I lost consciousness in its grip.

Eren checked both his arms and his legs. His cuffs and shackles were gone. Somebody had removed them.

"Looks like you finally woke up."

When Eren whirled around to face the sudden voice, a man was descending the stairs behind him. Though dressed more casually than during the battle with the Titans, it was unmistakable who it was. A white shirt, and at the base of his neck, an immaculate scarf. Boots gleaming dully under the cuffs of his beige pants.

"Captain Shikishima…"

"You're not hurt, are you?"

Fairly relieved to see a familiar face, Eren shook his head no.

Shikishima returned a smile. Perhaps because he was exhausted, he was breathing somewhat heavily. Sweat shone faintly on his forehead like evening dew.

"Where am I?"

"Let me explain in order." Shikishima let out a sigh and sat on the facing sofa with two cups of water. He placed one in front of Eren, offering it. "It's okay. The water is from a working well. It's clean."

Eren gave a small nod of thanks. Shikishima gulped down his water.

"Excuse me, please allow me to rest for a moment." After gathering his breath, Shikishima placed his cup back on the coffee table.

"You were about to be taken away by a Titan. You remember that much, yes?"

Eren nodded.

"After that, I immediately went after you. And I found the Titan that took you, a strange-looking one. It wasn't the usual variety."

"It had white skin."

Shikishima nodded. "We fought for a while, but eventually it got away."

"Got away…"

"It completely disappeared…I think. Well, no use speculating. In any case, I'm glad I was able to keep you safe. We are in a basement now, one that I thought would be a suitable hiding place. In any case, it is built very well. It was hardly damaged when the Titans attacked."

"A basement…where?"

"In Monzen."

Eren's eyes opened wide at the familiar name.

"What's more," Shikishima said with a hint of triumph, almost as if he were bragging, "it's the basement of the room of a man you knew well… His name was Souda."

"The old man's basement?"

"Well, it's not actually Souda's house. It was managed by an organization that he belonged to. To put it simply, it was their 'hideout.' Have you ever visited this place—'Souda's house'—before?"

"A few times…but he would never let me inside."

"I see. It seemed he kept you completely in the dark."

Eren detected actual info in the way Shikishima was telling the story. *The captain knows something about Souda and the so-called anti-government faction. Maybe he knows something even bigger.*

"Captain Shikishima," Eren said formally. "I-I don't know anything, and—"

"*You would like to know. Right?*" teased Shikishima, a bit meanly.

After thinking it over, Eren nodded. Shikishima returned the motion.

"I'm the kind of person who basically believes that anyone who says 'I want to know' should be offered as much information as possible. If you wish it, I will disclose what I know in as much detail as I can. At the same time, to gain knowledge, in some cases, is to take on considerable *pain*...though that's not how I like to look at it. Are you absolutely prepared to learn 'the truth'?"

Eren sensed the darkness in such a preface. It enfolded some dangerous bloom that didn't need to be, and shouldn't be, touched. But he had to move his head up and down.

"I think it would be a lie to say that I'm ready. Still, I can't go on like this, knowing nothing."

As if satisfied with Eren's answer, Shikishima smiled and closed his eyes. "Splendid." He crossed his legs. "In that case, I'm afraid you'll need to explain to me first what just happened in the hall. I'm sure you were interrogated by Kubal, but I also want to know what kind of intelligence you came by."

Eren launched into an overview of everything that happened in the hall, giving all the details he retained. With his eyes closed the entire time, Shikishima listened, grinning occasionally as if something was so funny that he could barely conceal his laughter. He uncrossed his legs and leaned forward over the coffee table when Eren finally finished.

"Thank you." Shikishima smiled again. "It was a very interesting story. Truly, this 'Kubal' person is a genius through and through."

"What do you mean?"

"Let me explain one thing at a time," Shikishima said, smoothly rising to his feet. He walked to the dust-covered bookshelf and carefully began to consider which book to grab. Examining the shelf, Eren realized all the books were government texts, banned books—so-called prohibited reading. The titles all sung of "history" and "truth," and he almost grew dizzy seeing them all lined up. Armin also owned prohibited reading, but only one volume whose contents weren't too deep. It wasn't an exaggeration to call it a children's book. Still, making sure its presence never came to light, he hid it strictly. That was how absolute their world's Designated Knowledge Confidentiality Law was.

Yet Souda had so many such books. Behind his bright, composed, smiling face lurked another aspect that Eren had never imagined. Still, somewhere in his soul, he couldn't bring himself to believe it.

"This one will do." Shikishima finally selected a book and placed it on the coffee table. "First, a history lesson. Do you know the details of why the Titans first appeared, or even why humans came to live behind walls?"

After organizing his thoughts, Eren answered. "Over a hundred years ago, the Titans appeared suddenly and began to attack us humans…in what's called the Great Titan War. The people who escaped the perils of the Great War built three walls and decided to live within them. We are their descendants… That's my understanding."

"The Great Titan War," Shikishima repeated as if to praise a clever joke. "Thanks to the cheap name, people are just flummoxed and don't even doubt it. It's rather well done, all told. It's almost as if... yes. As you said, we get the impression that a violent war occurred between these 'Titans that came from nowhere' and 'humanity.' It is an ingenious manipulation of the picture."

"But...that's not what happened?"

"Well, where do you think the Titans 'suddenly' came from?" Shikishima clicked the heel of his boot a few times against the floor. "From underground? Or perhaps," he went on, pointing his finger at the ceiling, "they came flying down from above? Either way, you understand that it's not realistic, don't you? Subjected to thought, it's something that anybody could see is impossible."

"So...how did the Titans appear?"

"You're quite impatient. There's no reason to rush." Shikishima waved his index finger. "I'll lead you neatly to the conclusion. Don't worry, just stay seated." He leaned his body fully against the back of the sofa.

"Though you believe that the Titans arrived only about a hundred years ago, in reality, the first Titan was created *two hundred and nine years ago.* It is clearly recorded in this book as well. And before the Titans arrived—or even for a while after they did—this world boasted a far more advanced civilization than what we're familiar with. This is something that you must already understand on some level, yes? After all, the motorized farming equipment and various other machines from the old civilization that the government hands down for a price aren't the kind of products that you could build yourselves. Think about the Designated Knowledge Confidentiality Law and the New Technology Suppression Act. We are clearly living in a civilization that is far more restricted than it was in the past. In the old era, even this place, Monzen, was a prospering city in its own right."

"Monzen was?" Eren's eyes widened. "A *city*, in a place like this… What kind of city? Like the city center of the Second Wall District?"

Shikishima laughed out loud and shook his head. "The comparison is charming. Measured against a city from the old civilization area, the Second Wall District center is a slum. Anyone from the past would say that such a place couldn't be called a 'city center.'" As he spoke, he began flipping through the pages of the book he was holding. When he found the page he was looking for, he placed the book on the coffee table and showed it to Eren. "Here's a photograph of this area two hundred years ago."

Eren looked down at the page, and rather than feeling shocked, he truly believed it was a lie. There was no way he could buy it; he could only conceive of it as a daydream from another dimension.

"It's not a fairy tale," Shikishima said, reading Eren's mind. "In those days, it wasn't only the military that had motorized vehicles, but also ordinary citizens. Structures taller than the First Wall were built all over the place, and the human population was hundreds of times what it is now. The city was always overflowing with people, and resources and food supplies were plenty. Nobody lived in abject poverty. *Monzen*, and *Omotemachi*, and *Yuki*, and *Iruma*—almost all of the current names are remnants from those days."

Though Eren's gaze was pinned for some time to the book, eventually he managed to tear his eyes away. Against his will he decided to swallow Shikishima's "truth." Getting hung up on the photo meant forgoing the rest of his story. Eren had to accept it before he could even understand it.

"Please go on."

Shikishima nodded easily. "Over two hundred years ago, humans were at war… 'Man' and 'man' were at war with each other. At the time, 'Titans' didn't even exist. The people at war were not the people of this country, our ancestors, but those from other nations. In those days there were quite a few, and multiple races… If I explained in too much detail I would only confuse you. For now, I'll spare you. Anyway, unrelated to our ancestors, some country was at war with some other country. Are you all right up to this point?"

Eren nodded.

"However, in the world back then, there was a pesky law relating to war—a law among nations. Called the Disarmament Treaty, it imposed a limit on arms you could own, how powerful they could be, how big they could be, and how frequently they could be used. The rules were minute enough to make people roll their eyes. Some bunch who loved peace had established the rules for the sake of peace. Well, in reality, you can't call it 'peace' if a war is occurring." Shikishima smiled ironically. "Anyway, the rules set by the peace-lovers grated on the war-wagers. Try as the latter might to swiftly defeat the enemy, 'international law' prohibited them from committing more powerful weapons, and there was no end in sight for the conflict. Meanwhile, because the war would not end, peace never came. It was a bit of a contradiction. And so our ancestors decided to extend a helping hand to one side. Though they didn't have much of a liking for direct combat, there was little public opposition to indirect participation."

Eren listened quietly as Shikishima spoke.

"Our ancestors deliberated. How would they help that one side win the war? What could they develop that would make that country happy—that is to say, make a purchase—from our ancestors? They thought, and thought, and thought. As a result, they arrived at an interesting conclusion."

"An interesting conclusion?"

"Indeed." Shikishima flashed a fearless smile. "Arms that wouldn't contravene the Disarmament Treaty… In other words, they needed to develop a weapon that wasn't a weapon. Something that was not a transport truck, or a tank, or a cannon, or a pistol. They could simply invent something that wouldn't be considered an armament, legally speaking, whatever its true nature. That invention was…"

"The Titans," Eren realized.

"Exactly," Shikishima confirmed with a broad grin. "Humans are humans, no matter how big or ferocious. Legally, they couldn't be categorized as weapons. At first glance, it seemed an extremely stupid idea, but our ancestors researched it in earnest, and miraculously created a certain chemical. If one ingests this substance, a person, a soldier, could turn into an invincible Titan. Of course, as you know, they left a weak spot at the nape. However, aside from that, the Titans were literally invincible. They were strong, and if their bodies were damaged, they could quickly use their own power to restore themselves. They were compelled by a state of extreme ferocity, and though impervious to emotions like fear, they could preserve their human reasoning and intelligence. Though they couldn't stay transformed for long, the chemically induced Titanization proved tremendously mighty. The drug was called Jaeger—the word means 'hunter'—and handily bestowed victory on the country that used it… And today too, there is someone who has been prescribed this substance.

"You," Shikishima said.

Eren's heart pounded furiously.

"You are without a doubt one of the humans that has gained the ability to transform into a Titan thanks to the power of this 'Jaeger.' Kubal's claim that anti-government organizations have been conducting studies on Titan transformation is entirely false. The drug Jaeger has existed for a very long time—from two hundred years ago."

Eren tried to pose a question to corral the info galloping around in his head, but he had no idea where to start and couldn't even open his mouth.

I'll lead you neatly to the conclusion. Don't worry, just stay seated.

Eren closed his mouth and decided to trust Shikishima.

"It was fine up to that point," the captain resumed. "However, it was at that time that someone had an unfortunate stroke of inspiration. A researcher from the defeated country performed a thorough examination of the Titans and, as a result, succeeded in developing another new drug. This second substance was named Wraith. Unfortunately, compared to Jaeger, it was much less sophisticated. People who took it transformed into Titans but couldn't turn back into humans. They lost all intellect and reason and were dominated by a cannibalistic drive. Because they lacked intelligence, their combat potential was inferior to the Jaeger Titans. Still, to a dreadful degree, they were 'human weapons.' Of course, there wasn't a single person crazy enough to ingest the drug. The people who developed Wraith did not administer it to their own troops. Instead, they sprayed it over enemy territory."

The air in the room grew tense.

"It can't be hard for you to imagine what happened next. As expected, the country that transformed into Titans began to eat one another, to slaughter themselves. With consummate efficiency, it fell into Titan hands in the blink of an eye. Even after that, Wraith was circulated in large quantities and used not only for war, but also for terrorism, for other crimes, and too many other ways over the course of time. Naturally, before long, humans found themselves unable to stop the Titans. Which brought about—"

"Today's world."

"It goes without saying that the Titans roaming around here are all humans from the old era who were given Wraith. But whether the Titan is a Jaeger or a Wraith, in the end it's quite simple."

Eren saw the next words coming but could only steel himself.

"They're all originally humans," Shikishima concluded plainly. He finished the water in his cup and sighed. "They call me 'the strongest man in the world,' but it's ironic, really, because the fact of the matter is that I'm just a mass murderer."

Shikishima snorted resentfully.

Eren, too, found himself thinking about the Titans that he had killed. He'd felled one with his VME, and as a Titan (though his memory was fuzzy) he'd ended a good number of them as well. All of them had been ordinary people once. Deep in his chest, he felt an uneasy feeling well up like a muddy stream.

"No use worrying about it," Shikishima advised blithely. "Anyhow, that's the truth of the Great Titan War. It's not like we were engaged in a war with the Titans. People fought amongst themselves, and as a result, the Titans were born. Those of us who managed to run and hide behind walls survived, while others who remained outside were all eaten and killed… Which brings us to now." Shikishima spread his hands out at the room, tying the story together.

Eren considered what thoughts to express, but immediately changed his mind. What he needed wasn't to express his thoughts but to obtain more information.

"Up until there, I understand," he said. "But why did the old man—I mean, Souda and the others—ally with the Titans to overturn the government? I don't see their reasoning for sabotaging the Outer Wall Restoration Operation."

As though tickled by this, Shikishima raised his eyebrows. "It seems there, your info is a little jumbled." Perhaps tired from all the talking, he loosened the scarf at the base of his neck. "I'll tell you the conclusion first. It wasn't Souda's organization that sabotaged the Outer Wall Restoration Operation."

"What?" Eren immediately groped for alternative scenarios but couldn't come up with anything that seemed obvious. *Then who could have done it? There were no other suspicious personnel as far as I know. I'm stumped.*

"The one who sabotaged the operation was…" Seeing how Eren was coming up empty, Shikishima spoke the answer firmly: "Kubal."

The transport truck traveled over a path chosen for its flatness and relatively good visibility. There was no threat of being suddenly attacked by a Titan lurking in the shadows of a building. Holding her binoculars, Mikasa kept watch. She spotted no Titans, but nor could she find what she truly sought. Calm fields of weeds continued endlessly as far as the eye could see.

"I'll switch with you, Mikasa."

It was Armin's voice. Still holding the binoculars, she said, "It's okay. Why don't you ask somebody on the other side?"

"Sasha just took over for Sannagi." Cautious of Titans, Armin spoke in as quiet a voice as possible. "Besides, I'm probably just the same as you."

"What do you mean?"

"I also want to find Eren."

Mikasa unintentionally lowered her binoculars, and then handed them to Armin. Smiling, he accepted them and quickly began his lookout.

"I'm relieved," Armin said, looking through the binoculars.

"At what?" asked Mikasa.

"That you're just like you were. Because of what you said, I thought maybe you'd actually changed… But sure enough, you're the same old Mikasa."

"I wonder," she mumbled as if she were addressing something inside of herself. "I thought I wanted to remain unchanged, but I think I did end up changing."

"That's not true."

"Eren hasn't…" Mikasa paused for a moment, uncertain if she should ask, but went ahead and did. "Eren hasn't changed?"

"Ha ha," Armin chuckled rather happily. "Of course not. Though I do feel like he's mellowed out a little bit. But still, Eren is Eren. The thick trunk at the bottom hasn't changed at all."

I see.

For some reason, Mikasa couldn't voice those words. Staring off in the same direction as Armin, she gave a small sigh, as carefully and silently as possible so he wouldn't notice.

Eren hadn't changed.

Armin's statement brought about conflicting emotions in Mikasa. One was the joy that Eren was the same old Eren. The other was a hopelessly petty pang of jealousy and despair that Eren had remained Eren even without her.

Eren is so important to me, such a big part of my life. Maybe on his side, I don't mean anything to him. Maybe I'm not even a "part" in his life at all. As she began to think this, her despair threatened to wrap up her entire body like a heavy overcoat. She bit the inside of her mouth to scold herself. She didn't have the right, and there was something else that she needed to focus on now.

"What kind of man is Captain Shikishima?" Armin asked as if the silence was too uncomfortable.

While Mikasa knew that his question didn't come from anywhere deep, she considered conveying her true feeling: *How should I know?*

The man's most salient characteristic, if she had to try, was that he was *unknowable*. Sometimes he was as tender and soft as silk. Sometimes he was astonishingly cold and aggressive. He seemed to overflow with fraternal love at times, but he could also be callously rational. No matter how much she tried to pin him down, she couldn't. Though he delved so deeply into her soul sometimes that she wanted to drive him out, he never let anybody into his. He was more dependable than anyone, but if you depended on him beyond a certain extent, he retaliated like barbed wire. She didn't dislike him.

She even trusted him. But if someone were to ask her if she understood the man, she could only answer:

I don't have a clue, either.

And also sometimes I feel guilty towards him. If I hadn't met this person called Shikishima, I probably would have gone straight to see Eren. The reason I didn't was that Shikishima's existence ate away at me. As to why... Well, that's an extremely simple story. It was because I overlaid him with someone else to deceive myself. And—

"He's my savior," replied Mikasa. There was no point in talking to what was inside of her any longer. She would just answer Armin's question, properly. "He taught me everything about fighting. As for the rest, he's a secretive man and hasn't told me much of anything."

"I wonder if there's some kind of knack to fighting. Of course, I'm sure it's not something you could explain easily. I just want to be of some use at least."

After thinking for a moment, Mikasa opened her mouth. "It's difficult to explain any kind of knack. But there's something he often said. A lesson, perhaps."

"That's good. Tell me."

It went...yes, something like...

"The only ones who can make a difference are those who can give up something that's important to them."

Armin remained still as though he were letting the words sink in. After a while, he slowly opened his mouth. "It's difficult, isn't it? I wonder what Captain Shikishima meant by those words."

"Who knows." *He never explained anything to me.*

"Ah!"

Mikasa lifted her face at Armin's exclamation.

It was coming into sight: that familiar scenery, and for the first time in so long. A green wind blew eternally, like a symbol of peace, over a dazzlingly bright patch of memories.

Missile Hill.

"Supervisor Kubal…sabotaged the operation?"

"To put it accurately, it wasn't just Kubal but the central government. It seems they just don't want to let the operation succeed."

As Shikishima spoke he rested his hand on the sofa's armrest and stared at Eren as if to test him.

Eren let his body sink into the silence of the gloomy basement. The captain's disclosures had already confused Eren to a great degree, and this bit of news was even more troubling. If an organization trying to overthrow the government had perpetrated the sabotage, that was one thing—no, actually, it was already baffling—but the central government disrupting a government-led operation…

"But why?" asked Eren.

"Oh…" Shikishima shrugged and wore a put-on look. "I don't know."

"You don't know…"

"But it's the truth. During this expedition, too—my advance detachment cleaned out all of the Titans en route to Omotemachi, and yet when the main force arrived, they came. From what I've heard, there were mysterious severed heads, even. That was courtesy of the government. Killing the lookouts at the relay point and allowing the ensuing attack of the Titans was also the government's handiwork.

Think about it carefully. To begin with, it's not easy for anyone aside from government personnel to leave the wall without permission. And yet, such an extensive trap was laid *outside*. The simple answer is that only the government could have accomplished the feat.

"I participated in the past two expeditions as well, and on both occasions, we faced the same kinds of obstacles. At one point, we were attacked by Titans at an odd moment and suffered a devastating defeat."

"Then how did the government summon the Titans?"

Shikishima's expression stiffened. "To be honest, we don't have a perfect understanding of how they do it. But we can basically surmise that the central government exercises immaculate control over the Titans roaming outside—over the movements of Wraiths."

"Control." Eren could only shake his head. "Unbelievable."

"Just as I said before, I don't understand the principle," Shikishima continued seamlessly. "Researchers theorized about controlling their actions using particular electromagnetic and high-frequency sonic waves. Others posited something more supernatural. But aside from government personnel, nobody knows the truth. It's all mere hypothesis... Still, you can without a doubt believe that the central government exerts perfect control over the Titans. Think about it from the beginning. Do you know the approximate circumference of the First Wall?"

Eren didn't.

"It's an estimate, but it's said to be two hundred fifty miles long." Shikishima raised a finger. "How do you think the central government built such a vast wall while the Titans were attacking?"

Eren felt an eerie draft of cool air on his body.

"We're struggling to close a hole less than forty feet tall and sacrifice nearly all of our troops each time. And yet, in the past, humans apparently built a wall two hundred fifty miles long and fifty yards high while being attacked by Titans. Well, you get it, don't you? It would have been absolutely impossible. This is the undeniable, simple proof that the central government can control the Titans. We were, after all, the technologically advanced country that gave birth to Jaeger. The knowledge of the workings of the Titans must be preserved to more than a considerable degree."

The government is controlling the Titans.

Eren frantically processed the words and arrived at an even bigger question. "Then why doesn't the government get rid of the Titans? If they can control their actions, it should be easy to beat them."

Shikishima's nod was the deepest yet. "There it is. *That* is the biggest question of this world." He cleared his throat. "Excuse me. Have you ever been inside the Third Wall?"

"Well…" Of course not. It was silly of the captain even to ask. In fact, hardly anyone had ever had a glimpse.

Absolutely no trespassing—the nobility's sanctuary.

"Right, I'm sorry." Shikishima laughed. "As of now, only the so-called nobility lives inside the Third Wall. Its population is a few thousand or so. However, if you think about the origins of this country, you can begin to guess their nature. They weren't hereditary royalty, nor did they have any aristocratic titles. They're simply the descendants of the officials who built the wall: the military authorities at the time, building contractors, scientists of the government research division who invented Jaeger. The descendants of their families retreated to the safest area and control this world to protect their own lives."

Shikishima sat up and leaned towards Eren to come on strong.

"The life that they alone enjoy behind the Third Wall is far sweeter and more elegant than whatever civilization offered them before the Great Titan War. So, even though they can eradicate the Titans, there's no way they will. Reason being, they don't want to change their own lives. To them, the Titans are able watchdogs. The denizens of the Second Wall, the First Wall, are obedient slaves under those watchdogs. The residents of the Third Wall are nobility if they just keep the world the way it is."

Eren had no words. Unable to speak in face of such an overwhelming truth, he sank into a whirlpool raging around him.

"Previously, you said something to me," Shikishima recalled. "'I'm not livestock.' That's not such a bad expression. However, if you would let me add a small twist, you aren't in danger of becoming livestock to the Titans, but to the nobility."

"But that's…" Unable to find the right words, Eren uttered a very simple one. "Horrible."

"Exactly. But just one person behind the Third Wall held that same conscientious view," asserted Shikishima, his voicing rising a little.

Eren lifted his face.

"That person was," the captain continued, pointing a finger at Eren, "your father."

"*What?*"

"Your father was a nobleman and a brilliant scientist. One day he acquired the government's secret formula for Jaeger and escaped to the Second Wall District. He founded an organization that aimed to overthrow the government and create an equal society. They were without a name and instead acted under a single emblem. It was the design of a gull with its wings spread. A free bird that flies over the sea."

"The design that old man Souda wore."

"That must be so, though I didn't see it firsthand." Shikishima took a breath as if to rest his throat. "In order to lend combat power to his organization, your father administered Jaeger to his two sons."

"*Two* sons?" Eren leaned forward. "I-I had a brother?"

Shikishima nodded. "Yes. Your older brother was a man named Haku."

"What is he doing now?"

"Unfortunately…" Shikishima paused before answering, simply, "he died, just a little while ago."

Casting his eyes on the floor, Eren tempered his heart. Fully aware that it must still be fluttering, Shikishima pressed on regardless.

"Haku was raised in the Second Wall East District, and you were raised here, in Monzen. It was the common opinion at the time that due to terrain, the Titans were mostly likely to attack from the north or the west. Thus it was believed that Monzen, at the southernmost tip, was a relatively safe town within the First Wall District. I'm sure that's why your father decided to leave you in Monzen. And the head of the organization's local branch hiding in Monzen happened to be a man whom you knew very well—Souda. However, here is what I cannot quite process. Why didn't this man called Souda brief you about the organization and the power of the drug administered to you? It's somewhat difficult to understand."

"Somehow…" Eren was surprised to find his tear ducts beginning to loosen. Still, his proud streak didn't allow him to cry. "Somehow, I feel like I know why the old man didn't tell me."

Eren remembered Souda's words from that day:

Your life is your life. It doesn't belong to anyone else. I only want you to live the life that you desire. But don't listen to what other people say. There's no need to try to carry what you think is your fate or your destiny on your shoulders.

Souda had wanted Eren to live freely.

So no matter what I did, he didn't restrict me, he didn't coerce me, and he didn't interfere excessively. And yet, back then, I'd do things like land a job and quit immediately, or get all excited about something and talk big but quickly lose interest and return to square one. I did that over and over again. What a way to waste the priceless freedom that the old man allowed me…

For Eren, it had been his first freedom. He felt bitter.

It's too late now. Souda already sacrificed himself. Kubal killed him because he tried to protect me, to keep me free. Eren clenched his fists on his knees. *How pathetic am I?*

"I want to avenge Souda."

At first, Eren wondered if his own thoughts had sprung from him, but it was Shikishima who had spoken.

"That's the kind of look I'm seeing on your face."

"I don't know," Eren said candidly. "Captain Shikishima, everything I just heard from you was so insane, I can't keep up with it. As for the old man, I'm frustrated and angry. But still, as for what I should do, I really can't decide right away. I…"

Finally he was seeing himself.

I acted so tough, like I knew something. I made fun of others, felt like I was better. I pretended to be something different and vented my feelings and blamed other people for my actions. But it all boils down to one thing.

I am so weak.

I wanted to pretend I was brave, but I was just acting. And now, having discovered my Titan strength, I see that I don't have the strength to decide anything. So…

"I don't know."

"In that case…" Shikishima's expression grew stern as if to supplement the weakness in Eren, as his mentor. Deftly using words as a lifeline, the captain began to lift Eren's heart from the sea floor.

"Serve with me."

Eren's heart leapt.

"There is a reason why I was able to obtain this much info. Know that I, too, was once a Gull."

"You were the old man's comrade?"

"Indeed. However, it's a little different now." Nodding with a confident smile, Shikishima pulled a handkerchief from his pocket and placed it on the surface of the coffee table. On the handkerchief was a symbol very similar to the one that he had called a "gull" embedded inside Souda's uniform.

"This is…"

"I've met the man—pardon me, your father before," Shikishima said, holding off Eren's question. "However, for better or for worse, he was a simple and naive person. The Gulls aimed to amass combat potential like yours everywhere but to rely on negotiations—a bloodless revolution. How boring. You understand, don't you? The central government is not going to give up their vested interests so easily. It's past the time for leisurely talks."

Shikishima poked twice at the design on the handkerchief.

"This is the design of the Falcons."

"The Falcons?"

"A brand-new anti-government organization that I started. The ideological foundation is largely similar to that of the Gulls. However, unlike them, a Falcon doesn't tediously drift through the sky but sometimes also bares its talons and hunts its prey. We bare our talons at this hopelessly unequal and rotten world. We hone our beaks to overthrow the government… It seemed that Kubal did not guess that I was one of the rebellious elements."

Eren blinked several times.

"Eren," Shikishima stared into Eren's eyes, right into the depths of his soul. "*We can do it now.*"

Eren gulped.

"I want your cooperation. I want your power." Shikishima weaved his words sharply as though to pierce Eren's soul. "Your father still lives on the run, awaiting the chance to overthrow the government. However, as you just saw, they lost Souda and a couple of other members, and the organization is slowly weakening. For several years now, members have been smoked out one after another and either incarcerated or executed. The Gulls are finished. Walk with me, Eren."

"I don't know if I can make much of a difference."

"Don't doubt yourself." Shikishima laughed and pointed his finger right at Eren's chest. "*You have to live to live.* And to do that, you have to fight. End the era of the slaves and usher in a new epoch.

Don't betray the hero inside of you."

"Hero…"

Suddenly a hard sound echoed in the room—*thunk thunk*. Somebody was knocking on the entrance above ground.

"Oops, it's already time!" Shikishima stood up and fixed the position of his scarf.

"Who is it?"

"Come."

The captain strode across the room and swiftly donned the uniform that was hanging from the wall. The stagnant air of the basement shifted and flowed at the new wind.

Outside, there were over twenty soldiers standing alert. At first, Eren assumed they were part of the expedition but soon realized that he didn't recognize anyone. The team wore VMEs, and some carried rifles. Unable to process the situation, Eren didn't speak.

"The Titans?" Shikishima asked one of the soldiers.

"Based on the lookout's report, four in the distance. They are headed east."

"Then they are not a problem." Confirming this, Shikishima turned around towards Eren.

"Who are these people?"

"They share my intentions. They are part of my organization."

Eren surveyed the soldiers again. The uniforms they wore all bore the Wings of Freedom. In other words, they were dressed like the Outer Wall Restoration Operation, in the outfit of all the members except the MPs and medic/cooks. However, when Eren thought about it carefully, that was strange as well. This team who stood before him was definitely not part of the expedition, and there was no other ongoing operation that they could belong to. There was only one explanation for the soldiers and their uniforms.

"Troops...from the past expeditions?"

"Good guess," replied Shikishima, adjusting his gear. "Almost all of them are Survey Corps regulars from before the breaching of the First Wall. They participated in the 1st and 2nd Outer Wall Restoration Operation."

"But they all died..."

"Camouflage. To throw off the government," Shikishima divulged proudly. "During the previous expeditions we established a base within Titan lands and had them hide out there, all for this moment. Of course, the government's official announcements state that they all died. As for the 3rd Outer Wall Restoration Operation, aside from Squad Leaders Kanaya and Mikasa, the Shikishima Advance Detachment was part of my organization."

So Mikasa doesn't know anything, the thought instantly occurred to Eren.

Then, from the other side of the road, a single transport truck approached. Eren watched it only for a moment before his surroundings stole his eyes. Though he only sensed it vaguely before, he was definitely in the town where he was born, near Souda's home. As if to draw some of it into him, Eren took a deep breath.

When the truck finally came to a halt, Eren's gaze was glued to the cargo bed.

"There's just one thing I have to apologize to you about," Shikishima said, smiling despite his words. "The ones sabotaging the operation are certainly Kubal and the central government. But he wasn't the one who stole the truck that carried the explosives."

"Those are…" Eren couldn't believe it. "The explosives from the relay point's basement."

"We weren't about to let the government lift our precious cargo," Shikishima's voice rang. "It was yours truly who absconded with them. Though it was unfortunate what I had to do to that girl. She was a necessary sacrifice."

"That girl?"

"Pardon me. That's between me and myself." Shikishima's eyes glazed over for a second before they quickly blinked. "We could certainly use more gunpowder to carry out our mission perfectly, but beggars can't be choosers. It seems we will have to make do with what we have."

"Oh! There *is* more." Eren recalled Armin's proposal in the hall. "On Missile Hill."

Shikishima and the troops surrounding him turned their attention towards Eren. He felt as though he'd finally struck upon something that would rouse him to action.

"I'll take you there," he offered confidently.

Shikishima nodded.

Eren had found his rightful place.

He realized that when he saw the captain's expression, which shook him. He would rise again, from Monzen.

An almost nostalgic, somehow fleeting, and cold wind swept past.

IX. THE SHORES OF ACHERON

The missile sat on top of the hill just as Armin remembered it. As expected, it was considerably heavy, and loading it on the truck was very difficult.

After Sannagi led the effort to excavate it, they carefully placed it onto the cargo bed. Since they couldn't afford to let a wayward impact set off the bomb, they used the snare nets and blankets stocked in the truck for padding.

"Well, I didn't think it would be quite this massive," Hange said, wiping the sweat from her forehead once they were done. "A bomb this big will definitely blow the wall to pieces. Unless we detonate it in the air, it might be too large of a blast for the wall."

"You think it won't work?" worried Armin.

"Hmm…it will be a matter of chance, I think. I'll certainly calculate the location of the bomb and the scale of the explosion as best I can so that we succeed… We also need to examine the cracks that they made in the wall."

The group returned to the transport and departed for the hole

in the First Wall. While Hange drove, Mikasa, who knew the streets
of Monzen well, sat in the passenger seat to navigate. Sasha and Jean
and Sannagi kept watch for Titans, and Armin sat in the cargo bed
to jerry-rig a detonator.

Fortunately, he had his oil extraction timer, so he decided to base
the device on it. He tuned the mechanism so that when the timer
reached zero, a large metal lever would activate, hit the fuse directly,
and detonate the bomb. As he engaged in the complicated task, he
began to fall into his old habit of losing track of his surroundings.
His vision narrowed, sounds faded into the background, and his
body melted into his own separate world. Thus, he didn't notice that
something was approaching them on the road.

The truck stopped suddenly, and Armin crashed into the bed's
edge. Before the pain of the impact had even left his body, Sannagi
shouted, "If it isn't Eren!"

Forgetting the pain, Armin stood up on the cargo bed to see Eren
atop another truck idling before them. It seemed that both vehicles
had slammed on the brakes to avoid a head-on collision.

When Eren, who was standing on the cargo bed just like Armin,
saw his old friend, he ran and jumped right onto Truck Two.

Mikasa gently climbed out from the passenger seat to gaze at
Eren in relief. When Armin smiled at her, however, she just sternly
knit her brows. She seemed almost ashamed.

"Thank goodness… You're okay."

"Yeah," breathed Eren. "I was saved by Captain Shikishima. I'm
glad you're all safe too."

Armin could see Shikishima sitting in the truck that Eren had
left. The captain cast a languid glance at them and seemed to sigh.

Behind him was yet another transport carrying over twenty soldiers.

"Who are they?"

"Apparently, they're from the past expeditions and are surviving Survey Corps regulars. They've been hiding all this time on Titan territory. They're all anti-Titan specialists."

Though Armin couldn't immediately grasp the situation, for the time being, he decided to rejoice at the reunion. Meanwhile, Shikishima climbed down from his truck's cargo bed and slowly approached Hange in the driver's seat. She got out as well.

"I heard about the unexploded missile from Eren. I understand that you retrieved it?" Shikishima asked point-blank.

"That is the case," Hange answered, staring suspiciously at Shikishima's truck. "Are those...explosives? Whoa! And those armaments! A prewar MGL and dear old Carl Gustav! What's going on?"

"I don't have time to explain in detail." Shikishima's expression didn't change. "I want you to hand over the missile."

"H-Huh?" Hange calmed down a little and tilted her head. "Whether or not we hand it over, we're all going to the same place. And as for planning the deployment of the explosives, I think we are more qualified."

"No, you should all return."

Everyone fell silent at Shikishima's words.

"We'll provide an escort, though we can spare only one. It'll be a little out of the way, but you should return to East Gate, Second Wall. We will take over the operation, with Eren."

As if a cold wind were leaking from the depths of some nearby cave, an uneasy chill began to spread amongst Armin and the others. Shikishima's logic made no sense.

Hange laughed deliberately to disperse the tension.

"No, no, no, what? We came all this way. We'll be there at the wall's restoration."

"Please don't waste our time."

Shikishima quietly glared at her. There was no obvious aggression, just a subtle, insidious flicker that flashed like a razor-sharp blade. It completely removed all traces of Hange's smile, and she looked almost solemn.

"Can I ask for an explanation?"

Shikishima only spoke after an uncomfortably long pause. "I want you to hand over the missile and retreat towards the Second Wall."

"You and your gang aren't going to carry out the Outer Wall Restoration Operation, are you?"

"I'm afraid not," Shikishima huffed impatiently. "We won't be repairing the wall."

Armin stared at Shikishima incredulously, unable to process his words. *They're not going to repair the wall?* Thinking Eren might know something, Armin looked over at his friend, but he stared back in surprise and shook his head. Apparently, Eren hadn't been told anything, either.

A gray fog seemed to hang in the air, and silence weighed down on them like lead. It seemed they were in some kind of deadlock.

Searching for an answer, Armin's side scanned the expressions of Shikishima's crew, who stood with their eyes lowered as if to deny the inspection.

"Please answer."

It was Mikasa who demanded this of the captain. He stared at her for a while before sighing with resignation.

"Even if I do explain, it's not likely you'll understand… So I was hoping we wouldn't run into you guys." Shikishima turned around towards his own transport. "Hey, you explain."

"Yes, sir."

A large man got out from the passenger seat, nodded, and began to speak. His voice was ample and lustrous. Perhaps he had held an important post in the true Survey Corps as well.

"We don't have much time so I'll keep it simple. We are going to use these explosives to blow up the South Gates of the Second and Third Walls to let the Titans invade."

"What?" Jean blurted out, his mouth agape.

Armin felt the same way though he remained silent. *What is this man saying? Does he know what he's saying?*

The large man ignored their reaction and continued to explain matter-of-factly:

"From the outset, the government had no intention of repairing the wall. They can control the actions of the Titans very precisely and orchestrated every attack suffered so far. It's all part of a scheme plotted by the nobility and the central government in the Third Wall. Under the gaze of their watchdogs, the Titans, we are being kept like pets behind walls. We are basically no more than slaves."

"E-Even so, do you have to break down the walls?" Jean plucked up his courage and inquired. "Why would you wanna do that?"

"Today," the large man declared, savoring his words, "we will carry out a coup d'état to overthrow the government."

"C-Coup d'état…" Armin swallowed his breath and parroted to himself.

"We've been waiting for this day for a long time," the large man said. "Kubal is no longer within the Third Wall. If we are going to attack, it has to be today. There are others awaiting orders inside the walls. The plan is for them to join us when we invade. Today we will take down the government and rebuild a new, free society."

The world was accelerating before their eyes. It was difficult enough to understand the plan, and in the first place, Armin was having trouble keeping up with the man's worldview. *The government can control the Titans? We are being controlled? We are the slaves of the nobility? Everything that Kubal said to me was complete nonsense?*

"Um, excuse me."

The deflating interruption came from Sannagi. He sluggishly raised his plump arm to draw attention to himself. Both Shikishima and the large man shifted their gazes to him.

"I think I take you all's point, if only vaguely." With his raised right arm, he rubbed the nape of his neck. "Just, why do you have to break down the inner walls to enact the coup? That's what I don't get. Rather than go through the trouble of doing that, can't you just fly over the Third Wall in your VMEs? The Titans invading would suck."

Shikishima glared at Sannagi menacingly, hoping perhaps to make the greenhorn retract his question. Yet Sannagi did no such thing, and Shikishima had no choice but to open his mouth.

"Of course," he replied, still glaring at Sannagi, "the world will be plunged into utter chaos the moment the Titans flood the interior. That is our biggest hope."

"Meaning?"

"Though the inhabitants of the Second Wall District are mere 'slaves' to the government, it's apparent that they are also valuable 'laborers.' The government looks down on them but finds them indispensable. As he"—Shikishima pointed his chin at the large man— "just said, the government can control the actions of the Titans with extreme precision. If they invade, the government will immediately rein them in to make sure they don't attack people, its labor force. If there is a hole in the *Third* Wall, then all the more so: to save their own lives they will have to control the Titans. And when the Titans halt their attack, retreat towards the First Wall District, or exhibit any other strange behavior, doubts will erupt among the people.

"We are going to vividly expose the reality of this regime. And eventually, the people will realize that they have been tricked. Then, after gaining the public as our ally, after instilling a crisis of faith in the government, we will strike at this country's center. These steps are essential. If we merely overthrow the government through violence, the *hearts* of the people will not follow. We want to take down the government after clear evidence of its true nature is submitted to the public. That is our plan."

"But I bet the government can't control the Titans right away?" questioned Sannagi. "What if they start attacking people before the government can call them off?"

"Of course, I'm sure there will be many casualties," Shikishima answered unflinchingly. "Residents in the vicinity of the invasion's entry point will come under attack. It might mean five thousand deaths, or even ten thousand. However, it's a sacrifice that cannot be avoided."

"A sacrifice that cannot be avoided…"

"The only ones who can make a difference are those who can give up something that's important to them. If we fear such a degree of consequence, we will never accomplish anything. Even if I continue to explain this to you, it will be beyond you, I am sure. As for us, however, up until two years ago, we were forced to repeat useless missions called Extramural Expeditions over and over again in the Survey Corps."

The ex-Survey Corpsmen on the truck behind Shikishima all seemed to wince when he said this.

"If we went too far, a mysterious withdrawal order would come down from the brass. If we discovered historic ruins from the old civilization era, by the next dispatch of troops those ruins would be destroyed without a trace. So many soldiers were killed mercilessly thanks to the government's obsession with 'designated knowledge.' What Survey Corps, what Wings of Liberty? There was nothing more stupid. We just continued to fling ourselves into the treacherous world outside of the wall, and little by little we lost our numbers to the scenarios that the government drew up for us. Compared to that… What, so this time the civilians will suffer casualties? It barely matters. *It's fine.* Great success requires certain losses. It's the price we pay for true freedom."

A dull silence. Only the wind blew, weakly, and aside from the soldiers who scanned the area for Titans, everybody was motionless, their bodies sinking where they stood. Gravity worked relentlessly; their legs felt heavy as if they might submerge into the ground. Even their breathing and other listless movements were locked up in a world that had no clear answer.

"I didn't…" It was Mikasa who opened her mouth. "I didn't hear anything about this."

Shikishima caught Mikasa's gaze and responded with a voice devoid of emotion. "I deemed it inappropriate to talk to you about it," he said, staring at her. "Both you and Kanaya just weren't right for this kind of fight. There was a chance that you would try to derail the coup."

"If I were against it, what would have happened?"

"It wouldn't have mattered," Shikishima concluded. "Our will is strong. No matter who objects, the plan will not be stopped. Thus, I avoided unnecessary friction with you." Shikishima raised his voice to speak not only to Mikasa but also to everyone on Truck Two. "Please do not delay us any further. For you, this might be an expedition that you happened to sign up for, but we have worked for this very day for a long time. This is the day of the rebellion—the momentous day on which we will gain true freedom. So please, hand over the missile, and leave us promptly."

"But," Eren, still confused, defied Shikishima, "I told you about the missile because I thought you were going to use it to repair the wall! It wasn't to cooperate with *that* mission!"

"This from you as well." Shikishima sighed in disgust. "That's why I hate children. No matter how kindly and carefully you explain the reality of the world, the moment it seems like their hands are going to get dirty, they throw a tantrum. They believe there's some flawless, correct solution floating around and only think about avoiding all risk. They're unable to think about the full picture and only understand what is happening before their eyes. They don't have any bright ideas of their own, and yet their objections are uselessly loud. Fine. I was wrong to think that you'd be up for the fight. You should return home with the rest of them."

"B-But—"

"Whether you stay or go, you don't have much sway anyway. While your power is valuable, we will carry out the plan without you. That was our original intent. So step aside. If you impede us more than you have, we will not hesitate to use force."

Armin watched the exchange, unable to say anything. His body had begun to shrink, and his posture crumpled in on itself. He had no idea who was right, who was wrong, what to believe, what to denounce. Honestly, he thought that destroying the Second and Third Walls was extremely inhumane and strictly inexcusable. At the same time, he couldn't outright repudiate Shikishima and his burden of conviction.

Armin could only stand in place.

"Okay, gotcha," Sannagi piped up.

Everyone turned to look at him. He got down from the cargo bed and slowly began walking towards Shikishima. Then, with a bright voice that might be used to say good morning, he spoke.

"I don't know too much, but please let me lend a hand."

"Huh?"

It wasn't only Jean, but also Sasha and Hange who reacted thus.

"Sannagi?" Armin called out doubtfully.

"What?" Sannagi laughed cheerfully and scratched his head. "Considering the situation, mine is the natural decision. Don't be so surprised. Excuse me, could you please show me the bed of that truck?"

Shikishima gave a small nod at this request. Returning it, Sannagi approached the truck and quickly turned over the black sheet that was covering the cargo. Though Armin couldn't see very well from where he was standing, it seemed to be tightly packed with explosives. Sannagi jumped back in surprise and nodded several times as if he'd come to some kind of an understanding.

"This is a lot of explosives. With this, the Second Wall will be in pieces, ha ha." Laughing, Sannagi turned back to Shikishima. "Captain Shikishima, though I'm not very skilled, please let me help. Will you let me join your group?"

"Can I take this to mean," Shikishima asked, "that you sympathize with my thinking?"

"Of course." Sannagi nodded deeply. "I was struck by your determination."

Shikishima's nod was perfunctory. "Splendid. I'm not expecting much. You can bring up the rear."

"Leave it to me."

"Wait, wait! Hey!" Shaking with anger, Jean confronted Sannagi. "What are you thinking, asshole? Have you gone nuts? Huh?"

"Hey, hey, calm down, Jean," Sannagi replied in an altogether playful tone. "If you look at it calmly, this is the only option. These people are the elite of the former Survey Corps. They are soldiers who all boast pretty much the same combat chops as Captain Shikishima. If we continue to block them with our useless pride and have to fight them as a result, we won't stand any kind of a chance…right?"

"What is this?" Sasha shook her head in disbelief. "You're saying we should give way because we can't win? That's not right. These folks are about to hurt innocent people with their rebellion."

Shikishima glared at Sasha, his eyes filling with silent anger. She was forced to look down at the ground in fear.

"What's going to happen to your little brothers and sisters?" Jean pressed, taking over for Sasha. "They're staying by South Gate waiting for you to return, aren't they? So is my father. He checked into a hotel in the area and is waiting for me. If the Titans get in, the very first ones to get attacked will be the people near South Gate. Do you understand?"

"Grow up, Jean," Sannagi admonished him. "I know that. Every correct solution holds risks. Weren't you listening to Captain Shikishima? To me, my brothers and sisters are more important than anything. It's not an exaggeration to say that they are more important than my own life. To protect my siblings, I'll do whatever it takes." Sannagi opened his right hand and began to slice the air sideways with it.

"What do you mean? What you're saying and what you're doing don't match up."

Armin stared at Sannagi, who was still moving his hand horizontally. As if to stress something, he slowly repeated the motion from right to left. Finally, Armin realized what Sannagi was trying to do.

He couldn't be serious. With an uneasy feeling growing in his chest, Armin spoke.

"It's not right, Sannagi."

"Armin, you're kind, but your head is just a little too stuffy." Sannagi gave a fleeting smile, perhaps seeing that he had gotten through to Armin. "Take the very best path."

"Sannagi, you're a kind person too...but I think you're being a *complete idiot.*"

"Ha, harsh. But this is the only choice, right?"

"Sannagi..."

Armin wanted to object but couldn't find the words, unable to discern any path other than the one Sannagi was trying to choose.

So that's what he means to do. That's the only thing he can do.

Armin bit his lip. He was filled with bitter frustration at his own uselessness, at leaving everything to Sannagi.

"Armin, you're kind, but your head is just a little too stuffy."… I got it, Sannagi. I'll follow your lead. Please curse me for only being able to support you.

Fighting tears, he faced the one person who wouldn't be able to read Sannagi's message: Mikasa. When he met her eyes, he motioned for her to return to the passenger seat with his gaze. Hange too, who had gotten out from the driver's seat, returned to Truck Two as naturally as possible.

"Um, I'm sorry, does anybody have a light? I'd like to smoke this."

Sannagi pulled a cigarette from the pocket of his uniform and held it between his index and middle fingers. At that point, Jean and Eren also realized what was happening.

Shikishima's soldiers muttered to one another as they groped around in their pockets. The first soldier to discover a lighter approached Sannagi and held it at his mouth.

"It's not lighting."

"You need to inhale, stupid," the soldier holding the lighter said impatiently. "If you don't inhale, it won't light. Have you never smoked before?"

"Haha, embarrassingly enough, no. I'm sorry, could you just let me use it?"

No doubt fed up with the newbie's clumsiness, the soldier flung the lighter into Sannagi's hand. Nodding and accepting the lighter,

Sannagi finally succeeded in lighting the cigarette.

"Ugh!" he coughed. "So this is how bad they taste. I can't do this."

With the cigarette still in his mouth, Sannagi grabbed something hanging from his hip and gazed at it lovingly. It was the doll that his sister had made to look like him.

"I'm sorry, Koyuki," Sannagi spoke to it. "Can you forgive your older brother for using your special doll? This is all I have. I'm really sorry."

Then, as gently as he could, Sannagi lit the doll on fire with the lighter. The flame caught onto the left foot then gradually rose to its upper half, which began to turn into black cinders.

Was it some ceremony to say goodbye to his siblings? Assuming that it must be, Shikishima's troops just gazed at Sannagi's strange behavior.

"Koyuki, Yae, Nobu, Kaname, Gou!" he shouted up at the sky.

In his hand, the doll was already covered in flames. Holding on to it must have been a challenge. Still, without releasing the doll, he continued his speech at the sky.

"Everyone, thank you! I'm sure you'll grow up healthy like your older brother! When you do, go back home and till the fields! I'm sure my friends will take back the First Wall District! Your big brother is going to protect you!"

Shikishima caught on to it at last.

"Stop him!"

But it was too late. Nobody could stop Sannagi.

"Hange! Reverse!"

"I know!"

Truck Two, which carried all of Sannagi's friends, drove backwards at full speed. Armin clung to the cargo bed as the engine breathed furiously like a bucking horse. In preparation for the explosion, he crouched down.

Sannagi's repeated lateral hand motion had been a signal, of course. The horizontal cut with an open palm was unmistakable. It was the hand sign that Squad Leader Yunohira had used as well: *Return to transport.*

Gripping onto the shaking truck, Armin peeked over the rail and spotted Sannagi. He was smiling and watching Truck Two grow more and more distant.

"I'm leaving the rest to you!"

With that yell, he tossed the burning doll at the explosives.

Shikishima's soldiers tried to stop him but didn't make it in time.

Burning a passionate red as if to signify its owner's determination, the doll fell.

The moment it touched the bed of the transport, there was a flash and a shock—an explosion like the world was being turned inside out.

Truck Two rocked violently. In an instant, Armin's vision was cloaked in dust, and he couldn't see more than three feet in front of him. Even as he gripped the bed like a madman, the transport threatened to flip over. Hange handled the steering wheel and somehow maintained balance—and maintaining it, drove through the blast's aftershock.

As if being pushed by the explosion, they sped on.

It seemed they had gone more than a couple of hundred yards. In an open field at the base of Missile Hill, the truck finally stopped. As the dust gradually cleared, Armin and the others checked on their injuries. Fortunately, they were all unharmed—excluding, of course, Sannagi. As the traces of the explosion faded, everyone was plunged into deep sorrow.

"That *idiot*." Jean leaned against the edge of the truck and hung his head.

Likewise, Armin and Sasha were overwhelmed with despair.

Although so many had died since the very beginning, they weren't getting used to it one bit. Despair, egalitarian, crawled like ivy into the corners of the heart and haunted the souls of those left behind.

"I wonder if Shikishima and the others were all killed by the explosion."

"Of course," Jean spat at Armin.

After taking a breath, Eren asked about Fukushi and Lil as if he had just remembered them. When Armin explained their last moments, Eren looked down and bit his lip. The hundred-strong of the 3rd Outer Wall Restoration Operation had been reduced to the mere six of them riding Truck Two.

At this point, Armin felt like surviving the incredible odds was some kind of punishment. What kind of fate was this?

It was with weary faces that Hange and Mikasa climbed up into the cargo bed. Mikasa's especially was distraught, and it was clear that she was lost deep in her thoughts.

"I wonder…if it was the right thing to do," Eren muttered as if to himself.

"Really, asshole?" Jean stood and approached him. "Sannagi was wrong?"

"No!" replied Eren, but his ambivalence showed on his lips. "Sannagi was right. He made the right choice from his perspective, but...Shikishima also believed in something."

"So Captain Shikishima was right?"

"That's what I don't know!" Eren seemed frustrated not at Jean, but himself. "I'm sorry. I lost my temper."

Jean was left hanging by the swift and sincere apology.

"And now," Hange said, "we resume the Outer Wall Restoration Operation... Is that about right?"

"'Course," Jean seconded immediately. "Sannagi gave his life so that we could succeed. We can't just quit!"

Both Armin and Sasha stiffened in surprise.

"Wh-What are you guys making that face for?"

"I-It's nothing." Sasha laughed wryly. "You're like a different person than you were in training."

"Shut up." Jean looked down as if embarrassed.

"But," Sasha added, "I agree that we should close the hole in the wall. It must be because I'm not very smart, but I didn't really get Captain Shikishima's aim and didn't see the justice of it. I don't think Sannagi's decision was wrong. We couldn't let those people carry out a plan that would sacrifice so many innocent people. You agree, don't you, Armin?"

"Y-Yes," Armin answered reflexively, but he gave it some thought.

In part, he deeply sympathized with Eren's ambivalence. Just moments ago, Eren had pleaded with Shikishima to use the missile to restore the wall and, at that point, seemed not to have been feeling any uncertainty. Calming down now, however, he was confronting the actual proposition. It hadn't been such a simple issue.

As Sasha said, Shikishima and his team had formed a plan that would harm many, many civilians. From the viewpoint of common morality, it was inarguably *wrong*. Whether Shikishima's option was definitely incorrect, though, Armin and the others shouldn't have been able to say for sure. It was the same with Sannagi's deed: his self-destruction saved many residents within the Second Wall but also killed many members of the Survey Corps.

Armin was growing keenly aware of the toughness of decision-making. The world was so complex and hard.

Perhaps the problem was that Eren and Armin didn't have anyone they wanted to protect within the Second Wall. If they had precious people, family, that they wanted to save, then like Sannagi and Jean, or Sasha, they might automatically reproach Shikishima and ratify their own behavior.

No, I can't answer.

The more he disregarded his emotions and tried to think rationally, the more problems arose. He sighed and raised his face as if to contemplate something else.

Then—

He couldn't believe his eyes.

"You're kidding me."

At Armin's words, everybody looked at the swirling dust that the blast had sent up. From out of it, as if to symbolize some new beginning, a shape was slowly approaching them.

It was a figure to betray anyone's expectations, a figure to unsettle all of their hearts.

Like proof of their despair, it had emerged, and as it grew closer, their hearts froze.

His uniform was charred black as if he had returned alive from hell, and sparks fell from him like the remains of hellfire. The scarf at the base of his neck wasn't clean and looked instead like some kind of prop to go with his sangfroid. As if to wake himself up, he shook his head. His black hair followed, waving from right to left. Then finally, as he made his way to Armin and the others, he smiled eerily.

"Well, look at what you did…"

The smile remained on his face.

"To think that I would lose my troops like this… A complete wipeout, apart from myself." Shikishima slowly raked his hair. "However, to be clear, I have no intention of aborting my plan."

Armin gulped.

"I have the determination to carry it out on my own and the strength to see it through. If only to destroy the Second Wall, I will have to take that missile. And you, I will punish for the injustice you perpetrated against my team."

Shikishima gently sat down. Then, he removed his blade and placed it against his chest. The edge touched the thin white shirt that was showing under his uniform.

Armin thought for a moment that the captain was about to end his own life, but as it turned out, that wasn't it. In fact, he was leaping to a point that was diametrically opposed to death. Glaring at Armin and the others, and without hesitation or reserve, Shikishima plunged the blade deep into his own heart. Fresh blood flowed, and he gritted his teeth in pain until some began to trickle from the corner of his mouth. The next moment, however, he began to glow with a strange light.

Armin unconsciously covered his face with his right arm. From under it, he watched the paranormal scene unfold.

Countless cloud-like clumps suddenly appeared above Shikishima's head and descended to engulf his body. They gathered together and began to rumble faintly with thunder. Crackling electricity reverberated outwards. To Armin and the others, it looked like some kind of creation scene.

Eventually Shikishima's body, enveloped by the clouds, rapidly began to *Titanize*.

It rose in height—ten feet, fifteen, thirty—and continued to enlarge.

Forty feet. When the transformation ceased, slowly, as if to indicate that the process was complete, the clouds began to drift and disperse like steam. As if the sun were rising, and the sky clearing, a vista opened.

What it showed made everybody gasp.

"What the…"

Jean, too, looked up at the thing they couldn't forget if they tried. The bane of so many soldiers in that hall, the final blow that all but wiped out the 3rd Outer Wall Restoration Operation—it was the White Titan.

"C-Captain Shikishima…is a Titan?" Sasha's voice spilled from her mouth.

As if to confirm that each part of his body was working properly, Shikishima, or rather the White Titan, looked at its own hands and moved each of its fingers one by one. Then it let out an earth-shaking roar.

Everybody crouched to endure the howl, which seemed to strike at their very hearts.

Gazing at the Titan's white skin, which reflected the sunlight with an oppressive glare, Armin scrambled to sort out his thoughts. Considering it calmly, yes, if Eren was able to turn into a Titan, it wasn't so strange that someone else had the same power.

The White Titan had been Captain Shikishima. No wonder it had intelligence. No wonder it had taken out Squad Three and Kanaya from the Shikishima Detachment (his own subordinate!) so readily in the hall. In order to avoid suspicion, he had stolen Eren away, turned back into a human, and returned to the hall, and even dissuaded Armin and the others from going after their friend. Then he had tried to recruit Eren to his own side for his own ambitions.

Almost reflexively, Armin checked to make sure his Vertical Maneuvering Equipment was in a functional state. They were going to do battle with the White Titan, which was endowed with overwhelming strength and an intellect. Armin's heart froze at the thought. Did they even stand a chance?

"Did you know?" Jean asked, glaring at Mikasa. "That he was a Titan?"

"Of course I didn't," she answered without looking at Jean, her eyes lost. "If I had known..." Unable to find any more words, she fell silent.

Hange got out of the cargo bed and hastily returned to the driver's seat. "W-We're gonna scram! Everyone hold on where you can!"

As she started the truck, an all-too-loud rumble began to echo around them. It wasn't that the White Titan was moving in. From across the clearing, new Titans were approaching. There were three of them—the normal kind. They were charging with their clumsy gaits.

"Really? Does it have to be now?" Jean grimaced.

Armin shouted at Hange who was in the driver's seat. "First, please get us to some buildings! We can't employ vertical maneuvers here!"

"Got it!" As Hange pressed down on the gas, the truck lurched forward and accelerated. Holding onto the railing, Armin stared at the approaching Titans. Unexpectedly, they didn't give the truck a single glance and instead charged for the White Titan at full speed.

"Right…just like with Eren. Regular Titans see it as an enemy."

As the White Titan tried to chase after the transport, the three Titans blocked its path. *Good. This will buy us some time,* Armin thought, but not for long.

Without encountering the slightest difficulty, the White Titan killed its three giant foes in the blink of an eye. It struck the first in the head with its fist, smashing the nape as well. It shot out its left arm at the base of the second's neck, skewering it, naturally piercing the nape as well—instant death. It knocked the third down onto its face and, as if scooping up sand, drew the nape up, killing it.

Its power was so overwhelming that the trio hadn't even served to slow it down. Its movements were extremely polished compared to Eren's movements as a Titan, and its disposition appeared to be quite unflappable. The perfect movements flowed together. The strongest man in the world was not merely the Titans' nemesis but also the strongest Titan in the world.

"A worst-case scenario," Armin murmured.

After taking out the regular Titans, the White Titan began to chase after the truck. Each of its steps shook the ground, raising goosebumps on the humans' arms.

"I see buildings."

As Sasha said, sure enough, a cluster of structures came into view ahead. If they reached it, they would be able to use their VMEs. Yet Armin found no solace in that. Even if they transitioned to vertical maneuvers, what were their odds? To begin with, Armin, Eren, and probably Mikasa had misgivings about this fight. Their morale had suffered, undeniably.

His eyes on the approaching White Titan, Armin furrowed his brow. There was no way this was going to end well. Their only chance of winning hinged on a faint possibility.

Eren would have to turn into a Titan again.

On top of the truck, Eren finished readying his VME and assumed his stance so he could fight at any moment. However, a shadow clouded his face, and he was clearly reluctant. If Eren did decide to turn into a Titan, how would he even do it? Was he supposed to pierce his chest with his blade like Shikishima? It seemed too dangerous an act to imitate when they weren't sure.

The White Titan's pace was breathtaking, and it rapidly closed the distance to the transport. They weren't going to outrun it.

"A-At any rate, let's scatter for this fight," Armin proposed as though to rally himself. There was no superior left to offer better tactics. "When the truck slides into town, we'll split to the right and left and transition to vertical maneuvers. From the right, Mikasa and I, and from the left, Eren, Jean, and Sasha. Is that okay?"

Everyone nodded. Though with a feeble motion, Mikasa quietly clasped her triggers too.

"Let's focus on evading its attacks. We'll find an opening eventually. If you feel unsafe, immediately return to the transport. It wants the dud, so as long as we're near the truck, it shouldn't be able to deal any massive blow."

Jean assented in a remarkably loud voice, and Sasha also nodded decisively. The two of them, particularly Jean, seemed to be greatly inspired by Sannagi's feat. They had never shown so much fight before.

At last, the truck entered the town.

"Now!"

They dispersed.

Gripping his triggers, Armin leapt from the moving truck. At the same time, he shot his anchor for a wall to the right and began to wind the wire. His body creaked against the intensifying gravity as he initiated vertical maneuvers. He clenched his jaw. Already, Mikasa had reached a higher altitude than him and was flying over him. What skill. From the left, Jean, Sasha, and Eren, in turn, took to the air. Simultaneously, from the right and left, they harassed their pursuer.

—The White Titan raised its left arm as it ran—

Instantly, Armin's heart sank. The arm's trajectory was headed for him. Releasing his anchor, reeling in his wire, and burning gas, he tried to alter his route. He shot his anchor again, hit his mark, and reeled in.

—The White Titan swung its arm, destroying the wall that Armin's anchor had pierced—

Damn... He was weightless. Having lost his support, he plummeted towards the ground. For Armin, who had been flying at a low altitude, the ground was right beyond his nose. *Uh oh.* Mikasa screamed his name from the sky. Somehow, using his gas, Armin managed to move his body up and shoot his anchor for a wall to his left—a hit—and reeled in. *Don't let it be too late!* He was already scraping against the ground. Due to his velocity, an intense pain shot through his back from the friction. A cry escaped him, but somehow he regained altitude.

His trajectory was stable, but he had fallen behind considerably. The back of the White Titan giving chase to the truck at full speed was already far away.

Shooting out his anchors alternatively at walls on both sides, he maneuvered as fast as he could to catch up. Wind cut at him from right and left as he advanced in large arcs.

Ahead of him, his friends were engaged in a heated battle but were hardly holding their own. Instead, it was the kind of fight that Armin had feared. Mikasa's movements were somehow sluggish and lackluster. She was wielding her blades but gave no sign of swinging them. Likewise, Eren's flight paths were half-hearted and wobbly, and his arcs dull as if he didn't want to choose. That was extremely risky. Meanwhile, it was the opposite with Jean and Sasha. Their trajectories were too linear. Consumed by anger and their desire to avenge Sannagi, they were forgetting to mesmerize their enemy. As for Armin, he had not even caught up to the fight.

Watching from the rear afforded him a painfully clear view of how the fight was unfolding. To expel his hopeless thoughts, he burned his fuel. He felt pressure on his hips as his body accelerated rudely.

—The White Titan raised its right arm—

Its target was…Jean. His trajectories got good marks in exams, but he tended to choose routes that were too straightforward. It was only natural that he was being targeted. *Dodge it, Jean. Please dodge it,* Armin prayed as he continued to progress. However, the Titan's speed was so great that he couldn't seem to get any closer.

—Its right arm swung down—

And swatted. Armin grimaced and almost started crying. A human figure went flying along the arc of the Titan's violent swing, but it wasn't Jean. Eren, sensing the risk, had pushed Jean out of the way just in time.

Thus, the one who had been struck by the Titan was...

"Eren!!" Armin shouted, but his voice was swallowed by the wind as his friend's body crashed into a nearby building and punched through it. Opening a hole in the wall, Eren disappeared from view. Armin sank into despair. *Why? How?*

As if a switch had been turned on, Mikasa banked intensely. With the vigor of a surging wave, she coursed around the White Titan. Armin burned his gas harder, groped around in his mind, and came to a realization.

That's it, I finally see it. He's lost his purpose, too, thought Armin, gazing at the White Titan—at Shikishima. The plan that he'd composed in such detail for this day had gone up in flames when Sannagi had given his life to obstruct it. He had lost his crew, his true power and potential. Coolness was all it took to see that. Even though Shikishima had the ability to transform into a Titan, that power alone wasn't enough to overthrow the government. Thus he had assembled a team and worked out a plan for today. Yet now he was resorting to brute force without any forethought. It was as if he'd short-circuited. Surely, the man didn't really believe that he could still pull off a coup under the circumstances. He was just looking for an outlet for his directionless emotions, and acting out.

Amidst the wind and the gravity, Armin was convinced.

We definitely have to stop that man. We can't lose to that man.

I'm still not sure about what Sannagi did, but us going down to the White Titan is exactly what the government would want. The Outer Wall unrestored, the anti-government faction failing at their halfway attempt at a coup. As a result, this world's reign over its slaves will go on for eternity. That isn't right.

Then, for the people of the Second Wall District, for Sannagi, for the soldiers who've fallen in this operation, and above all for Shikishima, we have to defeat that White Titan. There's no reason to hesitate, at all.

Armin finally closed in on the Titan's back. Somehow he had to find a gap and attack its vital spot. As he calculated his trajectory from behind the Titan, a loud impact reverberated suddenly.

The White Titan's left hand had caught something. A thread seemed to be hanging limply from its fist, which it held at shoulder height. Armin didn't even have to guess what it was. It was a VME wire. He immediately checked his surroundings and spotted Jean and Sasha on his right. Then the one who had been caught was…

Mikasa.

"It's not true…"

His voice shaking, Armin pierced his left anchor into a wall. He had to save her. Should he cut the tendon in its arm? Or should he continue to target its nape? Either way, he needed to hurry—because the next instant, the muscles in the Titan's left arm flexed. It was squeezing its fist, squeezing Mikasa to death.

"Please, stop!"

As if time itself stood still, Armin's world skidded to a halt. Vivid red blood sprayed from the Titan's left hand. As much as he abhorred the comparison, just like a ripe tomato being crushed.

"Ahh…"

How weak was he? Why was he such a dunce? Even when he mustered his resolve and hardened his heart, he simply lacked the power to see things through. He was so pathetic, he'd…

Rather just die.

"Crap," he muttered.

Then it came: intense vibrations from behind him.

A whirlwind.

When he turned around, there it was.

Collapsed on the ground, he tried raising his right arm. An intense pain penetrated his entire body, but he was able to move. He clenched his fist, opened it, and clenched it again. *It's okay, I'm still alive,* Eren confirmed and slowly raised his upper body.

It seemed he had been hurled into an abandoned building. Before him was a large hole in the wall which he must have opened. Because the impact had been so intense, his memory from the moment was a little faded. The wooden wall he'd broken through had deteriorated considerably due to rot and had functioned as a kind of cushion. Otherwise, he would be dead now.

Unable to fully stand because of the pain, he dragged his body towards the hole. He crawled like a bug, slowly, weakly, precariously. As he did so, he confronted the unclear emotions eddying in his heart.

Shikishima had devoted an oddly substantial amount of his time, offered a plethora of information, and followed up with an invitation to collaborate. Eren had behaved as though he'd consented. At that point, he fully believed that Shikishima was his new leader in addition to everything the man said. No, Eren had been *trying* to believe. He had learned about the reality of the world and of his own existence and, not knowing what to do, had decided to put faith in the person who would guide him, a reliable leader. And there, he'd felt that he'd made progress.

Faced with the dark streak in the man's ideas, however, Eren had rejected him. Shikishima's voice echoed in the back of his head. *The moment it seems like their hands are going to get dirty, they throw a tantrum.* Eren had no excuse. It was exactly as the captain said. The idea of sacrificing innocent people to overthrow the corrupt government had seemed too violent and extreme then, and Eren still thought so. There had to be a better way to win freedom that more people could subscribe to.

—*They don't have any bright ideas of their own, and yet their objections are uselessly loud.*

Too precisely, those words prodded Eren's aching soul. On the one hand, he understood Shikishima's desire to change the world, and on the other, he understood just as clearly Sannagi's desire to protect the inhabitants of the Second Wall District. Eren couldn't readily support one or criticize the other.

The world was built upon so many conflicts, so many difficult choices, just like that one. He understood that well now. He had once scorned the majority of Monzen's residents for living boring, mundane lives and considered them pathetic. *I don't want to become like them,* he'd told himself, and never doubted that he was already leading a superior life.

But now I know. I'm the same. In the end, no matter what I know, I'm unable to decide. I just stand around, and as everything around me is shoved around by someone else's hand, I suck on my thumb and wait. In Monzen I lived under Souda's protection, and after enlisting I followed the instructors' guidance, and during the operation, the orders of my superior, and since learning the truth, Shikishima... In the end, I can't decide for myself.

Enduring the pain, Eren finally reached the opening in the wall. Still unable to stand on his feet, his upper body leaning against the wall, he took in the battle on the other side of the hole. He could see the White Titan's receding back, and around it, the tiny movements of Mikasa and the others as they flew. Armin was chasing after them. They were clearly at a disadvantage however he looked at it.

Shikishima's movements, or the White Titan's, were certain, and Jean and Sasha's hands were full just trying to stay in the air. Their wire motions were too monotonous, the arcs too extended—it was easy to predict where they were going. Only Mikasa's maneuvers were swift, but just one person's efforts couldn't usher in a decisive opportunity. They couldn't attack.

It's a matter of time... As the thought flitted across his mind, Eren finally admitted, *Right, someone who can't choose will keep on losing. Lamenting that you can't decide and wallowing in disappointment might feel noble, but it's actually very easy. If I did that though, I would not only never gain anything but merely watch as everything dear to me gets taken away. Just as the Titans took Monzen and the First Wall District two years ago, just as the government stole freedom and equality from us, just as Kubal killed Souda, I'll go on losing everything if I don't stand up and choose.*

So what was he going to do? What was he supposed to do?

He didn't even need to think about it. His heart burned with passion.

He had to do it. He had to choose. If he didn't choose, he'd lose something again. If he didn't decide, then for all eternity—

"I'd never make a difference!"

Saying this aloud, he ignored his pain and forced himself to stand. Perhaps his internal organs had been damaged, and it was hard to breathe, and his vision wavered. Still, he gritted his teeth and stood. The worst outcome was in store if he didn't do something. He had one and only one way to prevent it.

Eren installed the blade on his right trigger and let out his breath to expel his doubts. He closed his eyes, calmed his mind, and slowly pressed the blade to his chest. He steadied the trigger with his left hand, gripping firmly so he could use all his strength. To say he wasn't scared would have been a lie. There was no definite proof that this would transform him into a Titan, but...

Every correct solution came with risks. Sannagi had been right about that.

Eren paid his respects to Sannagi—because his friend had gone ahead and chosen. He'd done what Eren couldn't. Sannagi had been an amazing guy.

Now it was Eren's turn, and he would gladly accept the risk. *Shikishima is wrong.* He was making that call. *Just call it, act, and fight—regret later. If you don't act, you'll never make a difference.*

In the distance, Eren saw the Titan grasp something, but he

wasn't going to let anyone else get killed.

I will master this power and gain everything.

Eren willed strength into both his hands. Then, in a single breath, he pierced his heart.

Armin hastened to a wall to his left. The sudden gust from behind pushed Jean and Sasha to opposite walls and whirled after the White Titan. It was another Titan, and it was wild, a picture of combativeness. Its every muscle was toned like a work of art, its mouth and gleaming eyes had a savage cast, and its fist swung like the wrathful iron hammer of a demon of justice. Armin, of course, recognized the sight.

"Eren!" he shouted.

Eren, who had turned into a Titan, bent his right arm and magnificently sank his fist into his adversary's head—a direct hit. Mikasa flew from the White Titan's left hand, and Armin saw that the spraying blood hadn't been hers but its own. Holding her blades, she evaded to a wall to her right and gathered her ragged breath. Almost belatedly, fat, pillar-like fingers sprinkled towards the ground. She had cut them off—this was Mikasa, after all.

Eren pressed his case. With a thunderous roar, he kicked the stunned White Titan's abdomen—a clean hit. Penetrating the hard armor-like skin, the blow seemed to reach the White Titan's core. Flying with the force of a cannon ball, its body collided with a nearby building and left a giant-shaped cavity. The area was engulfed in rubble and smoke, and the entire town shook from the outsized fight.

Taking advantage of the opening while the White Titan rose to its feet, Armin joined Mikasa and the others with one vertical maneuver.

"Everyone! Let's leave this to Eren and return to the truck! If we stay we'll just get in his way!"

Mikasa insisted that they should aid in the fight, but nothing could be less practical. A Titan fight left no room for human intervention, and the dance of wires might actually inhibit Eren. Finally persuaded, she retreated with Jean and Sasha to the transport, which was idling a few blocks away.

When Armin and the others returned, Hange jumped out excitedly from the driver's seat and said, "So Eren succeeded in turning into a Titan…"

"Yes. Though we don't know how he did it."

Meanwhile, a battle so intense it seemed to rock the world itself raged on. Each move rivaled a natural disaster in its ferocity and destruction. A single fist smashed a building, and the street cracked when either combatant fell to its knees. This was what a clash between Titans looked like. Though the transport was a few hundred yards away, the impacts still felt immediate. Gulping, they watched attentively, though it was by no means a pleasant spectacle.

Eren, who had landed the first blow, maintained his edge. He struck again and again, and the White Titan staggered and forgot its footwork. Still, as time passed—perhaps due to a "maturation" gap as Titans—Eren's opponent's blows began to fall more and more efficiently. The durability of the White Titan's thick skin bolstered both its offense and defense, and Eren was clearly getting worn down. He swung his fists less frequently and began to assume a more reactive posture. On his head, side, stomach, and thighs, the White Titan mercilessly rained down blows that would have finished a normal Titan. As if to indicate the limits of Eren's vitality, steam quietly rose from him like morning mist.

"Is this…it for him?" Jean murmured, scowling.

"No, something's off."

Armin had noticed the oddness of it. Even if Eren was just fending off blows, his movements were deteriorating too suddenly. Had some serious problem arisen when he'd transformed into a Titan? Otherwise, Eren was—well, that had to be it.

Eventually, Eren leaned his entire form against a building. Rubble fell heavily from it and shrouded his body in dust. Certain of victory, the White Titan seemed to relax a little, and its yellow eyes gazed for a while at Eren's steaming figure as though to register his anguish and take satisfaction in it.

At last the White Titan began to approach him. As if it were already relishing the hunt along with its intervals and afterglow, it spent an excruciating amount of time on each step. Then, it raised its right arm as high as it would go. It overlapped with the sun, and the alabaster skin reflected the rays. At that precise moment…

Eren moved suddenly and caught the White Titan off guard. He dodged its fist by a hair and countered, slipping his left arm all the way over to his opponent's face; he had tricked it.

The White Titan's right arm opened a hole in the building without touching Eren. Eren grabbed its face with his left hand, yanked on its right arm, and at the same time trapped its right leg. Taken completely by surprise, the White Titan lost its balance and started falling backward towards the ground as intended.

"Th-That move…" Armin recalled. "It's Lil's."

Deprived of its equipoise, the White Titan had no way of fighting back. Eren's leg flashed and swung like a pendulum and scooped his opponent—with a devastating kick.

His strength, of course, was on a different order of magnitude from Lil's. As if gravity had forsaken it, the White Titan gently flew through the air. After an eerie silence, it landed on the back of its neck with a thunderous crash. A rumble that shook their walled world afflicted it.

"Go!" Jean shouted his prayer. "Do it!"

Eren raised his fist at the fallen White Titan and struck its face, pulverizing its head. Steam rose from it immediately. Then, grasping its legs and pushing all his muscles to their limits, he hurled the White Titan at a structure that stood thirty yards away. Speeding to its rendezvous point in a straight line rather than an arc, the giant form sliced through the air raising waves of wind. Then—the impact.

A gale reached Armin and the others where they stood. The White Titan's body was swallowed by the structure, which crumbled, unable to withstand the abuse. Countless pieces of rubble poured down endlessly to cover the White Titan's entire body. The five-story building melted away and was gone in an instant, leaving only a mountain of debris.

Then, quietly, a copious amount of steam erupted from the gaps.

Eren had been standing on guard so as not to be caught flatfooted. When he saw the vapors, though, his shoulders relaxed. Clenching both his fists he let out, as if to proclaim his victory, a howl that was as long as it was loud. It echoed exhilaratingly and refreshingly in the hearts of Armin and his friends.

"He…did it."

Jean laughed, showing all his teeth, rejoicing as if he had done it himself. Sasha and Hange also laughed, wearily, and Armin couldn't help but join in. Suddenly remembering Mikasa, he turned around. She had a faint, resigned smile on her face, and seeing that Armin wanted to know how she really felt, she shook her head and answered him.

"This is good." She sounded certain. "Eren did his best. This was good."

Armin nodded firmly.

X. SATAN AND BEATRICE

Over half a day had passed since the expedition had commenced, and finally, they arrived at their original destination. Just as Mikasa had witnessed on that day, Monzen's Outer Wall had a gaping hole forty feet tall and thirty feet wide. It was definitely sizable. Still, compared to the vast world, it was very small, no more than a nostril. This tiny aperture had been plaguing humanity.

Holding her hair as it blew in the wind, Mikasa turned towards the ruins of the Garrison base. The regimental outpost that Souda had belonged to was destroyed almost entirely. Pieces of concrete pillars remained like a skeleton, but she couldn't connect them very easily with her memory of the place.

It told of the severity of that day's debacle.

Everything started here, everything ended here.

Mikasa closed her eyes and sighed.

"E-Eren…can you hear me?"

When Armin spoke, Eren, still as a Titan, gave a small bark. It seemed that he somehow understood. Even though they knew that the Titan was Eren, getting across to a creature that had been considered the ultimate enemy had a hint of humor to it. Hange displayed extraordinary enthusiasm at communicating with Eren the Titan, but considering the circumstances she'd promptly decided to show some restraint. Mikasa felt that was the right choice.

"We want you to place this missile way up the wall," Armin instructed, craning his neck at Eren, who stood forty feet tall. "Strictly speaking, we want you to install it forty-two yards off the ground—the height is correct, right?" Armin glanced at Hange, who stood beside him.

She nodded. "Really it could be higher, but any higher and it probably won't be stable."

"Anyways." Armin looked up at Eren again. "When you get to the height where you need to install it, I'll give the signal. That's when we want you to put the missile in a suitable spot. Because the wall is so uneven, there should be several places where you could put it."

Eren barked.

"This seems kind of stupid, this conversation," Jean muttered as he stared up at Eren.

Sasha chided him briefly.

"This is the detonator." Armin held out the device he had made himself. "It's a timer, and just in case, I'm going to mount it on the missile. Eren, just be careful not to bump the fuse, the pointy end of the missile. It might explode before you place it."

When Armin finished explaining, everybody made preparations for transferring the missile. They wrapped the net that they had used earlier around Eren's shoulders and attached the missile to his back.

Because it was on his back, it wouldn't be in his way as he climbed the wall. As Eren had been told, vertical cracks ran up along either side of the hole. Stakes had been driven into the surface during the 2nd Outer Wall Restoration Operation. If the explosion did what it was supposed to, the wall would detach according to those cracks and slide down to close up the hole.

Mikasa didn't know if everything would go well. In terms of the physics, she could only trust Armin and Hange. As for the first problem of installing the missile properly, she had to rely on Eren. If either went wrong, the operation would amount to nothing. The worst-case scenario was that the missile would open an even bigger hole in the wall. The many sacrifices would have been for naught.

At last, when Eren was ready, he stood to the left of the hole. Then, with a look that seemed to show he'd come to a firm decision (Of course, expressions were faint on Titans' faces. Still, Mikasa could discern the subtleties of Eren's.) he looked up at the wall. The sight of Eren staring gravely up at the sky somehow seemed linked to that day two years earlier. To her immense happiness, and slight disappointment, Eren hadn't changed.

To his left, Mikasa shot her anchor up at the halfway point. Further to the left, Armin did the same. On the right side, Jean and Sasha also fired their anchors, aiming for the top of the wall.

Hange stood alert at the transport. She was supposed to release a signal flare immediately upon noticing incoming Titans or any other development.

Until then, Eren would continue climbing up to the target spot. And that was all.

Finally, Eren stretched his right hand to the first ledge, and slowly, he lifted his body. Though the wall gave a slight creak, it gave no signs of crumbling. Just like that, right leg, left hand, left leg, right hand, he continued to climb, patiently, deliberately, double-checking every movement. Mikasa controlled her trigger to align her speed with Eren's and slowly reeled in her wire. The surface of the First Wall had countless rough patches that were far larger than Mikasa had imagined two years earlier. Small protuberances a few feet wide were common, and in certain places, there were even spaces in which a truck would have been able to park. Sometimes Jean completely put away his wires to rest atop the ledges.

Thus, Eren had many places to put his hands and no trouble finding footholds. He climbed easily. At that rate, as Armin said, he would be able to install the missile anywhere.

When Mikasa looked down after some time had passed, Hange had grown quite small. Mikasa couldn't see her in great detail but well enough to make out that she wasn't scrambling to fire the flare.

Everything is going well.

The moment she thought that, Mikasa felt a hot wind blowing at her face. She noticed a great amount of steam beginning to rise from Eren's body. As though stoked by heated iron plates, the white vapors welled up from him with no signs of stopping. His movements pulling himself up were sluggish, the animal grunts intermittently rising from his throat frail and sparse.

"Looks like he's getting tired…" She could hear Armin's voice from her left. "Come on, Eren!"

Please, Eren, Mikasa wished fervently with Armin. *Just a little farther, you can do it.*

Then, as if recalling something, Eren suddenly turned to look at

Mikasa. He stared at her for a little while and abruptly released his left hand from the wall. He began to swing his arm, towards Mikasa.

No… A cold shudder ran through her.

She hastily released her anchor and kicked away from the surface. As she feared, Eren had lost it. His left hand struck where Mikasa had been just moments earlier. The First Wall shook violently, and fragments fell to the ground.

With their anchors attached, Jean and Sasha clung to the wall. Armin used wire action to get a little distance from Eren. The falling Mikasa shot her anchor anew and hit the wall. As she wound it, she felt an intense sense of discomfort, and her face twisted in pain. She clung to the wall and stared down at her right leg. She couldn't tell at a glance, but it seemed that she had sprained her right ankle. It hurt so badly that she couldn't even keep her right foot on the wall. She'd made a stupid mistake.

Mikasa bit her lip and looked up at Eren, who was still hanging high up on the wall.

Just like when he'd first turned into a Titan, he was going berserk. He had also lost his balance trying to hit Mikasa and wasn't holding on properly. He slid down, his limbs digging into stone. Debris and dust rained incessantly down at Mikasa. Finally, he came to a stop. On a large arc, Armin arrived next to her.

"Are you okay?"

"I twisted my foot a little."

Armin looked up at Eren. "Perhaps staying transformed for too long takes its toll. It was the same the other time."

As Mikasa watched Eren struggling, she hardened her heart and declared, "I'll do something." Without waiting for Armin's response, she climbed with her VME. Her sprained ankle only felt worse, and when she fired her anchor, the subtle vibrations of winding the wire tormented her foot cruelly enough that she almost cried out. Bearing the pain, Mikasa ascended and purposefully passed before Eren's eyes.

"Eren!" she shouted. "Do you recognize me? I'm Mikasa. We were apart for two years, but I'm your…" For a moment, she considered her words. The ones that she eventually spoke felt quite appropriate. "I'm your family! You have to take the bomb up. So many people are depending on you. Please, Eren!"

He stared at Mikasa with his red eyes and barked loudly. Once again, he lifted his left hand and tried to hit her. *No.* She burned her gas to dodge him. When his hand struck, the wall heaved. She released her anchor. Though her leg burned with pain, she wasn't about to give up. She feared that if she didn't guide Eren, she would lose too many things, yet again. Shooting her anchor, she moved to fall into Eren's sight.

"Stop! It's too late, get away!" Jean's voice came, but it didn't penetrate her heart.

"Eren!" Mikasa shouted. "You're human! Remember! Remember what you have to do!"

Eren again tried to lift his hand, but lost his balance and slid five yards down the surface. They couldn't go on like this. Mikasa held her breath to endure the pain and hurled herself through the air. Then, she shot her anchor near Eren's nape on purpose—a hit. Just like with normal Titans, he didn't seem to feel any discomfort at the anchor and went on hanging from the wall painfully as white steam rose from his body. She heard the others yelling that it was too dangerous, but determined, she ignored them. She reeled her wire and, tuning her movements with gas, alighted on Eren's nape. Somehow she was able to land without touching the missile. From up close she saw white steam rising endlessly from Eren's skin, and in an instant she was wrapped in a hot breeze. It was hard to breathe and hot enough to burn her.

"Mikasa! It's dangerous! What are you planning on doing?!"

Armin's cry was vague, lost in the sound of the hissing steam, and she couldn't pinpoint his location. "I'm going to talk to Eren!" she answered amidst the heat.

"That's absurd! Get away from there!"

Mikasa didn't bother to answer anymore. Instead, she was resorting to a last-ditch effort to awaken Eren. Pulling her blade from the right scabbard, she took a deep breath. She shot both her anchors at short range into Eren's neck to fix her body to him and prevent being flung off. She searched through her memory to recall the time Eren had emerged from the Titan's nape. From where had it been? Based on that, where was he concealed now? Surrounded by white smoke, Mikasa calculated carefully. The Titan's vulnerable spot went from the back of the skull to the neck, three feet tall, four inches wide. If she cut it off he would die. But if she just stimulated the area, it wouldn't be fatal. If she avoided the center, probably…

"A little pain is all," Mikasa murmured, almost like a prayer. She stood the blade on a point to the left half and stabbed him. The sensation, then silence.

The next moment, Eren began to flail. He barked loudly, smashed his head against the wall, and pummeled a ledge with both his fists. His body slid another five yards. Gripping both her wires, Mikasa braced herself to keep from being flung off.

"Eren!" she shouted louder than before. "Can you hear me? Eren!"

There was no shift in his demeanor, however, and he continued to flail around. To get through to him, Mikasa crouched and spoke directly into the nape, the heat against her face growing in intensity as she got closer to the skin.

"Eren! Listen, Eren!"

Nothing changed. It still wasn't enough—her voice didn't reach him. She dropped her stance even further and pressed her face against the blade she had inserted. A splitting pain ran across her cheek. Slowly her blood flowed, falling in drops from her chin.

This will do. Mikasa burned the pain on her cheek into her heart. "Eren!"

There was a clear shift. Eren suddenly rested his four limbs against the wall and remained perfectly still as if he'd just remembered something important.

"Eren…" Confirming that her voice had reached him, Mikasa spoke a little less loud. "Remember, Eren, remember what you have to do right now. Remember it well." She felt as though the eruption of steam had weakened a bit. "You promised—you promised, didn't you? That some day…" *I'm going to join the Survey Party and go find the Ocean. And after that, I'm going to take you there too. It's a promise.* "You were going to show me the Ocean… What happened to that? If we go on like this I won't be able to see the Ocean. If we can't take back the First Wall District, nobody will ever go outside. Please, Eren." Mikasa spoke with tears in her eyes. "A request from somebody like me might not be enough. After avoiding you for two years, and only thinking about myself, I might not be any kind of 'family' or 'friend' to you. You might say it's a lie, you might not believe me, but..."

Mikasa placed her hand on her left trigger and unwound the red cloth tied around the handle. She pulled off the scarf that Eren had wrapped around her neck back when she was little.

"I was with you all along, *all along*. Every day, day after day, I thought about you. I wanted to see you so badly I didn't know what to do. But the moment I considered it, I became scared and never took the chance to find you... More and more, I started to feel that I'd changed terribly, that I was ugly and dirty, and seeing you again felt so difficult. I thought I might disappoint you, and became so unhappy I couldn't even take the first step. But finally, just like you said that day you gave me the scarf..." *I'll let you have it. I don't want you to freeze to death if you run away from home again.* "I ran away, but I was able to come home without freezing to death."

Unable to wipe her tears away, Mikasa took a deep breath.

"Thank you for warming me with that scarf back then. Please, Eren, you need to come home too. Come home, and spend your days where I can see you again, okay? Wake up, Eren. Wake up, and..." *Save us all.*

Silence. The steam cleared, and Eren's skin, on which Mikasa rested, returned to normal. A grunt came from Eren's throat, and his right arm slowly stretched for a ledge above him.

"Yes!"

Armin had let out a jubilant cry. From the other side, Jean and Sasha did the same. Mikasa remained sitting as she was, atop Eren, as the tears continued to flow.

Thank you, Eren. Thank you.

The operation will succeed now, thank goodness... Hange, who was watching from below, tossed away her binoculars and began to applaud. Raising her fists, she jumped for joy on the empty truck.

Eren managed to climb to the forty-two-yard target point and reached nimbly for the missile around his back. Mikasa and the others watched with bated breath as he handled it with ginger fingers and deposited it, guided by Armin. When Armin waved his hand from high above to ask if the installation spot was fine, Hange returned the sign approvingly. It was about forty-two yards up, directly above the middle point of the hole. Without veering to the left or the right, it was in perfect accordance with her calculations. Originally she'd wanted to have it installed at a slightly higher point, but any higher and it wouldn't be stable. That was the best spot.

Perhaps relieved at fulfilling his objective, Eren began to emit more steam and rapidly slid down the wall. Using her blades, Mikasa sliced him out from the Titan's nape and flew with him to the ledge where the missile rested. It was fairly wide, and Armin, Jean, and Sasha stood there without using any wires.

"Ahh, I want to fly too," Hange murmured to herself, but immediately directed her attention at the Titan's body. The moment that Eren shed the giant husk, it began to dissolve into the air in a large amount of steam, just like when a normal Titan died. Then, obeying gravity, the body fell towards Hange, but before it could hit the ground, it fully evaporated into fog.

"Oh my, I'm learning so much!" Countless new questions rose in Hange's head about Eren's mind-body connection as a Titan, the mystery of mass materializing so suddenly, the relationship between the amount of steam and fatigue. She extracted her memo pad; she couldn't afford to forget. Then, when she finished taking notes, she raised her face again and examined the scene. Armin would be almost through with that detonator.

"Hmm?" Suddenly she froze. "What is that..."

Hange, whose vision wasn't very good to begin with, could not believe what her eyes were seeing. Because there was such a large chance that she was wrong, it was hard for her logical mind to accept it as the truth. She hastily found the binoculars that she had tossed away and studied the area in question halfway up the wall. She focused her eyes until she was certain.

She hadn't been wrong. *What's going on?*

"Right in the middle of the wall...a hole?" she blurted out, gripping her binoculars.

The hole Hange had found was incredibly small compared to the one they were trying to fill. Though it was only a visual estimate, it seemed to be about six feet tall and three feet wide. It was rectangular with beautiful straight lines and could not be natural.

She pondered the fact. Until just a moment earlier, there hadn't been any kind of a hole there. Why had one suddenly appeared in such a place? It was almost like a passageway.

Passageway—it can't be.

Just as the idea occurred to her, a dark shadow crossed the hole. In a frenzy, she grabbed the binoculars again and strained her eyes to try to determine the shadow's form. It had already completely disappeared except as a pale afterimage in her memory, but she was sure that what she had seen was *human*. Someone had passed through the passageway in the wall and gone to the other side. As Hange lowered her binoculars, she thought for a little while, holding the frames of her goggles. Why did the hole open? Who went through it? And why? As she tried to make sense of the strange phenomenon, her eyes glimpsed yet another mysterious occurrence.

She stiffened, murmuring to herself as it happened, "The hole... has closed."

As the wind petted his face, Eren lifted his heavy eyelids. He blinked twice, and as if cleaning up a cluttered room, one by one he gathered each memory leading up to when he'd lost consciousness. And when he remembered fully, he sat up, panicked.

"Careful!"

His body twitched at the sound of Mikasa's voice. When he looked directly beside himself, the ground was extremely far away. Eren realized he was on the edge of a ledge that protruded out from the First Wall. A heavy fatigue weighed down his body as if it were filled with lead. The aftermath of Titanization.

"What's the situation?" he turned around and asked Mikasa.

"How much do you remember?"

"I...threw Captain Shikishima. Then I carried the missile and decided to climb the wall. That's all."

"It's okay," Mikasa held her hair down against the strong wind and answered. "Everything went well. You installed the missile perfectly."

When he looked in the direction Mikasa motioned, sure enough, he could see the familiar missile. Armin was moving his hands restlessly as he configured the detonator. Jean and Sasha seemed to be driving something into the surface and fixing down the missile. Eren sighed and rested his eyes on the base of Mikasa's neck.

"That scarf…"

Mikasa looked away uneasily and brought her scarf up to her mouth to hide her expression. "I got a little cold."

"Right," was all Eren said before he shut his mouth. The scarf Mikasa was wearing was incredibly damaged, dirty, and worn out in places. Without some particular reason, it was in no state for anyone to actually use. Eren felt an uncharacteristic smile rising up to his face and quickly smoothed his expression. It felt like it had been a long time since he was able to have a regular conversation with Mikasa. It was fine when he wasn't self-conscious, but the moment he reflected on it, he began to feel shy.

"You really helped me earlier." When he said it out loud, Eren was astounded. It was a sincere thought that had suddenly crossed his mind, but he didn't know why he'd said it out loud. Mikasa's eyes, too, went round in surprise, and she pursed her lips.

"Somehow, I felt like I should say that." Eren scratched his head. "Thank you." As he looked down, he noticed the cloth wrapped around Mikasa's right ankle. It was bound tightly to restrict the movements of her leg.

"You're hurt…"

Mikasa looked down at the spot and shook her head exaggeratedly. "I'm okay. It's nothing."

"Did I do that?"

"Well…"

"No, it's okay. I know." Eren bit his lip. "I do remember, just a little. I'm sorry."

As Mikasa fell silent, a long pause descended upon them.

Unable to find the words to fill the space of two years, Eren resigned himself to it. The wind that caressed the First Wall seeped into Eren's soul as if to signify something. It rustled his hair, his clothes, and the seconds as they passed. Quietly, Eren began to converse with whatever it was that resided in him.

At the Omotemachi relay point, he had almost lost sight of his reason for enlisting. When Hiana asked him, he could only think about Mikasa and how she'd arrived with Shikishima, and hadn't been able to reply. After his dialogue with Shikishima, Eren knew that "Mikasa" wasn't the only reason he had joined. That was why he had been able to jump into the fight with the Titans and to cut away the chains that constricted his soul.

But now he reconsidered: *Though not the entire reason that I am here, a part of it is unmistakably related to Mikasa.* Eren felt like he was taking the final step with that realization.

It was so difficult to attempt something. It was so difficult to believe someone, and so difficult to doubt someone. It was difficult to believe in himself, it was difficult to make a choice, and it was difficult to understand it all. Yet now he finally understood.

Eren let out a deep long breath.

"Eren!" Armin must have finished his task and approached Eren, taking care not to lose his footing. "So you're awake!"

"Ah, somewhat."

"Your VME is right there. Jean just brought a spare up from the truck."

Nodding, Eren coaxed his body, which had grown extremely heavy from fatigue, and attached the Vertical Maneuvering Equipment to his body.

"I've finished setting the detonator. It's supposed to explode five minutes after I press the switch, so everybody get ready."

Finally, the operation would end. As if allowing his body to relax at long last, Eren closed his eyes and curled into himself.

"Come on, stand up!"

When he opened his eyes, Jean was stretching out his hand. Eren thought about teasing him for the unwonted gesture but thought it would be too immature and decided instead to politely take his hand. Then, relying on Jean, he slowly stood up.

"You saved me back there, didn't you? When I was almost swatted away by that White Titan," Jean said with a grin and a sigh. "A lot of stuff happened between us, but as of now, I don't hate you that much."

"Me too, from about an hour ago I don't hate you."

"Ha." Jean smiled. "No, actually I do hate you."

Eren returned the smile. As if agreeing to remember that moment, they exchanged a handshake. It wasn't a particularly firm one, but each of them felt warmth rising up in their hearts.

"Then, let's press the switch," Armin said.

It was when they seemed to come to the conclusion of the entire operation that it happened.

A high-pitched sound like a whistle reverberated behind them. When they turned around, they saw a single bright red cloud rising up from the ground. It was the signal flare. The person who had fired it was, of course, Hange. Red smoke—it signaled danger from something other than a Titan.

Eren and the others immediately tensed up and looked around, but they couldn't see anything. They looked back at the missile, but nothing seemed to be wrong. They checked each place one after another—their feet, the ground, the hills off in the distance—but spotted no danger.

"What's up, what happened?"

At Jean's words, a voice slowly answered, "I did, most likely." It was deep and low enough to make the earth tremble.

Eren and the others immediately glanced *up* at the voice they couldn't place. The anomaly that Hange had wanted to communicate was not around the missile or on the ground. Instead, it was above them.

At the top of the First Wall, they saw a man. He was seated, his crossed legs hanging in the air over the edge, his arms folded sternly. From where they stood, he was backlit, but they had undoubtedly seen the black silhouette before. The deep voice, the intimidating air. A head of white hair and a deeply etched face. His black uniform that rustled in the wind was definitely that of the Military Police. There was no mistaking him.

It was Kubal of the Public Order Administration.

"Supervisor Kubal!" Armin cried out in surprise. "B-But you died!"

"I'm alive," Kubal said, twisting his mouth as if that displeased him. "Because I'm alive, I'm here. You know, ironically, I'm not so brittle a man."

Sasha examined Kubal's surroundings with a puzzled gaze. "H-How did you get up there?"

"There's a little bit of a passageway, in the wall. It's a piece of 'designated knowledge' so there's no reason for you to be aware of it, but...in truth, it has been two years since it was used."

There were only a dozen feet between where Eren and the others were standing and where Kubal was sitting. They could speak to him without even raising their voices, and the wind didn't even get in the way of the conversation. Still, somehow, the dozen feet seemed to Eren like an endless distance. It was an extremely uncomfortable separation.

"Your actions, to be honest, exceeded my expectations." Furrowing his brow, Kubal was staring somewhere far away. "To think that only six people could manage to install a bomb—I'm very impressed. It's enough to make me want to openly praise you. However...I have my own plans. I'm so sorry, but can I ask you one favor?"

Nobody answered. Kubal continued.

"Could you maybe return to the Second Wall without exploding that bomb?" His civil words sounded strangely authoritative. Upon first glance, it didn't look as if Kubal was carrying anything like a weapon. In terms of their headcount, too, Eren and his friends were in an advantageous position. So why did it seem like Kubal controlled the situation? Perhaps that was the very illusion that "height" fomented.

Without answering yes or no, Armin asked a question instead to deflect the request. "Was it you who was trying to lead the operation to failure?"

"Mm," Kubal replied, closing his eyes and nodding. "From

whom did you hear such excessive talk? This is rather terrible news. Though I tried to be completely airtight, some noise seems to have escaped. Almost like a gas leak."

"Please answer."

"Well...I suppose I can say, 'That is correct.'" Kubal laughed as if he'd given up. "From the beginning, we had no intention of closing up the hole. For that reason, we set a few traps for the operation... It is just as you said."

"Why would you do that?"

Kubal sighed and lifted his hands as if surrendering. "I understand. Then let's do it like this," he said. "I will explain the 'truth' of this world. I will tell you the secret of all secrets, what society deems 'designated knowledge,' the intelligence closed away in a black box. Then after you listen to all of it, I will give you two options. If you would, please pick the choice that suits you. Let's end it there. A peaceful resolution."

Unable to react, Eren and the others remained silent, which Kubal took as an affirmation.

"I'll start from the conclusion. First of all, we, the people of the so-called government, hardly need the First Wall District anymore."

"You don't...need it?" Eren blurted out.

"For us—and by 'us' I mean the people within the Third Wall— the First District used to be the production area for our precious food. The crops that the inhabitants of the First Wall District cultivated were brought to us as taxes, to satisfy our stomachs and our lifestyle. You should know this too. The First Wall District, and its citizens with it, were once indispensable to our lives."

Kubal paused before he continued, "However, a few years ago

there was a little bit of a technological innovation in the Third Wall District. We completely stopped needing the First Wall District's modest harvests. On even a narrow plot of land, in a short amount of time, we could consistently and efficiently produce high-quality fare. We no longer needed farmers to go through the trouble of working the First Wall District's meager soil. Didn't you think it was strange as well?" the supervisor asked. "That even though we lost the First Wall District that provided for seven tenths of the entire population, no matter how much you ate, the supplies didn't run out—and for two years? No matter how privileged soldiers might be, lavish feasts are not something we could have sustained amidst a food shortage. Even putting military personnel aside, how many residents of the Second Wall District starved to death during those two years? The food problem…does not exist."

Armin's voice spilled out in anger. "Then—then why did my grandfather have to go on the recovery mission to reduce the population?"

"That, I will explain shortly," Kubal said with a sneer. "By the way, Private Third Class Armin, your home was a canola oil store, wasn't it? Unfortunately, within the Third Wall, there is now not a single person who uses canola oil. The truck parked down there," Kubal said, pointing towards the ground where Hange stood, "doesn't even run on canola oil. Thanks to technological innovations, what we call biodiesel fuel has been reduced to a relic of the past. Although it was hauled to the Third District as a tax, most of it was disposed of untouched. Almost all of the heavy taxes from the citizens are burned upon arrival. How very sad."

Eren heard Armin grit his teeth.

Kubal went on. "So far, so good. Well, maybe 'good' isn't the right word, but the First Wall District was merely unnecessary, and there was no reason to actively discard it. If the citizens of the First Wall District went on meaninglessly producing crops, meaninglessly paying taxes, meaninglessly living, that was fine… But it wasn't meant to be. They were trying to put in motion a plan that could disrupt this world."

"What do you mean by that?" Jean demanded.

"With Monzen as the headquarters, a bewildering citizen movement was trying to get off the ground. Unlike the anti-government organizations, it didn't even espouse specific ideals, so it was such a handful."

"I see…"

Eren remembered that day two years ago. Souda, generally open-minded, had reproached Eren without discussion and denied his request. The old man who said Eren could do anything had banned him from one thing: joining a certain movement that had arisen with Monzen as its center and that hoped to exit the wall.

"The Citizen Survey Party…"

"Ahhhh," Kubal exaggerated his surprise as he looked at Eren. "I thought you were an imbecile cast off by the anti-government faction, but you're pretty quick. Precisely." As if he had suddenly fallen into a foul mood, Kubal narrowed his eyes. "After hearing about the stirrings of this 'Citizen Survey Party,' we knew it in our bones. Ultimate *peace*, the order and balance that embody this world's absolute *equality*, would be smashed by a lack of fear."

"This world is…*peaceful and equal?*"

"Certainly, at first glance, it doesn't seem so…especially to children such as yourselves," Kubal answered indifferently. "However, unfortunately, the reality is that this world is more peaceful and more equal than it has ever been in the history of humanity. A nearly ideal society has in fact been realized."

"How is it peaceful? The Titans devour people," Jean spat.

Kubal's expression was cool. "It is as you say. However, think about it calmly. Until two years ago—before the attack of the Colossal Titan—how many humans had been killed at the Titans' hands?"

Jean couldn't answer. He didn't know.

"In a hundred years, only a few hundred people have been killed by Titans, and all from the Survey Corps. If you do the math, we're talking about just two to three fatalities a year. As you know, for over a hundred years, the wall was never breached… The public was never in danger of coming in contact with the Titans. Before the Great Titan War, the world was exposed to war after war after war. How many humans do you think died in those wars? Of course, it wasn't two or three people a year. Thousands, tens of thousands, hundreds of thousands of people meaninglessly lost their lives in stupid disputes. If you think about it like that, kid…you'll see how peaceful this world is.

"Since the Titans arrived, there hasn't been a single instance where men have combated fellow men. The thing that people endlessly desire, a *warless world*, has been accomplished right here. And still, stupid people began to emerge who couldn't recognize this peaceful world as *peaceful*. Instead of believing the wall was *protecting* them, they began to hold the wild delusion that the wall was *imprisoning* them. This or that, it all relates to a lack of fear."

Kubal sighed and shook his head to the side as if to toss

something away.

"The 'Titan' that had been a common enemy and an overwhelming source of fear to the public began to be treated as a creature of the imagination. People doubted the existence of the Titans and began to recklessly claim that they could live outside the wall. It was a grave situation. The biggest factor supporting this world began to lose its function—and so." Kubal cleared his throat. "Though it was a painful emergency decision, we decided to remind them."

"Remind them…" Armin repeated softly.

"Yes." Kubal nodded. "That the Titans were not a thing of fantasy. That the Titans were terrifying, that they were creatures of devastating 'terror' that could never in all eternity be conquered by humans. That they were unyielding, supreme masters that could not be fought. So nobody would ever forget again, we decided to display the hopeless extent of the terror of the Titans. We wanted the fear to get passed down through many generations and become a permanent part of oral tradition. We decided to sacrifice the First Wall District, which had become conveniently unnecessary, to lay the foundations of peace."

Eren's eyes widened in sync with his heartbeat. Kubal, however, continued to speak without any emotion as if he were giving an administrative report.

"That was the attack of the Colossal Titan two years ago. The plan progressed as smoothly as we had hoped. We lost the First Wall District, and many people perished at the hands of the Titans. Humans became afraid of the monstrosities just as they had been before. The 'Reclamation Operation' that your grandfather had to join— that, too, was part of the plan. Of course, it wasn't intended to 'take back the wall' or to 'cut down on mouths to feed.' It was purely an operation to 'rekindle fear in people' and to have them 'recognize anew their lowly existence.' Even you, Private Third Class Armin. When you lost your grandfather in that operation, how did you feel? Didn't you resent the Titans?"

"Give me a break."

Kubal laughed mockingly. "It was all part of a policy to make people fear the Titans and feel direct hostility towards them. However, at that point in the operation, we began to see a few suspicious shadows, evidence of the existence of an anti-government faction." Kubal crossed his legs the other way. "From just before we lost the First Wall District, they became active. It seemed the Survey Corps was swimming a little too freely. To think even Shikishima had been waylaid by unnecessary delusions... Well, no matter. Anyway, their existence got to be a bit of an eyesore for us. Then, through what we called the Outer Wall Restoration Operation, we decided to tease out their members and to erase them one by one. Formerly I even had you collaborate." Kubal looked at Armin and smiled. "Thanks for that. We were calling on soldiers that seemed to have good judgment. We didn't want to reveal our *true intentions*."

Armin's shoulders trembled a little, but he didn't reply.

"Be that as it may, as a result, we almost flushed out all members of the anti-government faction. Imagine our relief. For a little while, the peace and equilibrium of the world would be safeguarded. To the very end, I would be able to protect this amazing world that I can't stop loving."

"What do you mean, amazing world..." Eren's anger came from the pit of his stomach. "Only people who live in the Third Wall

District and drink the sweet honey of this world can say that it's an amazing world! You have us living like livestock—"

"What's wrong with livestock?"

Kubal's query resonated harshly in Eren's heart like the sound of a giant bell. Eren did his best to endure the churning sensation and glared sharply at the man as though to push back against his words. Yet Kubal's gaze was the stronger.

"There's no reason to feel ashamed. What's wrong with livestock? Everybody is somebody's livestock. Children are livestock to their parents, and sometimes parents are livestock to their children. There are those who become livestock to their lovers, or to their siblings. Office workers are livestock to their place of work, and companies are livestock to their profits. The government and I—we are livestock to this country, and the country is in a wider sense livestock to the citizens. The Titans are livestock to the government, and you are livestock to the Titans. And so the world is built. There is not a single person who is not a part of this system. What part of that do you deny? What more do you want? History is proof that a world without disparity cannot ever be achieved. Thus, a system that is *not aware* of clear, established disparities becomes key. And now, that has been achieved here. What is it about this world that does not satisfy you?"

Kubal's words were suddenly taking on heat. His delivery grew rough even as he waxed eloquent.

"It is the privilege of youth to believe in the word 'freedom.' You can indulge in it as you like. Myself as well, I was almost taken by the sweet sound of 'freedom' when I was young. However, I soon realized that such a thing doesn't exist anywhere in this world. Even if it did, perfect freedom is nothing more than ultimate un-freedom. Think about it. Which do you think is more wonderful? Hmm? The ultimate freedom of being thrown out into the wasteland, or the un-freedom of being provided with a safe dwelling, and clothes, food, and work? The option of perfect freedom comes with conflicts and difficulties that are enough to tear you apart and will lay waste to your very bodies. What do you think, ladies and gentlemen? What kind of choices did you make to come all the way to the outer wall? How much agony have you suffered thus far? Compared to that, how wonderful a life without choices is!"

Eren felt a pain like a nail in his heart. He couldn't entirely deny Kubal's words. In fact, Eren partially agreed. He might find himself nodding along if he wasn't careful.

"In your confusion, you are all expressing anger at the truth of this world!" Kubal wouldn't stop. As if wielding a blade, he carved his words before Eren. "It's because you learned the truth. If you were ignorant of it, you could have been satisfied with your predicament. For example, if a certain man never found out that canola oil was a useless commodity, and sold it diligently, with spirit, and died after spending his last years being cared for by his family, wouldn't he say, 'I had a very fulfilling life. How happy am I?' If that's the case, is there any reason to tell him about the uselessness of canola oil? Even if it is true, if somebody will suffer from a certain piece of information, then it should be concealed… Being livestock is splendid! It isn't freedom that is important to human happiness. It is being content with the present situation. Thus, we always gave the people adequate resources, adequate tasks, adequate wants, and adequate joys. Thus, we maintained peace and harmony for over a hundred years. What reason do we have to let that crumble? In times past, the Disarmament Treaty, which was supposed to bring peace, instead gave birth to the Titans and led to great chaos. On the other hand, by succumbing to their fearsome dominion, humans were able to attain a supreme peace. It's an incredible contradiction and coincidence, but why is there any reason to throw away all of that?"

Kubal took a big breath and uncrossed his legs. Then, as if to finish his story, he spread his arms wide.

"I want you to feel relieved." True to his words, Kubal displayed an exaggeratedly gentle expression. "With this attempt, the 3rd Outer Wall Restoration Operation, our mission is complete. We have no plans for any more forays. After this, we will never again spill the blood of innocent citizens. If nobody tries to go outside the wall, if they don't try to determine the truth behind the Titans, this is an absolute promise. The people have no doubt been reminded enough. The fear of the Titans, the strength of the Titans, and the cruelty of the Titans, has been stamped into their very bodies. No more blood will be spilled."

As Kubal finished, he gently closed his mouth and dropped his hands. The dark aroma of his words lingered and drifted amidst the youths, and silence reigned for a while. It was hard to dispel, stubbornly clinging to the air as if it had adhered. And with every breath, it gradually settled into their bodies.

Realizing eventually that Kubal's speech wouldn't resume, Jean tore open the silence as though he were throwing open a heavy door. "So, what is it that you want us to do anyway? You said there were two options, right?"

Kubal let out a tiny sigh, gave a nod, and answered with his earlier composure, perhaps having calmed down. "The first is as I said earlier. I want you to return without operating that detonator, without filling the hole in the wall, and to leave the First Wall District as the Titans' territory... If you do that, I promise to offer all of you a place in the Third Wall District. Just the six of you, we can easily accommodate. The Third Wall District is safe, of course, but more than that it is exceedingly comfortable, and the standard of culture is exceptionally different. Private Third Class Armin. You, for example, would able to perform the most sophisticated research using cutting-edge technology. You will no longer be content to work with canola oil timers or anything like that."

Armin glowered at Kubal. Eren could say for sure that his friend had never looked more aggravated, ferocious, or barbaric. It was almost as if he wasn't Armin. With his teeth clenched, Armin spoke from deep in his throat.

"Would you please tell us the other option."

"Hmph," Kubal snorted. He moved his neck from right to left, cracking his joints. "I don't care which option you choose, but if I have to say, this latter one is by far the more comfortable for me. Realistically, it would save me a little bit of work. It's simple," he said matter-of-factly. "*I have you die here.*"

The temperature seemed to dip, and the First Wall that should have been sturdy shook from its foundation, rattling Eren's brain. Of course it was an illusion, but one that felt all too real and imposing.

"There aren't that many of us..." Jean smiled bitterly. "But you think you can kill us so easily? We'll show you."

"Don't overestimate yourselves. Humans die easily. You do understand that well enough after taking part in this expedition?"

"Well…you are no different."

"I wonder. I'm not so brittle. I haven't survived to such a ripe age for no reason."

As Eren listened, he digested Kubal's words.

According to the supervisor, whether Eren and the others turned around then and there or were killed, the wall would not be restored. In other words, there was no need to get killed. In exchange for assisting in maintaining the world's structure, they would be able to live pleasant lives within the Third Wall. The first option was the more logical choice, but naturally, he couldn't think that way. Kubal's alternatives were in no way unacceptable.

"U-Um…" Sasha, who had been silent up to that point, could no longer keep her mouth shut. It twitched, and she furrowed her brow. "M-May I say a word?"

Kubal glanced at her, and she spoke.

"I completely…decline. And let me say…" She took a deep breath and said with all her strength, "*I barely understood any of it!* A society ruled by Titans is a happy one? It's equal? Peaceful? I don't think I'm smart, but aren't you a little dumber than I am? I don't know what it's like outside the wall. But right now there are many people who are still hoping to live in the First Wall District! When you think about that, it's only natural to close up this hole! That way the food will taste better, won't it? I, myself, want to return to the mountains where I'm from and quietly live out my 'peace.' And what are you? Until just now, you've been talking like you're superior without understanding anything, saying that it's all part of the system, going on and on about senseless things… But you've gotta know," Sasha uttered far more powerfully than Kubal, "people are alive! It's not like some board game. The government this, the system that, saying it's rational and whatnot—we can't just agree to let you move us around at your convenience!"

Kubal sighed and coolly stared at Sasha. "At times I'm envious of stupid people. Meaning, stupid people generally don't have what I call 'troubles.' They are just like animals that don't go on wondering about life and death. For all their lack of philosophy, they are simple and don't hesitate. Because they have only a narrow outlook, they lack judgment and are quick to decide. How I'd love to be reborn as a stupid creature."

"You just won't shut up!"

With that yell, Sasha pulled out the bow from her back and rapidly fired an arrow. It whistled through the air and skimmed past Kubal's right foot to stick deeply into the surface of the First Wall.

"Please leave!" she demanded, her bow at the ready. "We'll close up the hole. If you won't let us, I will shoot you the next time. And I don't hesitate."

Seeing Sasha in that state, Jean laughed loudly. "She's a real idiot, but that, right now, was the truth."

"I can't forgive you, either," Armin followed suit. "We'll close up the hole. As for which system is right for this world, I don't know. But I at least know that the only people who will be worse off if we close this wall are you people in the government."

"I see." Looking bored, Kubal glanced down at the ground before shifting his gaze to Eren. "And what about you?"

"I don't even have to tell you," Eren replied, unhesitant. "I have no obligation to listen to what you say... I more or less understand how the humans you talk about, who don't have choices, are content.

That's exactly why people need to make solid 'choices' if they ever want to grow. I know this now."

"Very touching. But I'm sure you would eventually see that, in this world, there are people who simply can't 'decide,' try as they might. Well, no matter…" Kubal sighed, and then looked at Mikasa. "You too?"

Without answering, Mikasa drew her blade, and the sunlight reflected off its sharp tip. For an instant, Kubal's face shone white.

Confirming their views, Kubal gave another deep sigh and nodded. "I understand." His expression had become clear and empty. "So I take it that you have chosen the latter option."

"No," Armin retorted. "We'll close the hole. Nobody will die here."

"It's the same thing." Kubal smiled eerily. "What's more, you replied just as I expected. If I really wanted to invite all of you into the Third Wall District, I would have chosen my words more carefully. Thanks for saving me the effort."

Kubal pulled out Sasha's arrow from the wall. When he slowly stood up, he looked even taller than before. The sun that shone behind him plunged his form into shadow, and his silhouette seemed like some kind of dark symbol.

"It really has been two years." The corners of his mouth curled up. "I wonder if it will go well."

The next moment, with the tip of Sasha's arrow, Kubal cut his left index finger. The wound looked deep, and in an instant, blood began to flow from it onto the wall, drop after drop. Satisfied with the result, Kubal began to retreat. Step by step, his eyes on Eren and the others, he moved backward. Then, as he reached the edge of the wall, he threw his body over the other side, kicking himself into a free fall. He vanished from sight instantly, and Eren and the others were silenced by the man's inexplicable deed.

Yet in a second they understood everything. Eerie thunderclouds began to gather in the sky. A black fog enveloped the area as if ash were being scattered through the air and cloaked their vision in darkness. Soon, a violent crackling came from the other side of the wall, and the premonition that had been smoldering inside of Eren became a reality.

So that's what, Eren murmured in his mind. White steam began to rise beyond the top of the wall. Suddenly the edifice began to quiver, but of course, it wasn't an earthquake. Clinging to the wall, Eren found himself in a mist that descended like drizzle. The temperature of the vapors that caressed their faces, the fragments that fell from the wall, and the gray scenery as the steam and dust covered the sun—it all flashed back.

That day from two years ago was being resurrected.

Before long, a huge red face emerged from the other side of the wall. Spewing out steam, and pulsing its exposed muscles, it contorted even more severely a savage expression that seemed to exist only to instill fear in the entire world.

It was the Colossal Titan.

"You gotta be kidding me," Jean muttered, looking up. "It's so huge."

"The Titan from two years ago…" Mikasa gazed up with wavering eyes.

"Supervisor Kubal is the Colossal Titan…" rose Armin's hoarse voice.

Armin looked up at the Colossal Titan's head, which was as big as the sun. It seemed that it was still in the midst of generating its Titan flesh, and in parts it was still incomplete. Pieces of bone were visible in certain spots, and its pupils hadn't yet filled with life. However, as if to clear away those blemishes, the waves of steam continued on and on to form its flesh. It was the same as with Shikishima.

Eren clenched his teeth so strongly with resolve and fight that his gums hurt. *The actual culprit who ruined our lives that day... It destroyed the First Wall, massacred all those people, and drove a wedge between Mikasa and me. It was the cause of everything, the root evil.*

"I'll kill it."

Eren took out and gripped his blades in both hands. He wanted to fire his anchors and fly at it as soon as he could, but the steam was so hot that he couldn't approach carelessly. It was quite hot even where Eren was standing. It would no doubt burn the flesh off of anyone who stood directly in front.

"When the steam clears let's attack immediately," Armin said. "Is everyone okay?"

Of course, nobody was in a perfect state. For nearly the entire half-day since the operation had started, they had worn their equipment and gone through several battles. Their stamina and willpower were exhausted to their limits—no, past them.

"Mikasa..."

Eren noticed that her face was drained snow white. An unusual amount of cold sweat coated her forehead. It wasn't so much that she was scared; the pain in her ankle was serious. Lifting her right leg slightly, she was trying to keep her foot from touching the ledge's surface. Even the tiniest vibration must have hurt. She was in no state to use the Vertical Maneuvering Equipment, which required balancing with one's soles.

"You go down to the ground first," Eren said.

"I'll fight too."

"You can't." Armin was shaking his head too. "You flip the detonator and just drop down to the ground with your wire. In that state, you won't be able to fight properly."

"But…"

"Please." With his eyes on Mikasa, Armin added, "It's important. There's a timer linked to the detonator, so take that and go down. We can't leave Hange alone, either. I want you two to watch the missile from the ground. Thirty seconds before the blast, fire the green signal flare. You can do that, right?"

Mikasa was about to object, but quickly shut her mouth. She felt the severity of the pain in her leg more than anyone. At last, biting her lip and with tears pooled in her eyes, she managed to speak. "I'm sorry that I can't fight with you at a time like this," she sniffled. "Just…please don't die."

"Of course not," Eren responded firmly.

Mikasa looked towards the missile to hide her tears. Then, pressing the switch on the detonator and grabbing the timer that would measure the remaining seconds, she descended to the ground.

Eren let out a huge sigh. *I have to grant Mikasa's request. I was the one who injured her. I have to defeat that thing and return alive. I'll fight for her as well.*

Again he looked at the Colossal Titan as it continued to belch steam. It seemed the vapors were subsiding and that they would soon be able to attack.

"H-How should we fight?" Sasha asked.

"We can only defeat it with mobility," Armin answered. "Going from two years ago, its movements are dull and slow compared to those of regular Titans. It hurts not to have Mikasa, but with superior speed, we have a good enough chance. Despite its size, its weak point is still only three feet tall and four inches wide… Eren shouldn't become a Titan. We can't rely on brute strength with the Colossal Titan as our opponent. In fact, the bigger the target we offer it, the greater our disadvantage. We have to aim for the nape with vertical maneuvers to the very end."

"Got it." Eren nodded.

So did Jean. "Okay…I'm feeling just a little hopeful. Armin, I thought you were just a creepy guy who always hung out with Eren, but your instructions are right on. As of now, I'm depending on you."

"Ha ha," Armin laughed weakly for a moment, but quickly stiffened his expression. "Anyway, in the five minutes until the blast, we just have to continue to protect the bomb. If the wall is sealed with the explosives, at least a part of our goal will be achieved—at the same time, we'll put down Supervisor Kubal. Until then, we each have to fly as irregularly as we can so the Colossal Titan doesn't catch us. Exercising your discretion, you have to target the nape if a gap opens up. Eren and Jean from the left, and Sasha and I from the right. Is that okay?"

Everybody nodded. In the momentary silence, Eren gulped. The steam was slowly thinning—it was time.

"Now!"

They spread out. As one, they fired their anchors and buried them at the top of the wall. Eren squeezed his trigger tightly and reeled in his wire and revved the gas. Feeling gravity wrap around his entire body, he ascended, gritted his teeth, and braced himself. Then, for the first time in his life, he flew over the First Wall into the Outside World.

The eyes of Kubal, the Colossal Titan, which seemed to have ripened, clearly noticed him. As Eren flew to the height of its face, its hugeness sank in anew. It couldn't be compared to any other Titan. It was so massive, so savage—a sixty-yard-plus Colossal Titan.

Eren released his anchor, and he was weightless. He floated for a moment through the air. The other side of the wall was cloaked in a thick fog from the steam, and visibility was exceedingly poor, but Eren didn't have the time to enjoy the scenery anyway. Unable to see anything below the Colossal Titan's chest, he focused on finding Armin and Sasha. It was as if he'd been plunged into the middle of a cloud. The vapors were still dense around his target, but fortunately, the temperature was only enough to make him sweat.

Eren shot his right anchor at the Colossal Titan's right shoulder. When it hit, he reeled in immediately. To maintain some distance, he swiveled around in a large arc, and Jean followed in a similar trajectory. On the other side, Armin and Sasha were maneuvering likewise.

Coming around to the Colossal Titan's flank, Eren released his anchor, switched, and fired his left anchor. When it pierced the upper right arm, he reeled in his wire. He rapidly turned his right wrist twice and adjusted the altitude with his gas to cut through the humid air. Gravity lightly tugged at him.

The Colossal Titan still gave no signs of attacking. Its movements seemed much slower than those of regular Titans just as Armin had suggested. At this rate, Eren and his friends might be able to end this quickly. They could do it, and they meant to.

He swung all the way around to its back. As vast as a crop field, it pulsated bright red like its face. Eren fired his anchor right at the center—a hit. Thirty feet beneath him, he could see Jean, who seemed to have decided to attack from below. It wasn't a bad idea. Their movements were well distributed. If they continued like this, the Colossal Titan wouldn't be able to pin them down. Satisfied, Eren rapidly closed in on their foe. He wound his wire as quickly as he could and darted straight for the Colossal Titan's back like a bullet. As he did, Jean climbed. To Eren's left, Armin swung around too, and Sasha followed.

Already altering his trajectory for the second time, Eren released his anchor and fired again. Though bile rose up into his throat from the sudden gravity, he forced himself to swallow it. He sprayed gas. Through the heavy wind he zeroed in on the nape—he could attack it with ease. He prepared his blades and quickly raised both his hands.

He released his anchor, and his momentum carried him towards the nape. He was ready to slash at it.

—The Colossal Titan howled—

As if it had been waiting for the perfect opportunity, it spewed steam from its entire body again. From the nape that Eren had been trying to gouge, too, the steam exploded, a red-hot wind. He reflexively covered his face. The exposed parts of his skin erupted in intense pain. As he cried out, he was swallowed up by gravity.

Below him, he could faintly see Jean in the steam, and to his left, he could see Sasha and Armin also plummeting. The Colossal Titan had been waiting for that moment, and confirming the efficacy of its tactic, it slowly lifted its right arm. It had finally begun to move.

When its arm was completely raised, as long and steady as a road, it stretched it over the wall. It meant to pick up the missile. That had been its target from the beginning.

Eren acted immediately. Though his face still prickled with pain, he hardly had the time to cry out. He just clambered upwards and shot an anchor at the Colossal Titan's hip—a hit. Winding the wire, he aimed for the undefended right armpit and fired his anchors three times in quick succession.

He got there. He had to put its arm out of commission. He was rocked by intense waves of gravity and almost lost his sense of direction, but didn't. To ensure that he hit the tendon, he brought both blades down as forcefully as he could. He felt the impact in his arms.

Eren had succeeded in damaging the tendon in the Colossal Titan's right armpit—but it was too shallow a cut. He hadn't fully robbed the right arm of all movement. Was the Colossal Titan capable of feeling pain? Hastily pulling its right arm back as if it did, it tried to swat Eren with the same motion.

Eren felt the wind pressure. He revved his engine and retreated, shooting his anchor into the First Wall and clinging to it as the attack swung past him. The massive arm took a long time to slice through the air and parted the white steam. In its wake a heavy wind blew against Eren's cheek.

Though it was certainly slow, the Colossal Titan commanded a destructive power beyond that of any of its lesser brethren. Eren's respiration was so strained that he almost couldn't breathe. His fatigue from turning into a Titan was still fairly pronounced. He wanted to avoid a lengthy battle.

Eren threw out his chipped blade and exchanged it for a new

one. He kicked the surface of the wall and entered a trajectory that orbited the Colossal Titan. Then, in the white mist, he caught a glimpse of Sasha and Armin reaching the nape with a few clever wire movements.

That's it, you can do it. Eren couldn't help but smile widely, and to attract attention, he purposefully drew a flashy arc and passed before the Colossal Titan's eyes. As intended, its giant eyes followed Eren, and it began to lift its long left arm. But Sasha was quicker.

Yes. She raised her blades, and with all her strength, slashed at the exposed nape.

Eren hastily swallowed his shout of joy, because it was not the Colossal Titan's flesh but Sasha's blades that went flying. The dual-wielded weapons glittered in the light beautifully, almost out of place, before sinking into the steam that shrouded the earth. Armin swung his blades shortly afterward, but the result was the same. The broken swords fell away towards the earth.

No good. Neither Sasha nor Armin has the arm strength. Its skin is too thick. Eren clicked his tongue and descended to avoid the Colossal Titan's left arm. He banked, drove in another anchor, and gritted his teeth. His body was increasingly worn down by fatigue, and for just a moment, his memory seemed to skip, but somehow he regained consciousness a few seconds later. *I can't faint now. I can't die.*

He circled, dodging the Titan's attack, when below to the left, he saw Jean, who was looking at Eren in turn as if to tell him something. Eren understood: the long and short of it was that one of them, being stronger than Armin or Sasha, needed to slay the Titan. Eren signaled his assent with his gaze and proceeded to fire successive anchors into the gargantuan form.

Ascending through a violent match with gravity, he was attempting to catch the Colossal Titan by surprise. He would choose the most eccentric route possible, and then swing his blades through.

We have to. I have to.

The acceleration was intense.

—He blanked out, passed out—

Eren's consciousness broke off. Gravity had absconded with it. When he came to, his heart froze. Right before his eyes was the Colossal Titan's hand. A bright, red, clumsy palm had opened, and it was going to crush him any moment now. *Holy…*

Shit! As soon as he cursed inwardly, however, a gust billowed from behind and took Eren away.

"What are you doing, idiot?" Jean had come to grab him upon noticing Eren's dull flight.

The ace vertical maneuver student sped away from the Titan while Armin and Sasha whipped around before its eyes to gain its attention. Still carried by Jean, Eren shot an anchor at the wall.

Jean did too, and together, they clung to the surface. Staring at Eren, who was breathing so hard he was basically hyperventilating, Jean grimaced. His own face was scalded from the steam.

"You're exhausted from when you turned into a Titan?"

"Maybe…" Eren wheezed between breaths. "Don't worry… I'm fine."

"Don't push it. Nah, I can't tell you that. I'm sorry, but you have to fight to the death."

"I know…"

"You be the one to cut the nape," Jean offered. "I'll be the decoy. You're better at the gouging part."

A little surprised, Eren opened his eyes wide.

"It's true, isn't it?" Jean admitted with a forced laugh. "You're better qualified."

"Leave it to me," Eren replied assuredly, forcing a laugh back.

They kicked off the wall simultaneously and transitioned to vertical maneuvers. Armin and Sasha were trying to distract the Titan but weren't quite luring it away. They did their best to avoid getting hit, but glimpsing an opening, a massive hand rushed towards the other side of the wall. They couldn't let it touch the missile.

Then, from somewhere, they heard a faint sound that tickled their ears. A green pillar of smoke rose up on the other side of the wall. Mikasa had sent it up. There were only thirty seconds until the blast.

Eren flew once more towards the Colossal Titan's armpit.

At nearly the same time that Mikasa released the signal flare from the bed of the truck, the hand of the Colossal Titan came reaching inside the wall. Hange, who watched from beside her, instinctively let out a peculiar cry, and Mikasa also tensed up observing the hand.

In preparation for the explosion, the transport had been moved farther away from the wall. Still, they could easily see the missile and the Colossal Titan, and the unfolding scene made Mikasa gulp.

As if grabbing at something in a box, the Colossal Titan fumbled around in search of the bomb. Its fat fingers seemed unable to locate the missile tucked deep in the wall. Every time they scratched at the surface recklessly, rubble fell to the ground in clouds of dust. Praying,

Mikasa glanced at the timer that Armin had made. Fifteen seconds before the blast.

"Please hold out…" Hange murmured, her face twisting in a frown.

At last, however, the Colossal Titan's digits stopped moving as if they'd felt something. It seemed to have found the dud and started drawing out its hand, its fingers gingerly wrapped around it so as not to set if off. The bomb was lifted slowly into the air.

"Stop."

Then, the Colossal Titan pulled back its hand as if it had remembered something. Abandoned, the bomb tumbled wildly but settled back where it had been. Having bounced three times, it was facing slightly inward but remained on its ledge. The Colossal Titan's expression filled with intense fury as it returned to its battle stance outside the wall. Eren and the others had somehow succeeded in attacking its body.

Mikasa let out a sigh and glanced at the timer again—and for a moment doubted her eyes.

"What's wrong?"

"It's thirty seconds," answered Mikasa, "*past* the explosion."

Hange yelped in surprise and scratched her head. Mindful of the possibility of a lag between the detonator and the timer in their hands, they waited for a minute, but nothing changed; there was no sign of an explosion.

"The impact just now must have yanked the detonator loose," Hange lamented bitterly. "We need to reinstall it."

"I can do it," Mikasa said, gently standing up on the cargo bed, but her eyes widened as soon as she was reminded of the intense pain in her right leg. The sensation turned into a cold sweat that covered her entire body.

"It'll be hard in that state."

"But…" Mikasa bit back the pain. "You can't fly, can you?"

Hange lifted her head in reflection before drawing a knife from her hip. "Show me your right leg."

"What?"

"It's okay, I won't chop it off or anything. I'm just going to cut the harness that's wrapped around the bottom of your right foot a little shorter. The rest of the belt I'll gather and fasten above the knee. You won't be able to maintain your balance very well or have full use of your VME, but if you're just climbing up the wall with your wire, there will be less pressure on your bad ankle."

Mikasa complied and held out her leg. Hange severed the harness in a flash and skillfully gathered the belt above the knee just as she'd explained. Mikasa's ankle hurt like it was going to tear apart, but when the alteration was complete, her right leg was freer and the pain lessened considerably. Hange was a genuine engineer, and her handiness couldn't be matched by anyone.

"I'll take you close to the wall with the truck, and from there you can shoot your anchor."

Mikasa nodded, and the arms development squad leader got into the driver's seat and started the truck.

All the while, on the other side of the wall, an intense battle with the Colossal Titan was still raging. Every one of its motions sent a gust of wind and a large cloud of steam over the wall. Gazing up as though at a storm, Mikasa gripped her triggers. Then, when the transport was close enough to the wall, she ignored her pain and fired an anchor. It hit its mark, and she reeled in the wire. Slowly, grazing the surface of the wall, she rose towards the missile.

Eren twisted his body midair and shot an anchor into the raised right arm of the Colossal Titan. It landed near the wrist. He reeled in the wire completely, and on his own legs, ran across the arm straight for the nape. The Colossal Titan's skin was soft like damp earth and sucked at Eren's feet. Though faint, the eruption of steam didn't cease, and hot winds caressed his cheeks.

Running through the vapor, Eren turned his eyes towards the wall. A considerable amount of time had passed since the green flare, but there was no sign of an explosion whatsoever. Something was wrong. He hoped Mikasa and Hange could figure it out.

Jean and Sasha's maneuvers had captured the Colossal Titan's attention, but noticing Eren, it jerked its right arm to try to shake him off. He lost his footing and was thrown in the air but glared at the shoulder and fired his anchor. The moment it hit he reeled in at full strength and spiraled back towards the arm. When he'd gained enough speed, he released. He was aiming for the nape with his momentum, but another fountain of steam erupted from the Colossal Titan's skin and buffeted Eren, sending him plummeting towards the hip. It had happened again. He was getting nowhere. At this rate, his fatigue would only mount, and before long…

No. What am I thinking? I have to kill that thing.

He tensed his abdomen and fired an anchor once again. It sliced through the steam and stuck fast at the waist. Drawing a large arc, he returned to the wall to collect himself. As he clung to the surface, Armin flew over to hang beside him.

"I'll go check on the bomb." Armin was also short of breath. "I need you guys to hold out for a little while."

"Got it."

"Also, it seems that the Titan needs time to recharge before shooting off steam. It still hasn't done so consecutively."

"I see…which means…"

"Because it just erupted, now might be the chance."

They dispersed simultaneously. Armin climbed to the top of the First Wall, while Eren turned towards the Colossal Titan and flew up, trusting his friend's words. *If now is my chance then I don't have time to rest. A longer battle will only worsen our physical disadvantage.* The triggers were light—he knew that there wasn't much gas left. Either way, he couldn't fight for long. He would risk it all on this moment.

Burning gas freely, Eren sped to the Colossal Titan's nape. He hopped from the wrist, upper arm, and chest to the left side of the head, and circled twice. Performing complex maneuvers, he didn't let his foe acquire him. Up, down, left, right, from every direction, ruinous gravity jostled his guts. Still, he could take it. He wouldn't let his consciousness slip away. He would win.

Jean and Sasha moved intricately to distract the Colossal Titan.

It flailed its arms to resist Eren, but the movements were less tight than before, and he was starting to see gaps between them. It even turned towards Jean and Sasha, who were maneuvering flashily to pester it, to give them all of its attention.

I got this.

Eren chose a path that would remove him completely from the

Colossal Titan's view. He went by way of the hip and shot up without stopping. The next moment, however, the Colossal Titan swung down its left hand and hit something. It was Sasha.

She flew towards the ground at the speed of a cannonball. The white steam smoothly parted to make way for her, and the streak of clean air seemed to be guiding her down. Perhaps because she had passed out, her limbs didn't seem to have any strength in them. Eren immediately made to go after her, but his target, the nape, was already right in front of him.

What do I do? What am I supposed to do?

Even as he prevaricated, Sasha's body disappeared beyond the fog. He grunted and looked at the Colossal Titan's nape again. He had to set his priorities once and for all.

I'm the only one who can cut off the nape, and my gas is running out. Now is the only time that the Colossal Titan can't erupt in steam. That means the only thing I can do is believe Sasha is okay and pour all I have into what I need to do. Life is a series of conflicts and choices, but that's why I can't run away from the painful ones, and I better accept them straight up. That's what it takes to beat Kubal. That's why I have to make a choice with no regrets.

He accelerated even more. With two wire motions, he passed the Colossal Titan's shoulder blade and continued to climb. He tightened his grip on his triggers, which were slick with sweat. His blades glinted and shone.

In a moment, his eyes settled on the nape, and he soared, brandishing his blades—but that was when the Colossal Titan started to turn around. It had noticed Eren, and his innards went cold.

If the Colossal Titan finds me, it's over. If I miss this opportunity, the gas, my stamina, another blast of steam—whichever factor comes into play, I won't get another chance. Everything we've done so far will have been in vain.

Then, for some reason, as if the Colossal Titan had heard Eren's prayer, it halted. Instead of facing Eren, it froze midway, its eyes pinned to something.

What is it? he wondered for a moment, but soon saw what the Colossal Titan did.

Beyond its head, at the end of its line of sight, was Jean.

He was descending quietly right in front of the Titan's eyes. He showed no sign of shooting his anchor at anything or burning his gas. In fact, his right and left wires were tangled up in each other, and he couldn't reel them in. He was helpless in that state. He could only obey gravity.

That idiot…

Their gazes met. Jean was making fretful motions, but Eren realized it was all just an act. Seemingly focused on something far away, the guy's eyes were staring firmly at Eren. An elementary blunder like tangling your wires was something that only happened during the first month of training. After that, nobody made such a newbie mistake. Not to mention, Jean led his class in vertical maneuvers. There was no mistake. This was his last-ditch measure for grabbing the Titan's attention. He had tangled his wires on purpose to bait it. It was all so Eren could go for the nape. It was all to take down Kubal. It was all for the mission.

Jean.

Eren tensed his stomach to bear the moment. Right away, without hesitation, the Colossal Titan grabbed Jean, who was struggling in the air like a moth that had lost its wings, and crushed him.

His right arm, alone, leapt out of the Colossal Titan's grip, while blood dribbled down as though from a squeezed fruit. What had been Jean just moments ago rained upon the earth.

The thick despair that wafted in the white mist was simply too much, and Eren shut off his heart. Without screaming, without weeping, without letting his emotions take over, he focused entirely on the target in front of him.

I have to slice it.

I have to gouge it out.

That nape, that meat, the man inside, I'll take him down.

Absolutely, unconditionally, completely—I'll take him down.

I won't let Jean's sacrifice go to waste.

I'll end it all here.

Eren swung his blades.

Dragging her leg, Mikasa finally reached the unexploded missile where it lay. As expected, the detonator devised by Armin had detached from the dud, probably thanks to bouncing a few times after leaving the Colossal Titan's hand.

Putting away her wire and kneeling down, she tried to repair the device. It was clear, though, that she wasn't up to it. The mechanism was more complicated than she imagined, and certain parts were completely damaged. Several pieces had been disconnected, and the timer itself looked flattened. There was nothing she could do. She considered the best course of action.

"You should strike the fuse."

Mikasa jumped in surprise at the voice—*which wasn't Armin's.*

Almost crawling, the man slowly approached Mikasa on the ledge.

"If you hit the fuse, it will explode…and of course, you with it."

Unable to decide how to greet him, she just opened and closed her mouth.

"But if you explode a bomb of this size here, the wall itself will be blown to bits. If the cracks function well, perhaps you'll succeed, but I can't say it's a good plan. If you really want to close the hole, you should explode it at a much higher elevation, whether or not that is actually feasible."

"Captain Shikishima," Mikasa managed to say. "I beg you… don't try to interfere with the operation anymore."

Shikishima gave an exhausted chuckle and scratched his disheveled hair. The shirt he was wearing had frayed and torn nearly beyond recognition and was blackened with blood. Mikasa saw the stiffness in his body; it seemed his injuries were severe. He was alive, but it was a mystery as to how.

"I thought I'd court you one last time, but I guess I've fallen out of your favor."

"I'm grateful towards you… Please, let us be."

"Begging on your knees? How unlike you," Shikishima said, raising his face to look up at the top of the wall. "It seems that I'm someone who can never *completely* attract others."

Mikasa had no words, and Shikishima continued anyway.

"The Survey Corps, Eren, and of course, yourself. At the most crucial moment, I couldn't keep people attached to me. Our organization actually used to have many more members. Due to differences in points of view, to disagreements, one by one they left me. It was all thanks to my lack of charm... Really, to the very end, that was what I suffered from. Whenever I tried to be charismatic, a definite rift separated me from the world. I am hopelessly *lacking* in something. No matter what, I can't tear down the wall between myself and other—don't move!"

Surprised, Mikasa followed Shikishima's gaze. On top of the wall was Armin. No doubt having come to check on the bomb, he looked down towards them. When his eyes met Shikishima's, his body froze.

"It'll be over soon! Just stay put for a little while! Or else, I'll kill her!"

Shikishima got out his blade and pointed it towards Mikasa, but she felt oddly safe.

This man would never hurt me.

She told Armin that she was going to be fine, but he remained standing vigilantly on top of the wall.

"At times..." Shikishima watched Mikasa with his blade pointed at her. "I enjoyed the illusion that your heart was turning towards me. At least, you must have understood how I felt. And yet—no, because of that, you set something like a boundary in your dealings with me. But as seldom as it was, I could entertain the illusion that you were really looking at me. That mystery...now I think I know." Shikishima sighed. "You were looking at the 'Eren' in me. After meeting him, I finally understood. We are, indeed, hopelessly similar. You imposed on me the image of the precious presence that you had lost two years ago. It was only at such moments that I enjoyed the strange illusion and a fleeting euphoria. Really, it's ironic."

Mikasa kept her mouth shut. She couldn't deny Shikishima's words.

"If I'm someone who abandoned 'peace' for the sake of 'freedom,' then, on the contrary, Kubal is a man who abandoned 'freedom' for the sake of 'peace.' Eren, too, might learn one day that you can't obtain everything equally. We might seem to be motivated by completely different ideals, but the truth is that all ways of thinking exist on the same plane. I'm sure Eren will eventually turn into me, and that I will eventually turn into Kubal. It's not about who is right, or who is wrong. The question is merely at what stage you decide to take action. That's all there is to it."

"Why…didn't you tell me anything?"

"Let's see… Maybe that was how serious I was about you. I didn't want to speak carelessly and have you leave me. Even if what you saw was somebody else, if your eyes were turned towards me, then that was enough. So long as you overlaid me with Eren, and thus sympathized with me, I believed that you wouldn't go away. How terribly pathetic of me."

Shikishima looked up at the sky. As if a revelation had come to him, he sighed. He looked refreshed when he returned his blade to his sheath with a gentle metallic clink. He smiled beautifully.

"You be the one to guide Eren." Shikishima's words pierced through Mikasa's soul. "I know you don't need to be told, but I'm counting on you. Eren must be very important to me, too."

"Captain Shikishima…"

"Please. I no longer merit that title." Shikishima looked up again and let out a long, deep sigh. "From the day I met you, the day I decided to stand before 'Mikasa,' I decided to call myself 'Shikishima.'

Having cast off that burden, I will reassume a name that should have died already. 'Haku'—it sounds so hopelessly miserable and weak."

As Shikishima neared the bomb, he affectionately touched its body. "Now, I guess I'll do something at least a little bit brotherly." He shut his eyes and donned a caustic smile. "The loser must nourish the winner. May the choice direct what will follow. Here, today, the world is meeting its end."

"Thank you…for everything." The words spilled out of Mikasa's trembling throat at Shikishima's resolve.

His profile as he snorted in response did remind her of Eren.

He carefully gauged the angle of his right arm, his left arm, and raised both, his tendons fully stretched. With all his strength, he would deliver an ultimate blow.

The steam dissipated as if it were shying away from Eren's fury. His eyes gleamed intensely as though to burn the Colossal Titan's neck. Everything he had was devoted to slicing off the Colossal Titan's flesh. Gravity sucked his body down towards the nape.

Eren let out a war cry. Roaring, he swung his blades. He didn't care if making this strike killed him. If it brought death to the Colossal Titan, he didn't need anything else. Everything was for this blow, this moment. He was going to cut, simply and purely.

With his entire being, he sliced.

However—the sensation in his hands wasn't what it should have been. Frantically, he turned around.

When he looked, the Colossal Titan's nape had indeed been

gouged out. In accordance with Eren's slash, a piece of meat was flying through the air, turning into steam, and melting into the mist. But it was clearly a small piece. The wound wouldn't be fatal.

The moment he came to that realization, intense pain overtook him as if he had collided with a huge piece of debris. All of his bones were whacked together, his brain shook in his skull, and just breathing was painful. His exhausted body was ready to give up in face of this merciless punishment.

Amidst the pain, Eren finally realized that something was wrapped around his body. It was the Colossal Titan's right hand.

It got me—it's over.

Gripping Eren, the Colossal Titan slowly brought him to its face for a closer look. Its all too savage eyes stared for some time.

In his fading mind, Eren was sinking into despair. And he thought about the journey that had brought him to that moment:

Hiana had died, never to see her beloved daughter again or to find a reason for living, regretful. Her story had posed some meaningful questions for Eren. She had been such a human person.

Fukushi and Lil had died too. They had lived in this world by supplementing each other. At times their excessive lovey-dovey antics had been annoying, but they had been irreplaceable classmates.

Sannagi had died too. He had cared for his classmates more than anyone, been more cheerful than anyone, been more dependable than anyone. To protect his little brothers and sisters, he had surrendered himself to a ball of fire, entrusting Eren and the others with restoring the wall.

And Jean had died too—just when Eren was getting to know him, just when Eren thought they could fight together. Leaving everything to him, Jean had died.

Everyone had been killed.

And the one who understood me best and tried to grant me freedom, old man Souda, and PFC Yunohira, and all my other classmates, and the squad leaders, everyone. Everyone fell in this operation. I want to avenge them. I want to, but...

The Colossal Titan slowly opened its large mouth.

It looks like it's planning on eating me.

His hazy vision couldn't even make out the shape of the Colossal Titan's mouth. Everything had lost its outline, its reality. As proof that the mouth was thrown open, however, a warm and heavy wind blew against Eren. The tepid air coiled around his hair with a strange stickiness and coiled into the deep parts of his soul.

Though he struggled to move his limbs, they didn't budge an inch. In fact, the Colossal Titan's grip was so powerful that the hand tightened even further at Eren's every faint effort. A pain too intense to allow him even to scream racked his entire body, and a dry creaking sound came from his bones. He barely had the strength to twist his face in pain.

It's the end... So this is the end. But I wonder, thought Eren. *Maybe I did okay. I've grown so much compared to two years ago, when I was utterly helpless. While most of the soldiers died without accomplishing anything, I was able to survive and defeat my enemies until now. I installed the bomb. I did everything that I could.*

The Colossal Titan brought Eren closer and closer to its mouth.

Make it quick and crunch my head.

Just then, the Colossal Titan grimaced. At the same time, as if it had lost its balance, it slowly sank to the ground. Like a large building collapsing, the Titan lowered its body at a leisurely pace. It seemed to have fallen to its knees, and the impact ran through Eren's body as well.

The Colossal Titan looked down to see what had happened. Eren did too, and there, though it was incredibly small, through the gap in the steam, he could definitely see a human form. Two blades were gripped in its hand. Standing there, having cut the Achilles tendon of the Colossal Titan, was Sasha.

She looked up at Eren and shouted something. Although her mouth was moving, he couldn't make out the words with his fading mind—no, even if it were perfectly clear, he might not have been able to at that distance.

Still, Sasha's voice reached Eren, and it pried open something in him with a hard clang.

Exactly, Sasha. I was wrong.

Opening his eyes wide, Eren drew up his last drops of vitality and resisted as best he could.

I can't die at a place like this. I have to live to live. Even if I'm handed a die with sixes on all sides, I just strongly will to roll a one and cast it. If I do that, then maybe—no, for sure—I will get my one.

"RAHHHHHH!"

An impact.

In unison with Eren's scream, a deafening sound rang out from behind him. He tried to turn around but was squeezed so tightly that he couldn't. The Colossal Titan's eyes were wide with surprise.

What is it? What happened?

The next moment, the Colossal Titan let go of Eren. Gravity pulled him out of its hand.

From then on, it was as if he was floating in some other world. Everything moved in slow motion. As if time had been forgotten, the scene unfolded vividly but lethargically.

What entered Eren's sight, blocking the sun as he fell, was...

The White Titan.

Using the top of the wall as a steppingstone, the White Titan made a long, beautiful stride. It flew towards the Colossal Titan's face. In its right hand, it held a large cylinder. There was no mistaking what it was.

The White Titan was holding the unexploded missile.

Eren was still falling. The wind rushed over him as he cut through the steam, his eyes pinned to the almost supernatural encounter between the two Titans.

The White Titan lifted the missile high and—shoved it into the Colossal Titan's mouth.

The Colossal Titan frantically tried to brush it away, but not in time. Clinging to the Colossal Titan's face, the White Titan pushed the missile, which was still peeking out of its opponent's mouth, further down its throat. A deep sound rumbled as if a giant switch that existed somewhere in the world had been flipped. The next moment, a blinding flash of white filled Eren's vision.

Everything was swallowed up. Sound, light, voices, the blast—it all converged to a point and met their end.

It was the end of the world.

Along with the whirlwind of white light, the deafening sound of the explosion engulfed Eren's body. Helpless in the wind, he was bathed in the blast. As if to fling him away, it blew at him intensely, majestically, yet somehow didn't feel violent. Instead, as if to bless and welcome him like the strong, warm tolling of a joyous bell that echoed everywhere, it retained a sweet tenderness.

Before long the white world melted away, and "reality" began to reappear.

The Colossal Titan emerged before Eren's eyes. It had lost everything from the neck up. There was no need to confirm the details; it had cleanly disappeared down to its nape. Signaling its demise, steam spewed up from its body where it stood. As if it were dissolving into the vapors, the Colossal Titan's body—Kubal's—crumbled in midair. The muscles vanished, the tendons vanished, the bones vanished.

As gravity washed over Eren's body, he couldn't help but smile.

At the same time, something was happening to the wall's surface. Shaken by the strong explosion in the sky, an upper portion began to slide along the cracks that the previous expedition had made. As if to compete with Eren, guided by gravity, the cascade completely filled the hole underneath in no time.

It was *perfect*.

Tears spilled from Eren's eyes at the good fortune that had literally rained down from above. Instead of falling, his tears seemed to rise up. One, two, three. Continuously, as if to carry blessings to the heavens, they soared into the sky. He thought again about his friends who had fallen in battle, and his heart grew full. It was done. Everything was about to end, the way he'd wished it to.

Eren gripped his triggers and tried to fire an anchor at the wall, but there was no response. When he checked on the muzzles at his hip, he realized they had been utterly crushed by the Titan's hand. He didn't despair, though, and was able to accept it all. For them to be intact after being squeezed so hard would have been unnatural.

Eren surrendered himself to gravity all the more.

This is good, he thought. *This is good. I lived to live. I cast the die and rolled a number that wasn't even on it. I should hardly be punished for getting swallowed up by the earth and consummating my life. No one can blame me for dying.*

—ren—

From somewhere, he heard a voice. No, it was probably just his imagination.

—*Eren*—

Believing it was a hallucination, Eren slowly closed his eyes.

In moments, this body will hit the ground. There's no need to struggle. I'll just leave everything to heaven. I don't have any strength left to struggle. Let it end here.

"Eren!!"

His body was jolted suddenly. Yanked up from his hip, he was defying gravity. The abrupt reversal scrambled his sense of direction, and he was unable to tell heaven from earth, left from right. The world had turned upside down. His eyes snapped open.

"I'm glad... I'm so glad."

A tearful voice enwrapped Eren.

"Hold on tight," Mikasa murmured as if in prayer, embracing him.

Unable to say anything, Eren just let her. A wire hung down from above as if to offer him salvation. Mikasa must have stuck her anchor in a part of the wall that hadn't fallen. She wound her wire slowly to maintain her balance. Her leg must have hurt, but without betraying an iota of pain, she warily watched the end of the wire.

Eren closed his eyes again and rose up into the steam and dust that clouded the world.

They were approaching the top of the wall.

Armin landed on the ground and headed to where Hange waited with the truck. Raising her arms jubilantly, she smiled at him with her entire face from the cargo bed. As he ran, Armin couldn't help but look back several times at the spot that used to be a forty-foot hole.

"It's closed!" Armin found himself shouting what they already knew. "It's closed!"

"It's closed!" Hange, too, had to shout it out. "It's closed!"

Armin let his elated soul carry his body to Hange. They exchanged a firm handshake and congratulated each other on the fight for a minute.

"Can I join in?"

When they turned around in surprise at the voice, Sasha was standing behind them. She smiled somewhat shyly and scratched her head.

"After I sliced the Titan's ankle, I escaped through the hole before it closed to come over to this side. I'm glad I wasn't flattened by the rubble."

When Hange asked if everyone else was okay, Sasha's smile faded, and she said that Eren and Mikasa were probably okay but that Jean had sacrificed himself. Hange took in the news with a resigned look.

Then she sighed and said, "I was also prepared for death… I didn't think I would end up surviving…"

"Really?" asked Armin.

Hange opened her arms wide and laughed. "Why not? I'm a lab worker who's useless on an expedition. I can't even use the VME, I was just luggage. And to think that even then, I was assigned to it. Politics must have been behind it." Hange removed her goggles and continued, sounding almost carefree. "I secretly kept Titans as pets in the library. I did whatever I wanted. My Titans were slain by someone, and I figured I was getting the 'mysteriously killed in action' treatment. I thought I would be offed by a government agent during this expedition…"

"And you still came?" asked Sasha.

"It's not like I could refuse, right? It was an order from above." Hange shrugged. "And besides, well, in truth, I also wanted to try going on an expedition. I just had to see Titans in the wild, walking around with their own legs."

"Ha ha," Armin chuckled. "You have a death wish, don't you?"

Hange laughed to plead guilty and turned again towards the hole that was no more. "Beautifully blocked," she couldn't help but marvel. "The 3rd Outer Wall Restoration Operation…has succeeded."

Armin nodded and looked again as well. He didn't think he'd ever get tired of staring at the sight. As planned, the wall had slid towards the ground like a closing gate along the cracks made during the 2nd Outer Wall Restoration Operation. There was no sign of the hole whatsoever. Some additional cracks had come into existence around twenty yards up and light faintly leaked through, but it didn't seem like a huge problem.

As Hange said, the operation was hereby successful.

Tears gushed from Armin's eyes, and he knelt down. Then, to

everyone who had been chased out from the First Wall District—his parents, his grandfather, Sannagi, all the refugees waiting in the Second Wall District—he announced with all his soul:

"We finally took it back!"

Placing both her hands on her hips and puffing out her chest, Sasha said just a little hoarsely, "All right, everyone, let's go home and…"

At that point her voice nearly drowned in her tears.

"…Eat tons of delicious chow."

Mikasa brought Eren to the top of the First Wall and laid him down gently. Unable even to tell her thanks, Eren got on all fours and tried to catch his breath. Various thoughts, stirring up various emotions, consumed him.

He had a definite sense of accomplishment. He couldn't not feel proud and had shed tears just moments ago. Yet too many things had changed too much for him to show that honest reaction on his face or in words. So many of his friends had died. So many had had their hopes crushed. So many sacrifices underlay the fulfillment of his wish and decision.

In the process he had learned the truth about his world. He had learned of the diverse commitments to it. Having undergone so many "trials and tribulations," he was having trouble finding the right emotions to express. He just hung his head and rested his body. That was all he could do.

"Eren…"

He couldn't even respond to Mikasa's voice.

"Eren," Mikasa patiently called to him. "Look up, Eren."

Still Eren kept his eyes on the wall. All he could do was stare intently at the inorganic grayness.

"Eren," Mikasa said just a little more firmly. "Please look up... If you don't, *you'll probably regret it.*"

At that strange request, finally, as if waking up for the first time in his life, Eren slowly raised his head. When he saw what Mikasa saw, he couldn't help but utter: "What. The. Hell."

He couldn't look away.

The Outside World that had been concealed by the steam emitted by the Colossal Titan revealed itself before Eren. Whatever words or form of expression he used, he was certain that he wouldn't be able to convey this picture precisely.

The earth continued for a little while on the other side of the wall. Some areas were thick with trees, while others were bald, open terrain. The scenery wasn't so different from what Eren had vaguely imagined of the Outside World. Beyond that, however, a couple of miles past the First Wall, the earth broke off suddenly as if to proclaim an *edge*. From there on, like a kind of eternity, stretching endlessly...

Water.

On and on, blue on blue, it extended infinitely.

No matter how much he focused his eyes, no matter how many times he blinked, the scene showed no signs of changing. It was like some kind of dream. Yet it was the sure reality. The light sparkled. The line between sky and water was a breathtaking, vivid arc. It was what Eren had wished fervently to see back on that day.

"The Ocean."

Eren swallowed his breath. Just like Armin's book said, it was far vaster than land and girded the world limitlessly. As if to welcome the sun, it glittered now and then; as if to accept all things, it undulated calmly in the wind. The "largeness" that he'd felt upon seeing a Titan for the first time was relegated to a miniature world.

This was authentic grandeur. Authentic immensity.

The authentic world.

"It was…this close to us." Eren tried to smile but instead began to cry again. "It was this close to us and we never knew."

His tears wouldn't stop. As to what he was crying for, Eren himself didn't know for sure. Perhaps he was deeply moved by a scene that his eyes were beholding for the first time. Perhaps he was realizing the weight of what he had lost. Perhaps he was overwhelmed by the truth of the world. Perhaps he was angry that information had been kept from him. All of those things seemed correct, and yet all of them seemed to miss the mark.

The one truth in Eren's world at that moment was summarized by what Mikasa said next.

"It's beautiful."

Eren wiped his tears. He wiped, wiped, and wiped again. Still they flowed. He didn't know a single thing—what to do from now on, whether what he had done was really correct, or what was right for the world. Because he didn't, Eren continued to gaze at the Ocean.

Before the world ended, before the world changed, before the world forced another choice upon him—he stared out at the Ocean.

"From here."

Eren spoke firmly, as if to convince himself.

"From here."

Three gulls flew off towards the horizon.

Vividly, beautifully, as if to symbolize the world's vastness—

Smoothly, as if they were gliding, and farther and farther—

They flew on.

THE END